VENGEANCE OF THE BLACK ROSE

LEGEND OF THE BLACK ROSE 3

A.W. HART

WOLFPACK PUBLISHING
— EST 2013 —

WOLFPACK
PUBLISHING
— EST 2013 —

Published in the United States by Wolfpack Publishing, Las Vegas

Wolfpack Publishing
6032 Wheat Penny Avenue
Las Vegas, NV 89122

wolfpackpublishing.com

Paperback ISBN: 978-1-64734-086-5
eBook ISBN: 978-1-64734-085-8

VENGEANCE OF

THE BLACK ROSE

CHAPTER 1

The moonlit night had a dark heart. Its name was Catalina Christiana Rivera — the Black Rose. She rested on her haunches behind a large prickly pear cactus, a shadow among shadows, studying a circle of six wagons about a hundred yards upwind from her. Four other women squatted in similar postures within a dozen feet of her, but the Black Rose was clearly the fulcrum that moved them.

Two sentries stood near the wagons, talking quietly and smoking. Each carried a rifle and pistol. They did not seem particularly alert but neither did they look like they'd be moving anytime soon. And the wagon they stood nearest was the wagon the Black Rose wanted.

The Black Rose, or Lina as she generally thought of herself, cupped her hands near her mouth and vented a sound. The chilling howl of a hunting wolf reverberated across the desert. It was followed by the howls of true wolves in the distance and much closer, by the cackle of coyotes. The two sentries startled, glanced at each other with frightened eyes. By mutual agreement, they stepped back through the circle of wagons and closer to the illusory safety of the fire within.

Lina made a gesture with her hand high over her head. Two of the other women rose from their crouches and worked their way forward, taking up positions that bracketed the wagon circle. Sofia Lee and Adeline O'Malley, members of the religious order of the Sisters of Señora Maria and now of an inner circle of that group known as the Order of the Black Rose, were not wearing their habits this evening. Their black cotton trousers and long-sleeved shirts melded into their surroundings. They'd streaked their faces with greasepaint and even the blades they carried had been rubbed with coal dust to disguise any gleam of steel.

Lina made another gesture and Sister Mary Rosetta worked her way to Lina's side. The ginger-haired woman wore the same costume as the others. Only Lina's outfit was different. Her pants were of leather and she'd added a dark cloak and hood. The grease on her face resembled a crimson and black cross done in the pattern of Apache war paint. The two of them crept silently forward, with the last member of their band — Sister Caroline Harp — trailing them from a distance of a dozen yards.

The wagon Lina was interested in resembled a Gypsy wagon, though the rest of the six conveyances did not. The wagoneers, while a mixed lot, were certainly not of the wandering people commonly known as the Roma. Lina was sure the wagon, like its contents, had been stolen from some group of Roma.

The two women reached the wagon without being noticed. Lina took up a defensive position while Sister Mary selected two small metal tools from the pouch at her belt and went to work on the door lock. In a matter of seconds, the lock gave an almost noiseless click and came open.

Now, Sister Mary took up a defensive position while Lina moved to the wagon's door. Slowly, she drew it open and peered within. The interior smelled musty, as if it hadn't been aired out in a long time. Dirty clothes and jumbled baggage cluttered it. Bright curtains at the windows suggested happier times that were long gone. A single candle burned on a small table, with a narrow cot to either side of it. One cot held two small children who clung together — a boy and a girl.

These were Roma, with brown skin, dark black hair, and olive dark eyes. Their pupils were dilated with fear. Lina smelled their sweat; both needed baths. The boy, who was about five years old, trembled. His sister, a couple of years older, held him protectively, though she also shook.

Lina held a finger to her lips to signal the children to silence, then made a Romani gesture to indicate friend. The girl made a motion back. A question. Lina repeated her gesture of friend and added one of "help." The girl nodded and when Lina beckoned the two toward her, they came with caution.

Lina met the children's wide gazes, striving to convey her intentions through her eyes. It must have worked because the little boy let go of his sister and held his arms out to her. She scooped him up, patted him, and carefully passed him to Sister Mary. The little girl seemed worried mostly about her brother; her gaze followed him. She hesitated when Lina held out her arms, but after a gentle stroke on her cheek, the girl's long lashes gathered tears and she let herself be picked up. Sister Caroline Harp came to cuddle her.

"Get the children back to Santo Tomas," Lina whispered to her companions. They could all see the lights of that small settlement and mission in the distance. "Take Sofia and Adeline with you. I'll be along shortly."

"What are you going to do?" Mary Rosetta demanded.

"Business. I won't be long. Relock the door behind me."

Mary started to protest but Sister Caroline grasped her arm and gave it a gentle push. Mary moved off, with the Roma boy nestled in her arms. Caroline waited, holding the girl. Lina gave them each a smile and nod before slipping into the wagon and drawing the door closed behind her. The lock clicked; Lina was shut inside to await whatever might come.

******

An hour passed. Lina listened to men's voices outside, to curses and arguments and boasts. Finally, footsteps approached. The single candle had burned low, leaving the wagon's interior a dim clutter. Lina stepped into the back left corner, where a draped curtain of muslin created a sheltered alcove in which to hide and spy.

The lock rattled and opened. A man ducked through the low doorway, accompanied by the odor of rye whiskey. The man was taller than Lina, a couple of inches over six feet and broad shouldered. A faded cotton shirt stretched taut across his muscled back. His wool trousers and drooping felt hat smelled sour. A grimy-handled Bowie knife hung at his right hip.

Lina had the skill of disappearing into her surroundings and she wore no perfume that might catch the man's attention. He stepped past her hiding place, toward the cots where she had tucked pillows under the blankets to simulate sleeping children. The fellow huffed softly as he stared at the beds. He reached up and took off his hat.

Lina stepped free of the curtained alcove. She held a knife in her right hand. In her left she carried a modified sasumata, a man-catcher, a tool Sister Mary had introduced her to. This was a short stick with a leather loop on the end. She whipped this over the head of the man and twisted it around his throat, jerking him against her as she pressed the tip of the knife against his back at the level of the kidney.

"Silence buys your life," she murmured into the man's ear.

He went very still.

"Now, Chico," Lina said. "I'll ask a few questions. Answer truthfully and you may live through this. The children's family, where are they?"

The man's voice came out hoarse from the constriction of the leather thong around his neck, but he sounded calm as he spoke. "How did you know they were here?"

Lina had known because the fellow had visited Santo Tomas this day for supplies but had not allowed his men to come too, even though they surely would have been eager for a drink and at least a glimpse of a woman. Curious about what the traveler was hiding, she'd followed him, spied from a distance. She'd seen the children being led on leashes to their toilets and had known them for prisoners of bandits. However, she felt no need to share that information with her prisoner.

Instead, she pushed the knife harder into the fellow's back. He winced. "You asked a question," Lina said. "Your first mistake. Don't make another. Where...is...the family?"

"They're...they're my children. My wife—"

Lina twisted the stick of the sasumata, tightening the leather loop to further constrict the man's breathing. She pressed harder with the knife and the razor-tipped blade sliced through the fellow's shirt and pricked the skin beneath to draw a tithe of blood. He vented a small cry of pain, but not loud enough to be heard outside the wagon.

"Your second mistake," Lina hissed. "And the last one I'll allow. The children are Roma. You're not. Tell me of their family!"

"D...dead!" the man said. Emotion had final broken through his calm.

"Finally, a truth," Lina said. "Did you kill them?"

"Bandits killed them."

"Your bandits," Lina snapped. "The men outside this wagon."

The man struggled for breath but managed a croaking answer. "If you know the answers why ask the questions?"

"I want to know the reason. Why take the children?"

The man gave no words back. His body shook, though whether it was from fear or anger, Lina couldn't be sure. It was certainly anger that spurred Lina now. She twisted the tip of the knife against the man's skin, let him feel it scrape.

"To sell, damn you!" the man snarled.

The man-catcher was an effective tool, but the bandit was big and strong and afraid for his life. Her voice told him she was a woman. Weaker, perhaps. Surely unused to violence, as he assumed of most women. He took a chance at overwhelming her, twisting his body away from the knife and slamming his elbow toward Lina's head at the same time. Lina was ready for such a gamble. She ducked under the elbow and gave the neck leash a savage yank to pull the man all the way around to face her.

He was off balance, his legs splayed. His mouth opened to shout for help as he flailed at her with his right arm. She caught the ineffective blow on her left shoulder. At the same time, she thrust the knife in her free hand up through the soft spot beneath the man's jaw and into the brain. He jerked in a seizure and Lina fought to hold him. His body sagged; he went limp.

Using both the knife and the sasumata as support, Lina lowered the dead man slowly to the rug covered floor. He was heavy, but Lina was muscled like a leopard and full of fury. She withdrew the knife with a faint snick of steel against bone, then unhooked the neck leash. After wiping her blade on the dead man's clothes, she stood staring down at him.

"If I am to be damned, so are you," she said. Thoughts of the imprisoned children and their murdered family made her spit on the corpse.

As her breath calmed, Lina took a look around the wagon. The lit candle still rested on its little table but was beginning to gutter. Reaching out, Lina tipped the candle into the bedclothes beside it. It smoldered for a moment before bursting into bright flame.

"For a child born of fire," the Black Rose muttered softly, as she recalled her own past.

Slipping silently from the wagon, Lina loped away in the darkness as the dead kidnapper's makeshift coffin began to burn.

CHAPTER 2

The town of Santo Tomas lay quiet under the falling moon as the Black Rose crossed its empty streets. She passed the village's only hotel, the Casa del Poeta. Through the windows of the upper story she saw the gleam of the building's electric chandelier. Next to the hotel stood the bank, and across from both rested the new train depot built by the Kansas City, Mexico and Orient Railroad. A little farther down, Lloyd's Cantina rocked with light and sound.

Many of the town's buildings had been damaged or partially burned only a year and a half ago by raiders out of Mexico. But the people of Santo Tomas had rebuilt. They were tough. Survivors. She was proud to be among them

Reaching the convent where she lived as a novitiate of the Sisters of Señora Maria, Lina bypassed the ornate oak gate, which was locked at this time of night and scaled the adobe wall. She dropped down near the granary into the mission's garden. To her right rose the holy sanctuary, a brooding edifice whose sense of permanence often provided a source of stability and comfort.

A cobblestone path struck through the garden and Lina took it. The scents of native cactus and yucca tingled her nostrils, along with the headier perfumes of imported and carefully nurtured roses and lilies. Even the air felt more humid. It was peaceful here, but the calm of the place could not claim her tonight. She passed among the flowers to her room, opened the door and entered. Shadows waited and one of the shadows spoke.

"You are tardier than usual this evening, Catalina."

Lina caught her breath, then relaxed. "Mother Superior," she said. "I had business to attend."

A rustle in the darkness. The click of glass on metal and the strike of a match. A flare of light from an oil lamp. Mother Mercy Justice, prioress of the convent and secretly Lina's aunt, hung the lantern she'd lit on a hook on the wall of Lina's room. She was not a tall woman but the blue habit and bandeau she wore lent her a sense of stature and gravitas. Her horn-rimmed spectacles suggested the scholar but the eyes of blue-ice that lay behind them indicated the passion that animated the stout older woman.

"Indeed," Mother Mercy said. "I spoke with Sister Caroline and the others. I saw the children." She smiled.

"So, you know what business I refer to," Lina said.

"Yes. And it was well done. Even though we

generally do not like to operate so close to the convent. We cannot afford for suspicion to be thrown upon us."

"There will be no suspicion," Lina said. "Only one man saw me. And he will not be speaking of what he saw."

Mother Mercy nodded. "The one who stole the children?"

"The one who orchestrated it."

"What of those who helped the 'orchestrator?'"

"I did not have time to kill them all," Lina said, unable to keep a touch of acid out of her voice.

"A harsh statement. But perhaps a necessary one," Mercy said. "They will be marked. And followed. Their fates will be determined."

"I'll do it," Lina said. She strode across the room to her dresser. Removing her hood and cloak, she flung them across a chair, then dipped a cloth into her water basin and began cleaning her face of war paint. "And I will find out what happened to the children's family," she continued. "To see if any survive."

"I'm afraid that will not be possible," Mother Mercy said.

Lina rounded on her superior, her mouth open to protest. She paused as the Prioress raised a pale hand with two fingers extended.

"I understand your wish, Lina," Mercy said. "It is a fine one and does you credit. But I will send others on that errand. There is something else I need from you."

"What is more important than those children's

wellbeing?" Lina demanded.

Mother Mercy shook her head. "Not *more* important, perhaps. But important, nevertheless. And something for which you are suited."

By an effort of will, Lina calmed herself. "What?" she asked, as she leaned over and began unlacing her knee-high boots.

"You know of the mission, San Javier del Amor, do you not?"

"Yes, of course. A small mission near the border west of here. A relatively new one, I believe. What of it?"

"I received a letter. They are struggling. I need you to shepherd a small wagon train of necessities to help them. Sister Caroline will go with you."

A surge of anger rose like bile in Lina's throat. She tried to fight it down. "That…. I do not know why such a task must fall to me. There are plenty here who could see to the delivery of…supplies."

"Yes," Mother Mercy said. "And if it were only the delivery of such, I would surely agree with you."

"There's more?"

An odd expression crossed the Mother Superior's face — part confusion and part concern, along with something darker. "I'm not sure," Mercy said. "But I believe so. There was a … strangeness to the letter. A mention of rumors. And my prayers this past few evenings have been disturbed. I fear that something ungodly may be happening there. Or will happen soon."

Lina slowly stripped off her leather vest and

the trousers she wore. She reached to her hair and unpinned it, letting it fall straight and black to well below her shoulders. Her fist closed around something she'd removed from the weave of her hair.

She took up the blue-grey habit she wore in the convent and pulled it on over her head. As the rough cloth fell around her waist, Lina hung the burnt rosary that she'd taken from her hair on the rope belt at the left side of the habit. There, it made a constant presence against her leg, just as its subtle scent of sandalwood and fire constantly tugged at her memory. The rosary was precious to her, the only thing she had to recall her mother — her birth mother.

For most of her life, Lina had known Theresa Estella Rivera as her mother and Aquiles Rivera as her father. Neither of those things had been true. Mother Mercy had revealed to her the facts. Her real mother's name had been Victoria, a young woman scarcely out of childhood who had become the captive of an evil man named Adrian Felipe Fino.

Fino was officially a member of the Federales, Mexico's state police. Unofficially, he was little more than a bandit, albeit a wealthy one. A little over a year ago, Fino had led the raid on Santa Tomas that nearly destroyed the town. The Black Rose had put a stop to that raid and she'd killed Adrian Fino when she did it. Without pity. Without regret.

"Wherever I'm needed, there I'll go," Lina said to Mother Mercy, her fingers caressing the beads of the rosary.

"And you can do what is necessary?" Mercy in-
quired.

Lina closed her mercurial eyes. "His will be done,"
she said.

******

In the final light of a holy day, twenty riders crossed
the Rio Grande into Texas. They rode with intent,
without distraction or delay. Their leader stood
apart, almost hidden in the shadow of a fur cloak.
His mount was a big bay stallion who did not seem
to enjoy its master's scent; it enjoyed the unusual
rowels on his footwear even less and did what it
was forced to.

Over the past few weeks, others had gone ahead
of these riders, to mix among the locals, to spread
tales and hints of tales. A wildfire of fear ran ahead
of the leader and his men. That was just the way
he liked it. Fear pushed people together, sent them
skittering for cover into the arms of their fellows —
where they could feel protected, feel safe.

Making them easy prey.

CHAPTER 3

Sister Lina Rivera, who was secretly the Black Rose, straightened on the seat of the wagon she was driving. Ahead in the late afternoon Texas sky, what looked like a small tornado of dark leaves swirled amid the wide blue. Lina knew what those leaves really were. Death had come to the mission of San Javier del Amor and brought with it the vultures who were its servants.

With a "gee yaw" to her six mules, Lina flicked the reins sharply across their backs. Maggie, the lead mule at the left front of the team was eighteen years old and well experienced. She leaned into the traces at Lina's command and the other mules followed. The wagon jolted forward through the day's heat.

Sister Caroline Harp, who dozed on the seat beside Lina, sat up with a quick intake of breath. "What, Sister?" she demanded, her sleepy dark eyes sharpening to alertness.

"In the sky. Up ahead," Lina said, snapping the

reigns again over the backs of her team.

Harp frowned, then spotted the vultures and the frown turned to concern. "No, no, no!" she said. "What could have happened?"

"We'll know soon enough," Lina said grimly, urging the mules on to even greater speed.

Behind her, Lina could hear the three other mule teams coming fast. Their drivers were calling out for explanations, but Lina didn't bother to give one that she didn't have. Off to her left, Lina saw Henri Moissant, the mule train's scout, spurring his gray gelding toward San Javier. He must have seen the vultures, too. He'd get there ahead of them all.

A few minutes later, Lina pulled her team to a halt in the courtyard of San Javier. Dust and ash swirled up around her. Sister Harp coughed raggedly but Lina merely locked the wagon wheels and looped the reins before leaping down from her seat. The pleated skirt of her blue-grey habit slapped against her legs.

San Javier sat close to the border between West Texas and Mexico. It was not a large or prosperous mission. It had no wall, only a church and a few adobe buildings built around a large central well. Some of it had been burned, although the fires had used up their fuel days before. Only tiny trickles of smoke here and there still reached weakly for the sun.

The past fires were the least of the mission's problems, however. A few yards in front of Lina, half a dozen vultures squabbled around a crumpled object on the ground. Caroline shook her head at the sight and turned away; Lina reached into a storage box on the side of the wagon seat and pulled out an eight-foot bullwhip. She never used it against mules or horses but she let it unfurl behind her now.

The glutted carrion birds barely paid Lina heed until she snapped the bullwhip forward and let the popper at the tip peel a thin lair of skin off one vulture's bald pink head. The big bird gave a screech and threw itself off the corpse it was standing on. Awkwardly, it flapped its way into the sky, followed by its fellows.

"Should have killed it," Sister Caroline said, spitting.

Lina shook her head. "These creatures aren't responsible for the deaths here. They're merely doing what God made them to do."

"Well, I still don't like them," Caroline said.

Ignoring the other woman, Lina coiled the whip and returned it to its box, then stepped forward to examine the body on which the vultures had been feasting. Death's smell was present but not overly strong outside in the dry air and there weren't as many buzzing flies as she would have expected. Perhaps the smoke from the fires had kept their numbers in check.

The torn and bloody religious outfit worn by the corpse gave the general identity away. It was a nun…had been a nun. She'd been dressed much like Lina and Caroline, who led this small party of four supply wagons. They'd expected to find a struggling new mission, not a slaughtered one.

Men and women from the other wagons began to gather. Sobs and wails and the occasional curse cracked the late afternoon air. Caroline turned to the crowd to offer comfort. Lina rose to her feet, started across the courtyard to meet Henri Moissant, who was walking toward her with a moue of distaste on his patrician's face.

"More bodies around?" Lina asked.

Henri nodded his head. "Plenty. How many people were stationed here?"

Lina shrugged. "I don't know. Four nuns. A priest. About a dozen cooks and carpenters and other workers. But there could have been anywhere from fifty to a hundred locals seeking food or comfort."

"I found the priest," Henri said. "His praying days are over. There's about a dozen more bodies. Two of them nuns, including that one." He jerked his chin toward the corpse Lina had just examined. "A couple of the Sisters seem to be missing."

Lina sighed. "Any...children among the dead?"

Henri's dark brown eyes sparked with relief. "No. And certainly no fifty to a hundred others. If there were that many here, most survived. But they're not here now."

"The question," Lina said, "is did they run away, or were they taken?"

"Right," Henri said. "I'll check for tracks."

Lina placed her hand on Henri's buckskin-clad shoulder. "Thank you," she said.

He nodded, turned away. Lina watched him walk off. Henri Moissant was still much of a mystery to her. She'd found the tall man wounded near death at a muddy watering hole some fifty miles north of Santo Tomas about four months back. She'd never found out why he was at that particular watering hole with the men who'd shot him. He wasn't one to volunteer much personal information.

By his buckskin clothing and long rifle and his occasional use of a specialized vocabulary, he was clearly a mountain man, more used to the high lonesome of the Rockies than to the arid landscapes of this part of southwest Texas. Yet, he was also educated. While he did speak French to go along with his French sounding name, his primary language was certainly English. His accent indicated the East Coast and his manners suggested he'd grown up in wealth and privilege. The few lines on his face and the lack of any gray in his dark hair marked him as a man in his early to mid-thirties.

"What did Henri say?" Sister Caroline Harp asked, coming up from behind and interrupting Lina's thoughts.

Lina turned. The drivers and passengers of the other supply wagons were overcoming their shock and starting to wander through the mission ruins. She wondered if she should tell them to leave everything alone, but then saw what Sister Harp was carrying and realized someone was already finding clues. Maybe they'd find something that would prove useful.

"The priest and two nuns are dead," Lina explained to Caroline. "Two others among our Sisters are missing. And there's no sign of any children. There should have been some here. Henri's checking for tracks. What's that in your hands?"

Sister Harp winced and offered Lina the item she held. "One of the drivers found it. He said it was Comanche. They must be the ones who did this."

Lina took the broken arrow and examined it. She knew the Comanche tongue and had walked among them. She recognized their symbols and their patterns.

"The arrow is Comanche, all right. But the Comanche didn't do this." She gestured around at the destroyed mission.

Sister Harp frowned. "That makes no sense. What about the arrow? And even I can see that many of the hoof prints of the raiders are unshod. Like Indians."

"I don't know about the arrow. Maybe it was planted to make the raid look like the work of Comanches. But," she held the arrow up for Sister Harp to see, "see the tip on this thing."

Caroline Harp studied the arrowhead a moment, then shrugged. "I have no idea what I'm looking at."

"The arrowhead is nearly perfect," Lina explained. "In fact, I don't think it's ever been used. Comanche might leave behind a broken shaft for an arrow but not a perfectly good point. And what about that?" Lina pointed toward three chickens scratching in the bone-dry dust around the central well.

"Chickens!" Harp said. "What does that have to do with anything?"

"Food!" Lina replied. "The chickens are still here.

And alive. I saw a cow as we were coming in. There's a couple of sows in the pig pen. The Comanche would either have taken them, or killed them."

"But…but the body lying there." Harp indicated the nun's corpse without looking at it. "Hasn't it been…scalped?"

Lina nodded. "Yes. But not like the Comanche take scalps. The cuts are ragged. Whoever did it either didn't know what they were doing, or they didn't care about the scalp itself, only the show."

"So, who are we searching for?"

Lina was about to shrug when a voice called for their attention.

"Sisters! If…if you will! Please to come here!"

A young Mexican man named Miguel stood near the pig shed, gesturing vigorously to them. He was new to the mission at Santo Tomas; Lina didn't know his last name. But he handled mules like he'd been born to the work. At this moment, though, he looked terrified.

Lina held up both palms toward Miguel, to calm the man, then strode quickly toward him with Sister Harp following.

"What is it?" Lina asked softly, leaning in close to Miguel so he wouldn't shout out anything that might further alarm the others.

"This…this way," he answered, picking up on Lina's concern and struggling to calm himself.

He led them around the corner of the pig shed, gestured with a shaky hand toward the ground. Sister Harp hissed in sympathetic pain at what lay there. The man must have tried to hide in a hay pile. He'd been discovered, dragged halfway into the open and pinned down with pitchforks before being left to die. Blood soaked the soil and the edges of the hay.

"His...hand!" Miguel said.

At first, Lina thought the man's dying agonies had caused him to tear at the ground with the fingers of his right hand. She quickly realized her error.

"He was writing something in the dirt!" she said. "What is that?"

Miguel desperately crossed himself. "Bestia!" he said. "Bestia!"

"Beast," Lina translated.

CHAPTER 4

Leaving Sister Caroline to calm Miguel, who'd begun to mutter about devils in the desert, Lina went in search of Henri Moissant. She discovered the tall man studying tracks just outside the settlement, with the afternoon sun casting his shadow long across scattered cactus and mesquite.

"I found some of your missing people," he said, as she stopped beside him. He pointed to a trail of marked ground heading southwest away from San Javier.

Lina studied the trail. She was no expert tracker but could read some of it. "Both shod and unshod horses, in two columns," she said. "With a line of people in the middle?"

"Yep. The folks in the center. They were bound together. I figure a yoke of some type. They're walking almost in each other's footprints. You can only tell them apart because of the different sized feet."

"A slave column?" Lina asked.

"Probably. Captives for sure."

"How many?"

Henri shrugged. "I'd say more than thirty but less than sixty. The prints overlap too much to count every individual."

Lina asked a question she was dreading hearing the answer to. "Children?"

Henri met her gaze and did not look away. "All sizes. Probably men, women, *and* children. But most of the feet are small."

Realizing that she was grinding her teeth together, Lina forced herself to calmness. "How long?"

"Trail's about three days old."

"You and I'll go after them," Lina said. "I can take your remount. We'll send Sister Caroline and the others on to get help."

"That help will be at least a week behind us. Probably more."

"We'll have to be enough until it arrives."

Henri nodded. He'd first met Lina as the Black Rose. He'd ridden with her before on short missions and kept her secret. Now he said, "Our friend who rides in black might be enough all by herself."

"She'll do her best."

"There's something else I have to show you," Henri said. "It's...weird. Not sure what to make of it."

"Lead on."

"It involves some unpleasantry."

Lina merely stared until the mountain man turned and walked off at a right angle from the trail they'd been studying. The ground here was mostly dirt and rock, with scattered mesquite, catclaw and cactus. The came up a small rise and Lina saw where they were headed.

A man had been staked down on his back over a rough hole in a rocky outcrop. His corpse was bent backward over the outcrop like a drawn bow; it was horribly swollen and discolored. His black robes had been mostly cut from his body, leaving only scraps that flapped in the occasional breeze. For some reason, there were no buzzards here.

"Close enough," Henri said, stopping.

"Why?" Lina asked, though she stopped as well.

"Listen!"

Henri stomped his boot on the ground. Instantly, an angry buzzing began from the rocks and bushes around. "Rattlers," he said.

Now Lina understood the lack of carrion birds. She wanted to spit but her mouth was bone dry. "They staked the priest here alive," she said. "Let the rattlers have him."

"The snakes were nesting in that hole beneath him," Henri said.

"This isn't what you wanted to show me, though," Lina said.

"Right," Henri replied. "It's over here."

The buckskin-clad scout led the way to a broad patch of wind-blown soil that had gathered in the lee of the outcrop. He pointed and Lina bent down to study the tracks she could see imprinted there.

A swift intake of breath signaled her agitation. She glanced up at Henri with a frown. "What is this?

Those aren't human tracks. They're clawed. A bob-cat. Or panther. Why are you showing me these?"

Henri shook his head. "Notice the size. You ever see a bobcat or panther that big?"

"No. But that doesn't mean there aren't any. Pan-thers at least."

"Look closer. This thing's not four-legged. It was standing on its hind limbs, watching the priest die.

"A bear?"

"Don't think so. It was standing like a man."

Lina blinked. "A beast," she said softly.

She was thinking of a word a dying man had scratched in the dirt with broken fingernails and his last breath.

******

Sister Caroline Harp opened her eyes, her hand reaching instinctively to pluck up the Kpinga at her side. This was a three-bladed throwing weapon from her ancestors' homeland, a tool with which she was adept. For a moment, her newly awakened thoughts were confused. Then she remembered — the mission of San Javier and the slaughter of many of its inhabitants. And, too, the word from Henri Moissant and Sister Lina Rivera that many others had been marched away as prisoners.

Caroline sat up. She couldn't have been sleeping long. Moonrise was due at nine but there was no sign of it yet through the holes in the roof of the half-burned adobe where she'd cast down her pallet. The pallet next to hers, where Lina Rivera had made her bed, lay empty.

A whisper of movement drew Caroline's gaze to the window. Someone leaned there, a shape shrouded in a midnight cloak. Caroline had no fear, however. She knew the silhouette.

"So," she said. "The Black Rose rides tonight."

The shape drifted toward Caroline. The dark-skinned woman's keen eyes picked out the sharp cheekbones and knife-blade jawline of Lina Rivera, accentuated rather than hidden by the black and red war paint that Lina wore. Lina squatted next to her.

"I'm riding with Henri after the prisoners taken from San Javier," Lina said.

Caroline pushed back her blankets. "I'll accompany you," she said. "My people know something of what it is like to be shackled. I would not wish it on anyone else."

Lina rested her hand on the other woman's shoulder, stalling her actions. "You can't," she said.

"If you expect me to stay behind in safety—" Caroline started to say hotly.

Lina shook her head, interrupting her companion's words. "I don't believe there is any safety here. Or on the trail. But we must move fast and we have only two horses. Our mules have to pull the wagons."

Caroline knew Lina's logic and accepted it, though she didn't like it. "What am I to do?"

"In the morning, lead the wagons to the nearest town with a telegraph. I think it must be Jacaranda. North of here. Get a message to Mother Mercy. Tell her what's happened and I know she'll send help. After that, it's up to you to decide how best to proceed."

Sister Caroline nodded reluctantly.

"You also," Lina continued, "will have the tough task of keeping the rest of our little wagon train calm. I was out just now. Checking on our sentries. And listening. The word Miguel found scratched in the dirt. 'Bestia!' Beast. Talk of it has spread like fire. Some of our people had family here. Or nearby. The beast seems to be a local legend. A local devil. Everyone's terrified. I heard talk of fleeing. There may be deserters from our ranks before morning."

Sister Caroline sighed, then slipped out from under Lina's hand and rose. "I'll go out. Nip it in the bud. If I can."

"Take care, Sister," Lina said.

Caroline turned toward Lina, gave her a hard hug although she knew such signs of affection discomfited the other woman. Lina bore it stoically.

Caroline broke the hug but left her hands gripping Lina's forearms. "It's you who must take care," she said. "We all depend on you. You don't know how much." With that, Sister Caroline released Lina's arms and swept out of the adobe to see to her duties.

CHAPTER 5

The Black Rose moved unseen and unheard through the ruins of San Javier. She reached what had once been the mission's stable, found Henri Moissant puffing on a cigarillo while he waited for her. Two saddled horses stomped the ground restlessly, as if they knew excitement lay ahead.

"There you are," Henri said. He dropped his smoke, toed it out. "The moon is on its way. I've got food and plenty of water packed."

Lina said nothing, only took the reins of the Appaloosa stallion Henri offered her. The other horse was a roan gelding. Henri commonly rode the gelding, reserving the Appaloosa for emergencies. The stallion was bigger, faster and could be dangerously aggressive to those he didn't recognize. He was familiar with Lina, though and had accepted her. Lina understood. Henri knew the stallion would give its all for her. He was doing his best to protect her. She didn't try to argue with him.

"Where did you get the extra saddle?" she asked.

"Left behind in the stable. One of the few things that wasn't burned. Here, take this too." He tossed her a rifle, a Winchester carbine in .44 caliber.

Catching the weapon, she checked it. It had been loaded and freshly serviced, its metal parts gleaming. She smelled gun oil and gave Henri a questioning glance.

"Found that in the stable too. Half buried in debris. You've probably got a hideout pistol or two tucked here and there but a long gun might come in handy. Cleaned it for you. One of the victims had it but it doesn't look like he had a chance to use it. Whatever happened here, it overwhelmed them quickly."

Lina nodded. The Sisters of the Black Rose, Lina included, preferred edged weapons to guns. But they all knew how to shoot. And sometimes one needed to strike from a distance. She slid the weapon into the rifle scabbard at the right side of her saddle, mounted and clucked to the horse as she urged it out of the stable. Henri followed and they threaded their way through the darkness until they reached the outskirts of the settlement.

The night scents of cactus blooms and morning glory perfumed the faint breeze. The moon peaked over the horizon. It would be nearly full tonight. Silver light began to spread, creeping first over rows of graves that had been dug only this past evening for the murdered. The light crawled farther, reached the wide track left by the raiders and their marching prisoners. Henri urged his roan alongside the trail and Lina joined him. They lifted their animals to a trot.

Henri sat relaxed in the saddle, as if he had no care to burden him and had never felt a moment's worry. But Lina remembered their first meeting some four months back when she'd found him in pain and near death.

Riding the desert night after completing a mission fifty miles north of Santo Tomas, she'd spotted the warmth of a campfire and some stray impulse had driven her toward it. She had no intention of stopping. Or so she told herself. It was only to have a short glimpse of someone else's life, perhaps a more normal life than the one she led.

The abrupt rattle of gunfire had notified her of her mistake. She topped a small rise, spotted a watering hole and a violent tableau below. Three men with rifles and drawn pistols stood over a fourth man who lay on the ground. One of the three standing gunmen, young and sandy haired, was wounded. Blood ran down his left arm and he whimpered as he swigged from a bottle of whiskey held in his good hand. Lina's approach had been nearly silent and the wounded man's moaning covered what little noise she made.

"He shot me!" the injured man said. "Can't believe he shot me! Knew we shoulda let the poison work longer."

"Shut up, Cal!" a second man said. This one had shaggy dark hair and a thick mustache. He was short but thick with muscle, and clearly the leader. He stared at the man on the ground, addressed him with, "You came a long way to die, Moissant. Glad it was me who put you in your grave."

Lina had a perfect vantage point to see Moissant's response. He'd been shot at least three or four times but showed no fear; his hand inched toward the shine of a Colt Peacemaker that lay nearby in the dirt.

The leader of the three chuckled. "Close but can't quite get there. The story of your life, Moissant." He lifted his own pistol, cocked it for effect. "See you in H—"

Lina's hand dropped to her waist, to what looked like a belt with a sword's hilt. She grasped the hilt, twisted it slightly and the "belt" snapped loose to become a flexible metal blade, a kind of hybrid of whip and sword called an urumi. She jerked it free, kicked her horse into motion down the rise into the camp. Her hand whipped forward; the flexible steel blades of her weapon snapped across the shaggy-haired gunman's wrist, slicing it the bone. His pistol went flying.

The shoulder of Lina's horse struck the sandy-haired outlaw, knocking him into the fire. He dropped his bottle. Whiskey sprayed everywhere, soaking his clothes and fireballed. The young man screamed as flames leaped up his body.

The last of the three outlaws spun, bringing up an old Spencer carbine he held. Lina was faster. She snapped her urumi across; the blades tore out his throat, sending blood spuming into the cool night air.

The shaggy-haired leader shouted an oath. His good hand scrabbled for a second revolver tucked with its barrel through his belt. Lina's urumi was out of position. Her left hand snaked into her vest. She pulled out the Remington over-and-under .41 that she'd started hiding there and pulled the trigger on the top barrel. The heavy slug smacked the outlaw in the chest. He stood, swaying, still trying to pull his own pistol. From the ground, the wounded Moissant swung a leg and swept the other man's feet from under him. The fellow crashed heavily to earth and did not rise.

The outlaw who'd fallen into the campfire struggled to his feet and fled screaming into the night with flames eating at his clothes and greasy hair. Lina let him run. The smoke from her derringer tingled her nostrils. She slid the weapon back home beneath her vest, feeling the heat of the steel barrel through her shirt and against her skin.

Dismounting, she approached the wounded man named Moissant. He was panting for breath. His face was a mottled gray; his eyes looked bruised. A red rheum leaked from three bullet holes spread across his upper body.

Lina folded the urumi back around her waist before kneeling beside the man. "Poison?" she asked.

He nodded weakly. "The coffee," he replied in a hoarse whisper. "Should...have known."

Lina glanced toward the campfire. The coffeepot sat on a flat stone near the flames. She kicked it over with a booted foot, watched the corrupted brew gurgle into the dirt. She glanced back at Moissant.

"This won't be pleasant," she said.

"Right."

She grasped the wounded man's shoulder, turned him on his side. He groaned with pain. Lina pinched his nostrils shut, and when he opened his mouth to breathe she stuck two long fingers down his throat. His eyes widened in shock; he gagged. Vomit exploded over Lina's hand but she kept her fingers pressed down against the base of his throat. He thrashed. His clotting wounds reopened and blood ran afresh. But more vomit came up until nothing but bile was left and Lina was sure the remnants of the poison had been expelled.

She eased the man down, found white cloth in one of the outlaw's saddlebags to clean him. After dressing his wounds, she built up the fire and made her own coffee. Through the long night she sat with Moissant, to see if he would live or die. He lived. And now he rode with her in service of her wishes and her mission for justice.

For a long time, the two rode in silence along the trail of captives.

"Are you worried at all about this 'Bestia'?" Lina finally asked Henri. "The thing that stands like a man but has claws on its feet?"

Lina saw her companion's teeth flash white with a grin in the night's silvery light.

"There's nothing more dangerous under the moon than a black rose," he said.

CHAPTER 6

When the moon fell, the two riders — Henri and the Black Rose — camped. They'd have to wait for morning's first light before they could see to follow the tracks of the mission prisoners and their captors. There wasn't much deep darkness left for them to share. Each slept for an hour while the other watched. After, they took up the trail again.

Mid-morning found the two coming into an area even more desolate than what they'd passed through before. The mesquite and cactus had thinned. The patches of bunch grass that had provided their horses with a little quick grazing were gone. All the world seemed made of dust and stone and scorched earth.

"We're gaining on them," Henri said. "The tracks are fresher."

"But our horses are tiring," Lina replied.

"They'll last," Henri said, though whether it was from surety or hope, Lina couldn't tell.

They crossed a long dry arroyo so old the sides were eroded to gentle slopes. As they topped out on the far bank, Lina pulled the Appaloosa to a stop. Henri brought his horse alongside hers, looked to where she pointed.

"That isn't natural," Lina said.

Reaching into his saddlebags, Henri drew out a pair of scuffed binoculars that might have seen use in the Civil War. He studied what lay ahead through the glasses before handing them to Lina.

A scratch across one lens of the binoculars didn't bother Lina as she gazed through them. About half a mile ahead stood what could only be described as an altar. It had been constructed from slabs of rock and consisted mostly of one long, relatively flat stone resting across stacks of rougher pieces. It was all of natural stone. Nothing had been hewn or shaped.

"Thrown together in a hurry," Lina said. "From whatever local rocks were available."

"Recent?" Henri asked.

"Probably," Lina replied. She handed the glasses back to Henri. "And whatever is lying on it is recent, for sure."

Henri studied the altar again, let out a deep breath. "Blue cloth," he said. "Missed that before. The sun hasn't faded it. The top of the altar is set at a bit of an angle. I can't tell if it's just cloth, or a body."

"You know it's a body," Lina said. She pointed to the sky where the black specks of several buzzards soared.

"Right."

"Spread out," Lina said. "We'll go in slowly." She didn't have to tell her companion to watch for traps.

Lina drew the Winchester from its scabbard and levered a shell. Henri tucked away his binoculars and pulled his own rifle into his arms. The big single shot 1874 Sharps was chambered for a .50-90 black powder cartridge — a bullet meant for hunting big prey. And humans if necessary. Lina had never seen Henri miss a shot.

Watching everything, the two rode forward. It soon became apparent that the altar's burden was indeed a body. Black hair fluttered on its head; blood had poured in rivulets down its side and down the sandy stone of the altar. Exposure to the sun had dried the blood and turned it a rusty shade.

"A man!" Henri called. "Dead for sure."

"Why aren't there any buzzards on the ground?" Lina shouted back.

Suddenly she knew why. The dead man wasn't the only unnatural thing here. She'd been carrying the Winchester with its butt resting on her thigh. She whipped the barrel down just as the ground around the altar exploded and four attackers came hurtling up from the small covered hollows where they'd hidden. Their bronzed skins were caked with dirt and sweat. They wore breechclouts and fur boots and feathered armbands. Two carried bows and arrows. The other two had long, thrusting spears with gleaming stone heads of obsidian — ancient weapons suited to ancient times.

Lina heard the bellow of Henri's Sharps even

as she triggered her own rifle. She saw one of the bowmen go down, his shoulder half torn from his body by Henri's shot. The other bowman released his arrow just as she fired at him. Her bullet caught him in the chest, flinging him back against the altar. His arrow whipped through Lina's cape at her left side, its punch nearly dragging her from the saddle.

Lina levered the action of the Winchester but had no time to shoot. The attackers were fast. One of the spearmen lunged toward her, lance glittering as he stabbed at her horse. She jerked the Appaloosa's head to one side, lashed out with a booted foot that kicked the spear up and away.

The Appaloosa reared in anger. Lina tried to swing her rifle around but the spearman leaped forward and grabbed her foot. He twisted and she came out of saddle, landing hard in the dirt but managing to hang onto her wind. The Winchester bounced away. The Appaloosa struck at the man with its teeth but missed as the man drew a knife from his breechclout and rushed Lina.

She rolled toward him rather than away. He stumbled over her, fell and by the time he regained his feet Lina was standing too and had freed her urumi. She whipped the weapon's tip toward him. It snapped across his hand, took two fingers and sent the fellow's knife spinning away.

Gunfire filled the world behind Lina but she dared not turn to search for Henri. Her attacker seemed not even to notice the fingers he'd lost. His chest heaved; his bulging eyes were shot through with swollen, purplish blood vessels. He looked mad. Not enraged mad, but insane. He charged her, screeching like some monstrous owl.

Lina snapped the urumi at the man's legs, cut them from under him. He hit dirt but instantly thrust himself upward and scrabbled toward her on hands and knees. She had no choice. Whipping the urumi up and over, she lifted onto her toes to put every ounce of strength she had into one blow. The weight of the flexible twelve-foot steel-edged blade crushed the man's skull and he collapsed as if struck with an axe. This time he did not move further.

Twisting around, Lina's gaze sought desperately for Henri. He'd dismounted from his gelding and stood with his legs braced against the earth. The empty Sharps lay a few steps away, but two Colt Peacemakers smoked in his hands. The second spearman lay nearly at his feet, shot to ribbons. Striding toward her companion, Lina let the length of the urumi trail like a snake behind her in the dust.

"The one you shot was still alive," Henri said, nodding toward the bowman that Lina had thought dead. "I had to put a couple more slugs in him."

"What about the last one? The one you shot."

Henri pointed. "Still alive, too. But the .50-90 seems to have persuaded him to stay down. These boys are tough but that round will knock a buffalo into next Sunday."

"I imagine so," Lina said.

She paused while Henri took a moment to fill his Colts with fresh cartridges. They started forward, toward the last surviving member of the band who'd attacked them. The man saw them coming. His glazed eyes brightened and he struggled to a seated position.

His right shoulder was destroyed; that arm hung like a broken wing at his side. He couldn't use his bow but drew a knife from his hide belt with his left hand. Before either Lina or Henri could guess his next move, the fellow slashed his own throat and flopped back, convulsing in death.

"I guess he really didn't want to answer our questions," Henri said.

"What was wrong with them?"

"What do you mean?"

"Their eyes. They looked...crazed."

"I noticed. Some kind of drug maybe. Not opium. Folks on that stuff act like they're half asleep or dreaming. Coulda been peyote, I guess. Or something similar."

"Maybe," Lina agreed. "Another question is, who are they? They look vaguely Indian but they're certainly not Comanche. You recognize the haircuts at all?"

All four of the dead warriors had similar hair styles, with the front half of the heads shaved and the remainder of their black hair pulled through a broad leather band and greased into an elaborate series of interwoven braids.

"Never saw any natives with that style," Henri said. "Could be a Mexican tribe, I suppose." He frowned. "Something's nagging at me but I can't recall it right now."

Lina made no acknowledgement, only strode over to the altar and stood staring down at the dead body adorning it. The face and arms were scratched and bloody but she forced herself to look at those areas rather than the chest region, which had been slashed open and the ribs pulled back.

"Helluva way to die," Henri said. "Is it one of the villagers from the mission?"

"Can't be absolutely sure but I imagine so," Lina said. "And the heart's missing."

"Kinda figured that," Henri said. "Why else cut open the chest like that?"

"The altar. The open chest. The heart. It's like some kind of religious ritual. Like a sacrifice."

"Not to any god I've ever heard of."

Lina shook her head. "You're wrong there. Plenty of ancient gods demanded this kind of sacrifice. In just about every tribe that ever existed. Yours included."

Henri drew in a deep breath, let it out. "I guess you're right."

An odd wink of light from within the dead man's ruined chest caught Lina's attention. She frowned, leaned in for a closer examination even though she didn't want to.

"What is it?" Henri asked.

Lina drew her knife, used the tip to push a lung aside. She reached in and plucked out a roughly oval-shaped object that gleamed like emerald through a sheen of blood.

"A stone!" she said. She wiped it clean with her

fingers and lifted it up to the sun. It drank the light, captured it and held it deep within — a jeweled heart about the size of a woman's fist.

"Is that jade?" Henri asked.

"I think so. With the major blood vessels indicated in threads of gold. An expensive work of art to leave behind in a dead man."

"Some religious meaning, I'm sure."

Lina nodded, then stepped around the altar and stood studying the ground. "You'll want to see this, too," she said.

Henri joined her. His gaze followed her pointing finger. Blood from the sacrifice had spilled into the dirt there, leaving behind a small stretch of mud. A single print was impressed deeply in that mud, which had dried to preserve it. It was the same beastly track they'd seen back at the mission.

"Guess that explains why the chest on this fellow looks *clawed* open," Henri said, pointing at the body.

"You still think the Black Rose is the deadliest thing out in this desert?" Lina asked.

Henri's brown eyes danced with strange light. "Maybe I'm rethinking that," he said. "And it's not a comforting thought."

CHAPTER 7

Lina and Henri buried the dead. It didn't take long. They put the four strange warriors back in the hidey holes they'd emerged from, then dug a shallow grave for the innocent man who'd been sacrificed. This they covered with stones torn from the altar. In half an hour they were ready for the trail again.

Lina saved the jade heart, storing it in her possibles bag. She did one other thing before they rode. She picked up one of their ambushers' bow and arrow sets and one of the obsidian-headed spears and tied them across her saddle roll. She wasn't quite sure why she grabbed the spear but she'd used bows before and liked how they let you strike from a distance without the noise of a gun.

Riding stirrup to stirrup, Lina and Henri made good progress. The tracks they were following grew fresher and fresher. Clouds began to build as the day passed. The sky darkened. A wind came.

"If it rains…" Henri said. He didn't complete the

sentence. Both knew that a hard rain in the desert would wash the trail away. The prisoners they sought to free would be lost to them.

Lina wanted to pick up the pace but the horses were tiring and had to be handled carefully. They alternated between cantering, trotting and walking. Lina chafed. Her mind churned. Finally, during one of the episodes of walking, she spoke some of her thoughts to Henri.

"The ambush at the altar bothers me."

"Right," Henri said. "Because, how did they know to leave it? How did they know we were following them?"

"Yes. The mission was isolated and they left no one behind who could track them. I can understand them watching their backtrail for some eventual posse, but to leave an ambush... Don't you have to *know* you're being followed for that?"

Henri shrugged. "A lot of strange things going on. That's not the strangest."

"So, how do you explain them? Or do you think it's the devil in the desert that Miguel spoke of back in San Javier?"

"You scoff at it?"

Lina frowned as she studied the man riding next to her. "Don't you?"

"Your sisters in the order certainly believe in the Devil," Henri replied.

"The Devil inside man," Lina said. "Evil takes a human form. Not a beast in the wild."

Henri said nothing. He looked lost in thought.

"Well?" Lina demanded.

Henri glanced at her. His eyes, reflecting the clouds, seemed gray rather than their normal brown today. When he spoke, his voice was hollow.

"I rode with a Cheyenne named Charlie Wolf once. We trapped all through Colorado and up into Wyoming. Even into Montana. One winter we didn't get out of the mountains in time. We were snowed in. But we built ourselves a snug little cabin. We had quite a bit of food and figured we could eat our burros if we had to. Maybe we would have, but we never got the chance.

"One morning early on, I went out to get firewood. Charlie was sick. Down on his back with fever. I wanted to get him some fresh meat. I'd set a few traps for rabbits. Caught one. But something got it. Tore it to shreds. And tore up all the other traps. There were no tracks in the snow. None except the rabbit's. You understand?"

"An owl, maybe," Lina said.

Henri nodded. "That's what I thought. At first. But something came sniffing around the cabin that night. Something big. Charlie was sound asleep in his fever but I figured it was just a bear. I went out next morning to see. This time there *were* tracks. But they were...wrong. I'd seen plenty of bear sign and this wasn't it. And there was a dead rabbit with a broken neck lying almost on our doorstep.

"Never one to look a gift horse in the mouth, I dressed the rabbit, cooked it up in a stew, fed Charlie on it. He ate heartily for the first time in a while.

Ate almost the whole thing. Started feeling better almost immediately.

"Two days later Charlie was up and around. I told him about the traps I'd set, about the bear that didn't leave tracks like a bear, about finding the rabbit left for us like a gift. Charlie was a pretty dark-skinned fellow but he turned pale and ashen. He began to sweat and shake. I thought his fever was coming back but he told me I'd made a bad mistake. He said I'd accepted a gift from the devil and would have to give something back or the devil would come and take whatever he wanted. And since Charlie had eaten most of the gift, even without realizing it, he said his payment would have to be much larger. I laughed at him."

Lina shivered. Maybe the darkening sky and the wind had chilled her sweat. Or maybe it was the strangeness of the story Henri was telling, a kind of tale she'd never heard him recite before.

"So?" she asked. "I think most people would laugh at something like that."

"Could be," Henri agreed, then continued. "Charlie told me several times that I needed to leave out a gift for the devil. Some salt or coffee. My timepiece. A few brass cartridges. He did, but I didn't. Didn't believe in the devil, you know. Early one morning when it was still dark, we heard a monstrous racket outside. We each had a horse and burro for packing furs and supplies. We'd built a little shed for them backed up against the cabin. The noise came from the shed.

"I ran outside with my gun. Charlie too. It was icy cold. The kind of cold that freezes your hair stiff. One corner of the shed was smashed in. The horses were gone. Run off. Never saw them again. The burros had been torn open, their innards spread around like strawberry jelly. Their heads had been taken. Both heads. I was enraged. There were the same tracks again. Odd. I followed them. Charlie refused to. I trailed them for miles. Came to a cave...."

"And?" Lina prompted.

"There was nothing there. The tracks in the snow led right up to the cave mouth. But when I went inside I found it empty. No bones of anything that might have been eaten there. No leaves or sticks that might have been dragged in for a nest. The cave looked as if it had never been touched by anything living."

"And no devil," Lina said.

"No," Henri said. "No devil."

"You must have felt pretty foolish."

Henri nodded. "A little. At the time. Then I turned around and went home."

"What did Charlie say when you returned?"

"He didn't say anything. The cabin door hung open. There was a horrible stench. I ran inside to find one of the burros' heads in the fireplace. Maybe the smell was the singed hair in such a closed place. But I'd smelled burned hair before. This...." Henri shook his head as Lina stared at him with wide eyes. "It smelled like nothing I can describe."

"What about Charlie?" Lina demanded.

"He was hanging upside down from the ceiling. His legs had been broken and hooked over one of the rafters. He was naked. So naked that even his skin had been taken off."

Lina winced. Her teeth clicked together. "That's... that's a horrible way to die."

"Oh, he wasn't dead. He lived for several more days. Screaming most of the time."

Lina swallowed though her mouth was dry. She wasn't normally much for offering comfort. She wasn't always sure how. But she leaned over in her saddle and reached out to squeeze Henri's hand.

"I'm sorry," she said. "Must have been Indians."

"My first suspicions were the Blackfeet. Or maybe the Crow."

"Did Charlie...talk at all?"

"Only gibberish. When he died, I put him in the snow. Left him until spring. When I was ready to walk out, I put him in the cabin and burned it and the shed until there was nothing left."

"What about the Indians?"

"It wasn't Indians. I searched all around the cabin. There would have been clear signs in all that snow. It was something else attacked our burros and killed Charlie."

"What? An animal of some kind? It couldn't be. No animal would hang a man up like that to die."

Henri shrugged.

"You're saying it was a devil?"

"I don't know what it was. Something I'd never seen before. The Cheyenne I knew back in those days claimed it *was* a devil. Years later, an old mountain man told me it must have been a wolverine. Maybe it was. They're like a badger. Only a whole lot bigger and meaner. This fellow told me that in the worst winters they raided human food caches. He said they'd been reported to hang their food up in trees to keep bears and other critters away. It's a beast. But not just a beast. Not quite."

"Perhaps," Lina said. "Did it come back?"

"Nope. Left me alone the rest of the winter."

"Any idea why?"

A faint smile with no humor in it twisted Henri's lips. "Well, I left it an offering. Like Charlie told me too."

A fresh chill goosebumped Lina's arms. "What offering?"

Henri lifted his left hand from the reins of his gelding and showed her the inside of his arm where a savage scar ran from the elbow to the wrist. "Blood for one," he said.

"For one!" Lina said. "What else?"

Henri shook his head and pointed to the darkening horizon ahead of them. "That'll have to wait," he said. "There's something up ahead we better pay attention to."

Lina lifted a hand to shield her eyes from windborne dust. Evening approached swiftly. Obscuring shadows gathered everywhere. The two riders were coming down a gentle slope and a couple of miles ahead Lina could see a dark brown stain covering the land.

"Looks almost like muddy water," she said. "Could there have been a flash flood through here?"

Henri pulled out his binoculars and studied the landscape. "Nope," he said after a moment. "It's an old lava flow. And that could be a problem."

Lina didn't have to ask what kind of problem. Bandits didn't leave tracks across rock. Neither did their prisoners. Lifting their mounts back to a canter, Lina and Henri soon approached the flow. It was ancient and broken, with mesquite and other bushes sprouting on it here and there like green mold growing on a crust of burnt bread.

Despite its age and the long erosion of wind and weather, the reddish black lava was jagged in enough places to cut a horse's legs to ribbons. Even people with good boots would struggle to make a safe passage through the whorls and folds of frozen stone. And if they tried it, their pace would be slow.

Henri pointed to the trail they'd been following. "Our kidnappers didn't try to cross it," he said. "That's good for us. The bad news is, they've split up. One set of tracks leads almost directly south. Mexico way. The other set turns back north toward New Mexico. We can't follow them both."

Lina chewed her lower lip. She dismounted, Henri with her and studied the tracks.

"The larger group went toward Mexico," Lina said.

"Yep, but from the size of the prints I'm seeing, most of the kids seem to be in the northern group."

Lina turned toward the north. Her eyes filled with anger and red spots of color flushed on her cheeks. Long fingers tapped at the rounded hilt of her urumi. Her voice, when it came, was rough with rage.

"North," she said. "The children come first."

"All right," Henri said, as he pulled saddlebags off his roan. "But first we rest the horses and get something in our bellies. The tracks here are the most recent yet. We've gained quite a bit. When the moon comes up we'll see if we can run them down."

"And kill everyone we have to," Lina added.

CHAPTER 8

Out of necessity, Henri had learned to cook decent food during his years in the mountains. Tonight he made biscuits for himself and Lina in their iron skillet. There was no butter but he whipped up a thin gravy from some simmered beef jerky. The two ate and Henri rolled in his blankets and slept for an hour.

Lina didn't sleep. She couldn't. She took care of the horses, giving them plenty of water and even pulling fresh bunches of grass for them from among the broken rubble of the lava field. She touched up her war paint after all the sweating she'd done today, and sewed up the tear in her cape where an ambusher's arrow had passed through. She cleaned up the dishes from their meal and repacked Henri's saddlebags. When the moon rose, she was ready and quickly awakened her companion.

The horses were rested and refreshed and Lina set a fast pace. The moon was still close to full and gave plenty of silvery light to see the trail by. And it didn't look like any attempt had been made by the kidnappers to hide their passage.

The two rested a little while during the darkest part of the early morning, when the moon was down and the sun not yet rising. But as soon as it was gray enough to detect the trail, they raced along it. The tracks were freshly turned now. At least twenty horses were with the bandit column, many traveling light. Only occasionally did they see a child's footprints and Henri suggested that the kids were being allowed to ride at points so they could move faster. It wasn't helping them much. Lina and Henri steadily closed the gap and about three hours after dawn they spotted something ahead. But it wasn't quite what they had hoped for.

In an open area that was mostly drifted sand, the companions spotted four seated children tied together in a circle with their backs to each other. The ground all around them had been churned up by hooves but there were no horses around and no sign of any kidnappers.

When the children sighted Lina and Henri they began to wail shrilly for help in a babble of Spanish and English. Lina shouted for the kids to calm down, using both languages. The babble eased but didn't stop. The kids were scared. Lina and Henri shucked their rifles and rode closer, but they were cautious. It felt too much like another trap and they both remembered the one they'd so recently sprung.

Henri studied the landscape all around through

his binoculars. "Looks flat," he said. "With no place to hide. But there could be an arroyo close by where they're waiting to ambush us as soon as we dismount."

"I don't think so," Lina said. "I think it's a different kind of trap. You know anything about mines?"

Henri frowned. "What?"

"Landmines. Buried bombs."

"Oh," Henri said. He turned his binoculars on the churned earth around the bound children. A moment later, he lowered the glasses with a curse. "You've got it," he said. "They're pretty well hidden but when you know what to look for you can see them. I'd say they're laid in a broad circle around the kids. Step on *one* of those and they'll all go off. Kill everyone within a hundred yards."

"Using the children as bait," Lina said, spitting in the dust.

"Bait for us?" Henri asked.

Lina shrugged. "Either they know we're still following and I don't know how that could be but don't think we can discount it. Or they're just being cautious and are willing to sacrifice children to protect their own safety. *Anyone* who stopped to help these little ones would likely be killed. Even a bird landing there might set the mines off."

"Wish I could get my hands on these scum," Henri said through clenched teeth.

Lina did not reply, only dismounted and stalked closer to the minefield. She made a circuit of the kids, with Henri following. The children began to call loudly again for help. Some were crying. Lina ignored it all as she studied the situation.

"There's a safe area right around the children," Lina said finally. "I guess so they wouldn't set it off accidentally. The circle of mines looks to be ten feet across. Maybe a little more."

"Not sure how that helps us," Henri said.

"It helps," Lina said.

The Black Rose turned away from Henri, took a few paces back toward the horses, then spun around without warning and sprinted toward the children. Just before her feet touched the edge of the mine-field, she leaped, soared. Her cape fluttered behind her like batwings as she came down with a thud of boots right next to the children.

Henri cried out in alarm. The kids screamed in surprise. But Lina dropped to one knee in front of them and began to offer a soothing voice and the comfort of her hands.

"What the Hell!" Henri yelled. "What do you think you're doing?"

Lina glanced toward her friend and smiled as her hands petted the little heads and shoulders of the frightened children. She leaned closer to them. "It's all right," she said. "All right. We're all going to get out of this alive. I promise."

******

Henri Moissant stared helplessly while the Black Rose soothed the four bound children. Finally, they quieted and Lina rose to her feet. Her gaze met Henri's. He wanted to yell at her but knew that wouldn't do any good.

"I hope you can catch," Lina called.

Henri had no idea what she was talking about until she cut one of the children free of his bonds and helped him stand. The boy was maybe eight years old, thin for his age. He had dark hair and eyes and wore ragged jeans with a blue cotton shirt. He looked to be in shock.

Lina placed her hands on the boy's shoulders and spoke slowly to him in Spanish. His eyes blinked; maybe he understood what she was saying. Henri couldn't tell. She grasped the back of his jeans and the front of his shirt and picked him up. Her lean muscles bulged under her shirt. The boy made no protest. Lina glanced toward Henri and he understood. He put his rifle down and rushed to the edge of the minefield.

Lina nodded at him. Without waiting any longer, she spun around three times in a circle to gain momentum, then hurled the lad like a sack of feed toward Henri. The boy cried out and his hands and feet flailed at the air. But he cleared the minefield by at least half a foot and thudded into Henri's arms. The mountain man caught him, held him, lowered him slowly to earth. The boy burst into tears and Henri hugged him.

Leading the boy over to his gelding, Henri pushed him gently down on the sand to sit. "Wait right here," he said. "We've got to get the others. It's going to be all right."

The boy gave an almost imperceptible nod but Henri took it for understanding. He returned to the edge of the minefield, nodded to Lina. She'd already cut a second child free. This time it was a girl with blonde curls and sharp little chin. She wore a knee-length yellow dress over a pair of shorts and was maybe six or seven.

Again, Lina talked to the child before picking her up. She grasped the girl by the shorts and the front of the dress. The child went limp and closed her eyes in expectation. Lina spun twice and hurled the girl toward Henri. She cleared the mines more easily than the boy and thudded down into the mountain man's arms.

The girl lay very still until Henri said, "You're safe."

The child opened deep blue eyes. "Thank you," she said politely.

Henri almost laughed from the release of tension. He put her down, told her to go sit beside the other boy. Turning back to Lina, Henri realized that the Black Rose was choosing the children based on size, from largest to smallest. The last two kids were both boys, both of Mexican descent and barely six years old, if that. They looked much alike. Lina hurled them across one at a time and Henri caught them and set them next to the others. Finally, he returned to the edge of the mines. His face became grim because now another problem asserted itself.

"How are you going to get across?" he called to Lina. "You can't jump ten feet from a standing start."

"I've been thinking about that," Lina said. "Bring me the spear tied on my saddle roll. The one I picked up at that ambush."

Henri fetched the spear as he'd been ordered. "Not sure what good this will do," he called, as he tossed the weapon across to Lina.

She caught the spear, promptly pushed the obsidian head into the sand and broke it off. She bent the spear shaft in her hands to test its give. Satisfied, she spoke to Henri. Her voice was soft but carried.

"Move the children and horses back. A couple of hundred yards at least."

Henri understood now what she was planning to do. "Wait," he said. "Maybe there's some other way. We need to think about it."

"No other way," she said. "Get the kids and yourself back!"

She fell to studying the minefield and Henri knew she was looking for a spot between two mines where she could put the tip of her pole. He turned and rushed back to the children, gathered them up under one arm. He took the horses' reins in his free hand. Leading the small band quickly away, he made sure to put several hundred yards between them and the Black Rose.

One of the things Henri always taught his horses was to lie down on command. He did this with the gelding and urged the kids into seated postures behind the big animal where they'd be sheltered. As for himself, he stood up by the Appaloosa and waved their readiness to Lina.

Lina waved back. Henri couldn't see her face but imagined it was a study in concentration. The woman had picked a place to rest her pole. She planted the tip carefully and stood holding the other end in both hands. Without hesitation, she stabbed the tip of the spear hard into the earth and pushed off with her legs, using the pole to lever her body into the air.

Henri held his breath as Lina swung forward. The spear bowed; Henri feared it would break, but it took the woman's weight and as she swung past it the bend released to act like a lever and give her added momentum. Her boots nearly brushed the sand over the last mines but she cleared the field and came down stamping on safe ground.

"Yes!" Henri shouted under his breath.

Lina came walking toward the others carrying the spear shaft in one hand. Henri got the gelding and the children up. He examined Lina's face when she reached them. She looked calm but he could see a faint quiver of the cloak over her shoulders. It had taken great courage to trust herself to that spear. Henri wanted to hug her but didn't think it was the time or place.

"Good work," he said.

Lina nodded. "Let's get going," she said. "But we can't leave those mines out here to kill some other traveler. Or any animals that might stumble through."

"Agreed," Henri said. "I'll take care of it." He'd already picked up his Sharps again before pulling back from the minefield. He drew it free of its scabbard on the gelding and folded up the rear sight.

Lina gathered the horses and the kids and led them farther away. Henri walked along behind. When they were almost six hundred yards clear of the mines, Henri brought the Sharps to his shoulder and sighted along it.

"Cover your ears," he told the others.

A wink of reflected light from one of the mines cast a metallic gleam into Henri's eyes. He fired. The world rang like a monstrous bell as the big rifle bullet struck the mine and set it off. An explosion geysered the earth. A chain reaction followed around the circle of mines in both directions. Detonation after detonation bludgeoned their ears, sending rock and soil soaring.

Despite being prepared, the children screamed. Lina hugged them to her, her cloak spreading over them like a mother crow's wings falling around her brood. The wave of concussions ended. The sound rumbled away into the distance. Sand rained down in a patter, followed by the thud of bigger chunks pelting into the earth. A smoking hole remained behind in the desert. But it had taken none of the victims it had been intended to claim.

CHAPTER 9

"What's your name?" Lina asked the little blonde girl, who seemed the only one of the four rescued children who was able, or at least willing, to talk.

"Perla Craft, if it pleases," the girl said, very properly. "And what is yours?"

Lina smiled. "I am called the Black Rose."

"Why?"

"It's a long story," Lina said. "And maybe someday I'll tell you. But right now I need to ask you some important questions. Lives could be at stake."

Perla folded her hands in her lap and nodded. After the explosion of the mines ended and the children had calmed down, Henri had brought them water. All were badly dehydrated and drank greedily. Now they were sitting in the dirt nibbling on strips of jerky. Lina squatted in front of them.

"The men that left you here," Lina said to Perla. "How many were there?"

"Five and a half," she said.

"Five. And a half?" Lina asked. Henri chuckled from where he stood behind her.

"One of them had a stick for a leg," Perla explained. "And a hook for a hand."

"I see," Lina said. "Good to know. What about the other children. How many other kids did they have with them?"

Perla shook her head. "No others. Just us."

Lina frowned. "We saw…a lot of tracks."

Perla looked blank, but the oldest boy spoke, the one who'd been in the deepest shock. It was the first words he'd said since being rescued.

"They had a wheel," the boy said.

"What kind of wheel?" Lina asked.

"One with feet."

Confused, Lina glanced up at Henri but the mountain man only shrugged.

"That's right," Perla added. "They had a wheel. They pulled it behind a horse sometimes. It had kid's shoes attached to it. It was kind of funny but I guess we didn't feel like laughing."

"Ah," Henri said. "Some kind of device to leave extra tracks. They tricked us. They wanted us to follow this group instead of the other."

Lina realized she was literally hissing with anger and forced herself to stop. They'd been fooled, but they had saved four children. That, at least, was a very good thing.

"The other group," Lina said to Perla. "The larger group. There were other children with them?"

Perla nodded, her curls bobbing.

"And...your parents?" Lina motioned around at the other children as well. "All of your parents?"

Perla glanced down as if to study the dirt. She no longer seemed to want to talk. "My mom," she said finally. "But I think they hurt her."

"What did they do, Perla?"

"They hit her. Really hard. When they were going to take me and she tried to fight."

Now it was Henri who gave a low hiss of anger.

Lina reached out and stroked Perla's shoulder. "We're going to go after them," she told the girl. "As soon as we get you and your friends to safety. In the meantime, I still need your help. What about the parents of your friends?" She motioned to the three boys.

Perla looked around. "That's Raul," she said, pointing to the older boy who'd mentioned the "wheel." "I don't know about his mother but they...well, they... took his father away and he didn't come back."

"They murdered him," Raul said, staring off into space and stating the fact flatly as if it were the time of day. "I know they did. We all heard him screaming." He turned away and lay down on his side in the dirt.

Again, Lina glanced at Henri. They both understood that the body they'd found on that altar must have been Raul's father.

"This is Juan and Carlos," Perla said, pointing at the two youngest boys. "They're brothers. Their parents were with us."

"What about your father?" Henri asked Perla.

The little girl glanced up; a quick smile danced across her face. "He's in the army. He'll come after Mommy and me." Her smile faded. "If...if he finds out."

"What's his name, honey?" Henri asked.

Perla shrugged. "Daddy."

"Right," Henri said. "Do you remember where he's at? Where he's stationed?"

Perla's face crinkled in concentration. "Mommy said it was a place that meant happy."

"Fort Bliss," Henri said. "Gotta be."

"Yes, yes," Perla said. "That's it."

"Good," Lina said. "We'll be able to get in touch with him soon. I just have one more question."

"All right," Perla said.

"In the big group. Was there a man who...looked strange? Maybe he had...claws on his feet?"

Raul moaned on his side.

Perla chewed her lower lip. Her eyes darted this way and that. "The tiger man," she said finally. "That's who you're talking about. I didn't like him. He likes to scare children. He told Juan and Carlos he was going to eat them unless they did what he told them."

The two young boys appeared confused at hearing their names until Perla interpreted. "El Tigre," she said to them.

The boys' eyes grew wide as saucers.

"Bestia," Carlos said.

"Diablo," Juan said.

"Muy Malo," they both added.

******

Sister Donna Marie, who had been — until very recently — the Mother Superior of San Javier del Amor mission, waited until the guard charged with giving them each a little water had passed. As soon as he did so, she leaned over the old man yoked behind her and let her swallow of water dribble into his mouth. His eyes brightened a little; he nodded weakly to her. She hoped he would make it. It their journey ended soon, he might. Otherwise, it wasn't likely.

Donna glanced up at the brutal sky, turned almost white from the hammer of the sun. She wasn't sure how long they'd been walking; she'd lost track since the morning when the raiders tore through her mission like a starving hound through dinner scraps. Before she could hardly think of resistance, she'd found herself stripped of her bandeau and coif and leashed by the neck to a line of other captives.

Not all of the people in her mission had been so lucky. She'd watched too many of them die while the bandits laughed. She'd heard Father Dominic scream. And he had been a strong man.

"Sister!" a voice said. She abandoned her troubling reveries to see who had spoken. One of the bandits stood in front of her. "The water was for you, Sister," the man said. "You are a healthy one. You need your strength. We have far yet to go and you will have much work once we arrive."

The man's smile seemed friendly. She tried to smile back.

"How...how much farther?" she asked. "We've already crossed the Rio Grande. How far do we travel?"

The man's smile broadened, just before he back-handed her across the face. She rocked in her bonds but could not fall over because of those constraints. The taste and scent of blood trickled into her mouth. The man's knuckles had cut her lip.

"You do not talk, Sister!" the fellow snarled. "Not to me or anyone. You drink your water and eat your biscuits when they are given. And you walk. That is all you do." He lifted his hand in position to strike her again. "Do you understand?"

She nodded quickly. The man still drew his knife. She tried to lift her hands but they were tied in front of her with a leather thong around her waist. The bandit stepped toward her; the old man she'd given water to kicked at the bandit as he shouted, "No!, No!"

The bandit snapped a knee into the old man's face, then grabbed a huge fistful of Sister Donna's shoulder length ash-blonde hair and started sawing through it with his blade. She cried out in pain, but the assault was over in an instant and he hurled the sheaf of hair into her lap.

"Now get up! All of you!"

People began struggling to their feet. The old man couldn't and the bandit jerked him upright. Sister Donna leaned into him, giving him as much support as she could without being able to use her hands. He smelled of sour sweat and sickness. She didn't imagine that she smelled much better.

And then they were moving again, staggering forward toward distant mountains that Donna could see to the south. She looked around, looking for the bandit leader, the man responsible for all this misery. Her gaze found him in his awful cloak. He sat astride a big horse maybe fifty yards away.

He watched her. Not like a man watches a woman. More like a carnivore studying a limping prey. Or like a devil counting a new soul as it enters Hell.

CHAPTER 10

Captain Caleb Jefferson of the United States Cavalry was on extended training maneuvers with three hundred mounted troopers southeast of El Paso when he saw dust making its way across the desert toward him. The dust contained a glitter of refracted light at its center, and soon the glitter revealed itself as a buckboard pulled by a single large mule. Jefferson was surprised to see that the driver was a woman — not only a woman, but apparently a nun. Intrigued by such an unusual sighting, Jefferson rode to meet the nun, leaving his men to rest in the shadows of a local sandstone bluff where one's brains did not broil quite as quickly as they did in the sun.

The nun's hands were deft on the mule's reins and she brought the buckboard smoothly to a stop beside Jefferson. Dust settled slowly on Jefferson's dark blue uniform and the nun's light blue habit. The woman was not exactly pretty, the Captain thought, but the word "striking" would fit. He glimpsed only a hint of dark hair behind her white bandeau and coif but her face was exposed. Her skin was tanned and taut across high cheekbones. Her nose appeared almost dainty but the chin was sharp. The eyes were formidable; he could not quite discern their color — blue, grey, green. The intensity of her gaze made him doff his hat and offer her a short bow.

"You are a captain of cavalry," she said, studying his rank insignia.

"Captain Caleb Jefferson. At your service."

"Are you out of Fort Bliss?"

"I am."

"That will save me the time of driving this buckboard all the way there."

"You have need of the army?" he asked, faintly amused.

"I don't. But there are others who do." She pointed back south the way she had come. "Have you heard of San Javier del Amor?"

"One of your Catholic missions, I take it?"

"Yes. It was sacked about a week ago. Many were killed. Others were taken prisoners and marched away by the raiders. There are women and children among them."

Amusement fled. Jefferson frowned. "You were there?"

"No. I came after. My companions and I followed. We were able to recover four children but there are more."

"How many more?"

"We estimate between thirty and fifty total prisoners. Ten to fifteen children."

"The children you rescued. Where are they now?"

"We took them to another mission. About fifteen miles from here. Santa Annabella. You know it?"

"Been there many times. To the town that surrounds it, at least. What about the raiders? Comanche?"

"No. There was some attempt to blame it on the Comanche but whoever did it made too many mistakes for that."

Jefferson didn't ask how the woman knew what she knew. He believed her. "Any idea where the raiders have gotten to?"

The woman hesitated. She looked young to be a nun, though Caleb had to admit he knew very little about nuns. He had pictured them all as old, however and perhaps mostly as "dried up prunes." This one certainly was not either of those things.

"We fear they may have already crossed into Mexico," she finally said.

"Ah," Jefferson mouthed. "You are aware of the... delicate state of affairs between the US and Mexico at the moment."

"I'm aware that it's always delicate along the border. I know there are raids. My order has treated the casualties of such. But this raid was far larger and more organized than any I've seen before. And the taking of large number of prisoners is new to me. Someone needs to take action to help those people."

Jefferson nodded. "What is your name, if I may

ask?"

"Catalina Christiana Rivera. I am a novitiate of
the Sisters of Señora Maria. In Santo Tomas."

"Well, Miss…Sister Rivera. Much as I would like
to ride immediately with my men to help, I can't
invade Mexico without orders from my superiors.
I'll speak with them, tell them what you've told me."

Sister Catalina's small resulting smile might have
been better described as a smirk. "And do you think
the appropriate orders will soon be forthcoming?"

Jefferson met the nun's gaze directly. "Unfortu-
nately, I do not."

"As I imagined." The woman lifted her reins and
clucked to her mule, who perked his ears up as he
awaited the command to move. "One more thing,"
Sister Catalina added. "Is there a man named Craft
among your troopers?"

Jefferson found himself startled by the abrupt
change in topic. "Why yes, there is," he answered.
"Why?"

"Does he have a family, do you know?"

"I believe he has a wife and dau—" Jefferson started, then stopped. "You don't mean…?"

"One of the children we saved. Her name is
Perla Craft. She said her father was a cavalryman
at Fort Bliss."

"Yes," Jefferson said. "Joseph Craft." The officer
nodded back over his shoulder. "He's among my
troopers right now."

"You might want to let him see his daughter. His
wife is still a captive of the raiders. If she's not dead."

Catalina Rivera clucked again to her mule and cracked the reins across the animal's withers. The buckboard rolled forward and she swung the conveyance into a wide turn to head back in the direction she'd been coming from.

Captain Jefferson stared after her, without a word in his head.

******

After her brief and opportune meeting with Captain Caleb Jefferson, Lina headed back toward the mission and town of Santa Annabella, where Henri remained with the rescued children. Although they'd sent telegraph messages to both Santa Tomas and Fort Bliss about the raid on San Javier and what they'd learned since, Lina's intent had been to put a face — of a nun no less — on the tragedy in hopes of stirring action by the military. She felt like she'd accomplished the "face" part with Captain Jefferson; not that she expected it to do any real good as far as intervention went.

She had to figure out what to do next, wait for help to arrive from Mother Mercy in Santa Tomas, or take Henri with her and pursue the raiders into Mexico on her own. She knew what Mother Mercy would counsel — wait. That wasn't her first choice, but Henri should have his say as well.

Lina had gone no more than a couple of miles when she heard the thud of hooves behind her. She turned to see a wide streak of dust quickly resolve itself into three riders. All wore cavalry blue. The one in front sat astride a bay gelding and passed her by with a faint twitch of his head. She could see little of him other than the lean frame and the short blond hair, but she was sure who it was — Joseph Craft, father of Perla. The others, no doubt, were escorts sent along by Captain Jefferson.

Lina cracked the reins to urge her mule on faster. A locked steel box slid on the floorboard by her feet. She glanced down, imagined the cloak and weapons it hid. It was almost time for the Black Rose to ride again.

CHAPTER 11

Lina reached Santa Annabella and returned the mule and buckboard she'd rented to the hostler. The town's Catholic mission stood at the northern end of the community. Henri and the children were there. And probably, by now, so too was Perla Craft's father. But Lina paused when she glanced to the south and spotted two men walking across the street from the hotel into the Horse Buckle Bar. Even at a distance, she could see that one of the men had a limp. A nagging suspicion bloomed.

Lina headed for the saloon and pushed through the beaded glass doors into the interior. About a dozen men sat at the bar or around at tables. They were dressed in a variety of clothing, from work overalls to fine suits with vests and ties. Many kinds of hats were in evidence — from flat crowns, to bowlers, to Stetsons and ten-gallons. Every one of them turned toward the door as Lina entered. She forced herself not to smile when all conversations among the patrons ceased.

The saloon had filled with late afternoon shadows. It was much cooler than outside under the sun. The only scents were of sawdust and lye, none of the beer and spilled whiskey she expected. Lina walked across to the bar, her habit swishing against her legs, her worn and comfortable shoes echoing on the floorboards in the quiet. The back, top edge of the bar, behind which the saloon keeper stood, was embedded with a row of belt buckles, all featuring images of horses.

Thus, the saloon's name, Lina figured. To the bartender, she said, "A sarsaparilla."

The barman's face was red. He wiped his hands continually on his spotless white apron. "Ma'am. Uh, Sister," he said. "We don't… That is, we can't…"

"The sooner you get me that drink, the sooner you'll be rid of me," Lina said.

The bartender hesitated for just a tad longer, then gave in and pulled a bottle of Log Cabin Sarsaparilla from beneath the bar and uncorked it. He set it on the bar in front of Lina and placed a glass beside it. She ignored the glass, picked up the bottle itself and had a deep swig. After wiping her mouth on the back of her hand, she turned to lean her back against the bar as she studied the saloon's patrons. They were staring at her as if she'd sprouted a couple of extra heads on her shoulders.

The two men that Lina had seen entering the saloon moments ago sat near the back of the room. One was tall, with a drooping mustache and a scar

on his left cheek below the eye. His clothing —
jeans, cotton shirt and vest, Stetson hat — were
typical of a cow puncher. No gun hung at his belt
but one might have been hidden under the ragged
duster he also wore.

The second man was of more interest to Lina. He
was the only one in the saloon not looking at her.
Short, maybe five foot four, he had a thick stubble
of black whiskers on his face. He wore a serape and
a sombrero, though he was not of Spanish descent.
His left leg had been replaced below the knee by a
peg. His left arm ended in a hook. Lina recalled Perla
Craft's comment about the man who 'had a stick for
a leg' and a hook for a hand."

"Sister," a well-dressed man in a gray suit and
wearing a bowler hat said. "Is there some reason
you're looking at us as if we were a boil under Sa-
tan's armpit?"

"I imagine there are some serious sinners among
this group," Lina replied. "I was just wondering if
the Lord were measuring your shrouds today."

The man chuckled, shuffled a deck of cards he
was holding with one hand without bothering to
look at them. *A gambler,* Lina surmised.

"The Lord has my measurements already," the
man said. "But I reckon he's holding off on the
shroud until he sees if I can remake my sordid life."
He held up the cards. "Speaking of which, would
you care to join us for a few hands of poker?" He
gestured around at the two other men who sat at
his table, both of whom looked like they might flee

at any sharp word.

"Another time," Lina said. "I fear I am about other business today."

"And that would be?" the gambler asked.

Lina looked past him, toward the table with the mustached cowboy and the fellow of 'stick' and 'hook.' "I'm wondering," she said, as if addressing them all, "if you men are aware of the atrocities being committed south of here."

The hook-handed man stared at Lina, his face expressionless but his eyes hooded with speculation.

The gambler frowned. "What atrocities are you talking about?"

Lina let her gaze focus on the hook-handed man, though her words answered the gambler's question. "A small mission called San Javier del Amor was raided a few days back. Many were killed. Many others taken and enslaved. Men, women, and children."

"Those damn Comanches," a fellow dressed like a merchant said.

Lina shook her head. "Not Comanches. And not Mexicans either. At least not all Mexicans. The mongrels who did it were mixed. And white men were among them. Murderous scum perfectly willing to slaughter innocents."

The merchant glanced down. For the first time, the man with the hook spoke. His words were soft and measured. "Sounds like a job for the army."

"I've spoken to the army," Lina said. "They've got to kick it upstream to their superiors. I figure they might reach a decision in a year. Or two."

The gambler added his words. "You saying you want us to ride after them, Sister?" he asked. "Don't reckon most of us are the fighting sort."

Lina smirked. She reached for her sarsaparilla and took another swig. "No," she said. "I don't reckon you are." She let her gaze scan the room one last time, letting it rest last on the hook-handed man and his companion. She stalked from the saloon with her bottle in hand.

******

"You what?" Henri asked.

After leaving the saloon, Lina had gone directly to the mission. She'd found Henri in the garden, leaning against an adobe wall beneath the mission's bell tower and smoking a quirley. Birds frolicked in a nearby fountain. Her opening words had surprised him.

"I saw the 'half-man' Perla Craft described," she repeated. "He's here in town."

"The man with the hook and the wooden leg?"

"Yes."

"Was he alone?" Henri asked.

"One man with him. But the others could be anywhere in town."

"That's...disturbing. Why would he end up here? At the same time we are?"

"I know. Maybe they're scouting missions for new targets. But the coincidence of finding them here doesn't seem likely."

Henri's voice sharpened and he stood up swiftly, dropping his cigarette.

"Could they be after the children again?"

Lina was already standing but her body stiffened at Henri's words. "Anyone watching them?"

"Perla's father is there. He came in over an hour ago. That's why I'm out here. Figured I'd leave them alone. Two troopers *were* with the father but I don't know if they're still around."

"Let's go," Lina said.

Henri hurried across the inner courtyard garden where evening's long shadows were beginning to stretch. Lina followed as they entered the mission and rushed down a long, cool, corridor to the convent's dining area. The children they'd rescued from the mine field were all there. The two youngest boys played in one corner with a nun watching over them. The older boy sat quietly with his hands in his lap. Food rested untouched on a plate in front of him. Perla Craft chattered excitedly with a lean, blond cavalryman —her father.

Joseph Craft's blue eyes were red-rimmed as he looked up at Lina and Henri's approach. It appeared he had been crying, or close to it. He noted the concern on their faces and jumped up, his hand dropping to the flap of his holster.

"What's wrong?" he demanded.

"You came in with two troopers," Lina said. "Where are they?"

Craft frowned. He glanced down at Perla, who gripped the yellow stripe running down the leg of his uniform with one hand. She looked confused, but not scared.

"I…I told 'em to get something to eat," Joseph said. "Is there a problem?"

"I think we'd like to get them back here," Henri said. "Just out of precaution." He pointed at Lina. "Sister Catalina spotted two men in town who might have been with the group who kidnapped your daughter and the others originally."

Craft stiffened; his voice took on a sharp edge of anger. "Where?" he demanded. His fingers unsnapped the leather flap over his army-issue pistol.

Henri lifted a hand, spread a palm. "We don't want to do anything to scare them off just yet," he said.

"They've still got my wife," Craft protested, his voice hoarse.

"All the more reason for caution," Henri said. "But we should get the other troopers back here."

The nun who'd been watching the two boys play had overheard much of the conversation. "They're in the kitchen," she said. "I'll fetch them."

"Thanks," Henri said, as the woman hurried off with a swish of her habit.

"Is your Captain Jefferson sending any more troopers here to Santa Annabella?" Lina asked Craft.

The cavalryman shook his head. "No. He let me go ahead because of Perla." He patted his daughter's curls. "He sent a couple of men to watch over me but he's turning back to Fort Bliss with the rest of the unit. I reckon to give our commander whatever message you gave him about the raid."

"I see," Lina said.

"What are we gonna do about these two outlaws you saw?" Craft demanded. He looked with pleading eyes from Lina to Henri. "Why not let me and the boys take 'em? We can question them. Find out where they took my wife...and the others."

"That isn't off the table," Lina said. "But other things first. I want to see if we can get an eye on their belongings. Perhaps find some information we can use."

The nun who'd left to fetch the other cavalry troopers returned with the men. Lina turned toward her. "Sister," she said. "Is there anyone at the mission who cleans rooms for the local hotel?"

"There is," the nun replied. "Marie Ortiz and her daughter. Why?"

"Would you fetch them for me? I think they might be able to help us save some lives."

CHAPTER 12

The rising moon lit the streets of Santa Annabella with pale light, but there were plenty of places in alleys and behind buildings for shadows to hide. In one narrow alley next to the town's sole hotel, the Black Rose made such a shadow. She waited patiently for a signal.

Henri Moissant came along the boardwalk and turned in to the Horse Buckle bar. Lina observed and when five minutes passed and Henri did not return to the street, she knew the signal was given. The hook-handed man and his friend were still in the saloon.

Lina already had a plan. She placed her hands against the hotel's outer wall, then pressed her feet, one after the other, against the wall of the mercantile next door. Up she went, walking with hands and feet up between the walls to the second floor where a decorative band of bricks extended out from the rest of the structure.

Grasping two of those bricks with her hands, she let her legs drop down and swung along the line of bricks to the iron balcony at the front of the hotel. In another moment she was up and over the rail and crouched on the balcony like a being made of ink. People passed in the street below her — on foot, or horseback, or in wagons. No one noticed her.

Just behind her was the window to room 23 of the hotel. According to Marie Ortiz, who worked as a maid for the hotel, this was the room of a man named Benjamin Bolanger, who had a peg leg and a hook for a hand. The window had been left unlocked by Marie. Lina eased it up and flowed inside.

No candle or lamp burned in the room but ambient light from the moon daubed the floor and walls and Lina's night vision was superb. She smelled gun oil and alcohol, and the musk of unwashed men. The two beds, cots really, had been freshly made, probably by Marie Ortiz or her daughter.

Lina ignored the beds, moved to the saddlebags that lay on the floor by each cot. She knelt to examine their contents, not particularly concerned if the men noticed any disturbance of their stuff when they returned. Not much they could do if they did. The bags held some clothes, a few weapons. She found no papers of any kind and nothing that might incriminate them in kidnapping and murder.

Frustrated, Lina systematically explored the rest of the room. A throw rug on the floor caught her notice. The pattern on it reminded her of a Navajo sand painting, a kind of mandala with a central sun that had been given slashes to represent eyes and a mouth.

The rug was just slightly askew. Moonlight through the window traced a line where darker colored floor planks met lighter ones. The darker ones must have been covered by the rug for some time while the lighter ones had been exposed to the sun. That meant the rug had been moved. Recently.

Lina went to one knee, folded the rug back. Beneath it, an image had been sketched on the floor with colored pigments. Lighting a match but keeping it close to the floor where it wouldn't be seen, Lina studied the drawing. It was stylized but appeared to be a man's body coupled with the head of a beast. Both the hands and feet were clawed. One fist held a heart dripping with blood. The figure's chest had a hole in it where the heart had been removed and replaced by a green stone like the one Lina and Henri had found in the ritually murdered sacrifice in the desert.

The beast-head of the image had fangs and a short muzzle. Lina was reminded of what little Perla Craft had said about, "the Tiger Man," or "El Tigre" as she'd named him in Spanish. This had to be an image of that figure. The head didn't really look like a tiger, though. More like...the word came to Lina suddenly.

"Jaguar," she murmured to herself.

Had the hook handed Bolanger or his companion drawn this thing here? They were white men and this seemed very much a native image. But the sketch was fresh. Lina could smell the pigments and the painted lines had smeared slightly when the rug had been placed over them. Bolanger and his friend had probably witnessed the desert sacrifice, as well and they traveled with this El Tigre. They must have been the source. But why?

Lina replaced the rug and rose to study the room some more. One other throw rug had only dust underneath it. She checked beneath the mattresses on the cots and found nothing. Putting everything back like it had been, Lina stood for a moment in indecision. A long, shrill whistle sounded from the street outside.

A signal! From Henri.

The men who rented this room had left the saloon, were on the way here. How long did she have? There was only one place left to check. A small table sat between the cots, with an unlit oil lamp on top of it. The table had a drawer. Lina rushed over to it, jerked it open. And nearly died.

The rattler coiled inside the drawer struck viciously. Only someone with the honed reflexes of The Black Rose could have avoided the snake's lunge. At the instant she glimpsed the spade shaped head darting toward her, Lina twisted her arm away. The reptile's upper body brushed across the underside of her wrist; she felt the cool smoothness of the scales. And before the snake could hit the floor, Lina swept her left hand over and snagged the creature behind the head.

The snake writhed, slapping at her arm and belly

with its tail. The rattle had been removed, she noted. That's why she hadn't heard it in the drawer. It had been a deadly trap set for whoever might search the room. Had Bolanger known to suspect such a search? Or was it the normal precaution of an evil man with secrets to hide?

The sound of somebody ascending the stairs came from outside the room. There were bootsteps and a thump, thump, thump, as if from a wooden leg. Lina had seconds to escape. She grasped the snake's lower body with her right hand, pushed the thing headfirst back into the drawer and slid it closed with a faint snick.

The footsteps were just outside the room now. Lina slid swiftly through the window she'd come in by, closed it gently and crouched on the balcony like a dark bird of prey. Horses and wagons moved along the dirt main street just below her. A drunk staggered out of the Horse Buckle saloon and fell on the boardwalk; another man stepped over him and continued on his way.

No one saw The Black Rose. The metal railing of the hotel balcony broke up her silhouette, left her nearly invisible even with the moon. She'd learned well how to become part of her surroundings. Her life had often depended on it. But if Bolanger or his companion entered the room and looked out the window, she would be spotted.

Lina considered her options. She could take what she knew to Henri, but she'd learned so little and had hoped for much more. She moved back to the window, opened it a bare crack at the bottom so she'd be able to hear any conversation in the room beyond. A key turned in the lock and men entered. Lina smelled whiskey and cigar smoke. Someone stumbled against the wall, then must have dropped onto his cot, which creaked under a weight. A man groaned.

"I told you not to drink so much," a man said, his words harsh. "You throw up on yourself, I'll let you lay in it." Bolanger had spoken to Lina in the saloon earlier today; she recognized his voice.

The other man slurred a response. "Ain't gonna throw upf. Kin...hol' my likker."

Light flared in the room as Bolanger lit the lantern. Lina shrank back against the balcony rail. She wondered if the man would notice any disturbance she'd left behind. He didn't appear to.

"You better just sleep," Bolanger said to his inebriated partner. "You'll need your wits about you tomorrow. What little you have of 'em."

"Go Hell!" the drunk man grunted.

Bolanger vented a harsh cackle. "Ain't no human hell for the likes of us," he said. "Not after all we've seen and done."

"Mebbe," the other man said, his words beginning to trail away. "Wish had me a lil heaven now, though. Like o' that purty nun came inna bar today. Whatta...waste."

Snores followed. Lina heard Bolanger sit down on his own cot. "Yeah, that nun," he muttered to himself. "Didn't like the way she looked at us. Or her comments. Like she knew something she ain't sposed to know." Lina recognized the next sound she heard, a steel knife blade sliding out of a leather scabbard. "May just have to conversate with her before we head back south."

A long breath followed and the creak of the bed as the man lay down. With nothing more to learn, Lina slipped over the balcony rail, dropped into the alley and became one with the shadows.

CHAPTER 13

Back at the mission and dressed once more as Sister Catalina Rivera, Lina sought out Henri Moissant in the mission's garden. The mountain man sat on a bench and smoked beneath a single post oak tree in which two lanterns had been hung. A moth battered against one of them. Lina joined Henri, shared her finding of the strange drawing in Benjamin Bolanger's room.

"A jaguar?" Henri asked.

"The head and claws anyway. The rest looked human. Well, except for the jade heart."

"Any idea what any of it means?"

"No. And they didn't let much drop in conversation. But it was clear my comments about the kidnappings in the saloon earlier today bothered them. That may also be why they set a trap for anyone who searched their room."

"A trap?" Henri asked, frowning. "What happened?"

Lina explained about the snake.

"These boys like rattlers," Henri said. And when Lina glanced at him with confusion he continued with, "Remember the priest back at del Amor. They staked him out and let the rattlers have him."

"You're right," Lina said. Her voice turned grim. "Maybe someday we can return the favor."

Henri didn't say anything for a moment. Then, "To bad we can't get Perla Craft a look at them. She could let us know for sure if they were among the kidnappers."

"Can't risk it, but I don't think there's any doubt. A big question is, where are the rest of the six that Perla mentioned? They don't seem to be here."

"Right," Henri said. "So what do we do now?"

"Yes," a new voice added. "What do we do now?"

Joseph Craft and his two fellow troopers came into the garden and crossed to where Lina and Henri waited. Lina examined them. All three had been cast from the same mold — tall, lean, ramrod straight. They wore the uniform of the United States Cavalry as if they'd been born to it.

"We watch them, is what we do," Lina said, answering Craft's question. "They made some mention of a 'thing' they need to do tomorrow. Maybe that will reveal a clue. Whatever it is."

"All right," Craft said. "We can take our turns on the watch." He gestured at himself and his fellows.

"Fine," Lina said. "You three can take the shifts tonight and into the morning. But don't let them see you. The stable has a loft. That would be a good place to watch from. You can see the hotel from there.

They're in room 23. Upper right corner facing the street. From the stable you can also keep an eye on their horses. They won't go anywhere without those."

"What kind of mounts do they have?" Craft asked.

"I checked on that," Henri said. "A black and a dappled gray."

"Done," Craft said. He nodded to Henri, tipped his cavalry hat to Lina and strode off with the other two behind him.

"That means we can get some sleep," Henri said, yawning. "We both need it."

"Yes," agreed Lina. "But check on them early."

"Will do."

Henri hesitated, as if he wanted to say something else. The night was warm, the moon bright. The oak tree whispered and water from the fountains chuckled and splashed like a pleasant memory of a lazy day. Yet, there was tension in Henri, a tautness of mouth and muscle.

"What is it?" Lina asked softly.

Henri released a quick breath. "Nothing really," he said. "You sleep well. Lina."

She smiled at him. "And you, Henri."

He nodded, turned and strode away. Lina watched him go. Taking a deep breath, smelling the heady perfume of the flowers, she let her air out slowly. The mountain man was attracted to her, she knew. He was a fine man, a reflective man. She wondered if, in another world, she'd be able to return his interest. But this was not such a world. And she was the Black Rose, with all that entailed.

******

Lina sat up as the door to her convent room slammed open and the whirlwind of a young woman stormed in. Silvia Ortiz had much curlier hair than her mother and it was in full disarray as she called out:

"Sister! Sister!"

"Silvia! What is it?" Lina demanded.

"Henri. Sir Henri. He is in the garden. He say come quick."

Lina threw back her covers and leaped to her feet. She threw on her habit and grabbed up her coif and bandeau as she rushed for the door. Silvia fled before her down the tiled corridor as Lina tried to follow and finish dressing at the same time.

The convent itself allowed no men within its hallways, but in moments they reached the garden. Silvia held the door while Lina passed through. Henri stood beneath the oak again, smoking and pacing. He turned as he heard Lina.

"What is it?" Lina asked.

"The cavalry troopers are gone. I think they have Bolanger with them."

Lina wasted no time in asking Henri if he was sure. He wouldn't be here otherwise.

"What about Bolanger's drunk friend?"

"Don't know. I went to the stable. Bolanger's black gelding is gone. The other horse is there, but no sign of any of the troopers. Bolanger's room in the hotel is empty, too. And no one there has seen Craft or his friend. I checked before I ran here."

"I want to examine the stable," Lina said. "Let's

go!" She turned and Henri grasped her arm. "What?" she demanded, spinning around in exasperation.

Henri was looking down at her feet, and despite the uncertainty of the situation a faint smile played on his face. "Ain't no telling what one might step in at a stable," he said. "Don't you think you should put some shoes on first?"

Lina glanced down to discover that her feet were bare even though she's managed to dress the rest of herself. She gave Henri a wry shake of her head. "Guess it's good I've got you around," she said. "I'll meet you outside the mission gate."

******

Ten minutes later, fully shod, Lina joined Henri outside the mission wall and they hurried through town toward the stable. Santa Annabella was in the process of waking up. A woman swept the boardwalk in front of the mercantile while her husband carried out wares to place on tables in front of the store. Someone turned the sign in the bank's window from "closed" to "open. The local gunsmith propped open the door to his establishment to capture the cool morning breeze. No one was in the stable when Lina and Henri entered, though.

"Did you see the livery man this morning?" Lina asked Henri as she looked around.

"No. And that's a bit odd."

"Maybe someone paid him to disappear," Lina suggested.

"I'll check the saloon later. Let's hope they didn't

hurt him."

Lina stopped in front of a stall that held a dappled gray mare. She pointed at it. "You said Bolanger's friend rode a dappled gray?"

"Yep. And that's the one. Bolanger's gelding was in that empty stall next to her."

"What about the cavalry mounts of Craft and his fellow troopers?"

Henri shrugged. "They weren't in stalls here. No government branded mounts. But there's a corral out back. They might have been there. They aren't now, though. I checked."

Lina closed her eyes, let her other senses take over from sight. She smelled horse manure and animal sweat, the fresher smells of hay and grain, a remnant sour odor of men who'd been drinking. Her ears picked up the swish of horsetails shooing flies, the crunch of hay in toothy mouths. She heard something else — a slow, slow drip.

Opening her eyes and following the sound, she came to the back of the stable. A wide double door stood open there, with the corral Henri had mentioned only a dozen yards away. Plenty of horses ambled around between its fences but not any that cavalry troopers were likely to ride.

The drip sounded again, and Lina and Henri immediately located its source. The stable's loft was above them. Through its floor planks, a viscous fluid slowly filtered, collecting into a red tear before plummeting to the earth below with a faint plop.

"Blood!" Henri exclaimed.

A ladder standing just in front of the back door led to the loft. Lina quickly grasped its rungs and climbed up. She found a body sprawled in the hay. The face was purple from strangulation, but she recognized Benjamin Bolanger's drunken companion from the night before. He'd also been stabbed three times in the chest by what might have been a cavalry saber.

"This explains where Bolanger's friend went," Lina called down to Henri. "One of the troopers must have killed him. Or maybe all of them."

"You want me to get the sheriff?" Henri asked.

"In a minute," Lina said.

She climbed the rest of the way into the loft, knelt beside the body. She felt in the man's pockets, looking for something; she didn't quite know what until she found it. In the inside pocket of his vest lay a thick, hard knot. She plucked it out, held up a jade heart threaded with gold veins. She carried it with her back down the ladder to show to Henri.

"I'd like to know just what these hearts are supposed to mean," Henri said.

"I've got a feeling that if we find out, we'll have a handle on this El Tigre and his raiders."

"And if Craft and his buddies have Bolanger, they've got the only source that might be able to give us what we want."

"Yes. Which means we have to go after them. We can't wait for help from Santa Tomas. Would you go tell the Sheriff about our dead man? Then get our horses ready to travel. We should have remounts as well." She paused as a thought occurred to her. "Might be a good idea to take that dappled gray mare with us. She's been where we want to go. Maybe, at least."

"Right," Henri said. "And you?"

"I'll have the sisters at the convent pack us supplies. And I need to talk to Perla Craft."

"All right," Henri said. "I'll meet you outside the back wall of the convent when I'm ready." He started to turn and Lina grasped his shoulder. Their gazes met.

"Thank you, Henri," Lina said. "I'm sorry to keep dragging you deeper into this mess. But there's no one else here I can trust."

"Whatever you need, Lina. Always."

CHAPTER 14

After sending a last, detailed telegram to Mother Mercy back at Santo Tomas, Lina returned to the convent and spoke to the Mother Superior there. The portly older woman offered to gather and pack all the supplies that would be needed for a long journey. This left Lina free to seek out little Perla Craft. She found the blonde girl in the convent's ample library, looking at a book on the lives of saints.

Perla sat in a well-padded chair with the book open on her lap. She mostly seemed to be studying the pictures. The soiled and tattered yellow dress she'd worn when Lina and Henri found her had been replaced by a frilly white frock donated by a local mother whose daughter had outgrown it. She even had white stockings and shiny black shoes. Her feet did not touch the ground.

Engrossed in the book, or in her thoughts, Perla didn't hear Lina enter the library. "Hello," Lina said.

Perla jumped a little, then blushed a pretty rose

color. "Oh, hi, Sister Catalina."

"Sorry I surprised you," Lina said.

"It's all right."

"I wanted to talk to you. If that's OK?"

"I guess," Perla said.

A lock of blonde hair curled over the girl's left eye and she brushed it back impatiently. Her blue irises looked a little more clouded this morning than they had over the last few days. Lina was pretty sure she knew the reason why.

"Your father," Lina began. "He's gone, isn't he?"

Perla didn't speak. Her left leg kicked and kicked. Lina could see the conflict on the girl's face. She liked all the sisters at the convent. She trusted Lina and wanted to help. But she didn't want to betray her father.

"Your father is not in trouble, Perla," Lina said. "Not with me. I imagine he's gone after your mother. And he's going to need help. From Henri and me. And, you know who. But we need to find him."

Perla stopped kicking. She fiddled with the pages of her book. Finally, though, she nodded at Lina's words and spoke, "He's gonna bring Mama back. And he will. Daddy always does what he says he's going to do."

"Do you know if he went to Fort Bliss first? For help? Or does he plan to go straight after your mother?"

"He said the army wouldn't help him. But...he has a friend."

"The two troopers who were here?"

Perla shook her head. She squirmed a little in her chair. "They had to go back. To the fort. Or they'd get in bad trouble."

"So, you don't know who his 'friend' is?"

Perla shrugged.

"He went straight after your mother?"

"Mexico. He said he had to go to Mexico. I told him about the Tiger Man. I told him he had to be careful. But I think he didn't believe me."

"Well, I believe you," Lina said. "I've seen a picture of this Tiger Man."

"Where?" Perla asked, her face crinkling with curiosity.

"Someone from the town drew it. Someone who I think is with your father now. I'm not sure if that's the 'friend' he mentioned. But this man may be just the person to lead us to your mother. If we can catch up to your father."

"Daddy always rides fast."

Lina smiled. "As do we."

Perla looked down at her book.

"You know," Lina said. "That picture. Of the Tiger Man. I think it's just a man in a mask. Not a real tiger."

Perla's cheeks puffed up with air. She blew it out again. "I know he's not a real tiger," she said. "I'm just a kid but I'm not stupid. But you didn't see him. You don't know what he is. I saw him. Raul saw him. Ask him. I don't think he's just a man either. I'm not sure…if my daddy can beat the Tiger Man. I don't know if anyone can. Even…" she let a solemn gaze rest on Lina, "the Black Rose."

Lina almost smiled. She'd been careful to keep her identities as Sister Catalina Rivera and as the Black Rose separate in front of Perla, and she looked so different when she was in war paint as opposed to her blue habit that only a very discerning eye would pick up any physical similarities. But, obviously, the girl had her suspicions. She was a bright young thing.

"I certainly know you're not stupid, Perla," Lina said finally. "You're a very intelligent young woman. And I assure you that neither I, nor Henri, nor the Black Rose will underestimate this Tiger Man."

Perla nodded, glancing down. Lina heard the drip of a single tear onto the pages of the girl's book. More tears followed and Perla's tiny shoulders shook. Lina stepped quickly across the room, plucked the child from her chair and hugged her tight against a shoulder.

The girl's book fell, banged on the floor and fell open on an image: Saint Ignatius of Antioch being fed to the lions in the Roman Coliseum.

******

Henri Moissant sat his gelding outside the back wall of the convent at Santa Annabella. A whistle caught his attention and he looked up as the Black Rose materialized on top of the wall. She tossed him two sets of heavily laden saddlebags, then slid over the wall and dropped to the ground.

Henri draped the saddlebags across his horse

while Lina stuck her foot in the stirrup of the Appaloosa's saddle and swung aboard with a swirl of her cape. She glanced at him. It was hard to read her feelings behind the black and red war paint that crossed her face, but Henri thought she was upset.

"Is everything OK?" he asked.

"Fine," she said. "Let's ride!"

She booted the Appaloosa forward and turned the animal to the south, heading off in a gallop. Henri followed on his gelding, leading two other horses behind him on trailing reins, a line back dun and the dappled gray mare that Benjamin Bolanger's now-dead companion had ridden.

For a while, the two riders pushed on swiftly. Henri was content to follow, to watch Lina's athletic form sway in the saddle in front of him as she adjusted instinctively to every movement of her mount. Lina was lithe and beautiful, aware and intelligent, a superb equestrian.

And superb at everything else she did, Henri had to admit. He knew he was falling in love with this woman, though he'd been careful to hide it from her. The Black Rose did not need the distraction of love, not with the risks she so often took. Besides, she was also his friend and he valued that very highly. Friendship was often more important than love when survival was at stake. He'd learned that in the Rocky Mountains.

After half an hour, though, Lina slowed her Appaloosa to a trot and Henri drew up beside her. He glanced over but did not speak. She gave him a nod.

"It's Perla," she said finally. "I'm…afraid for her. Her parents. She could lose them both."

"Maybe we can get there in time," Henri said.

"Joseph Craft has a head start and a guide. If he can get Bolanger to talk. I suspect he will. On the other hand, we don't even know where we're going. We'll have to try to pick up the trail at that lava field. But it's old now. And if there's been any rain…"

"We'll do our best," Henri said. "It's all we *can* do."

"Yes," Lina said. "We'll do our *best*." She almost spat the last word.

"There's one other thing we might ought to do on our way," Henri said.

"What?"

"Where we found that sacrifice. And buried the four warriors who tried to ambush us…."

"The jade hearts," Lina said, catching Henri's point immediately. "We didn't think to check whether the warriors carried them or not."

"It might be important," Henri said. "And we'll pass close by. This…'El Tigre,' or whoever it is who commands these raiders, seems to place importance on those stones. We need to understand why."

"Agreed," Lina said. She lifted her Appaloosa to a faster trot and for a while there was no more talking.

******

Lina and Henri rode cautiously down toward the site where a couple of days earlier they'd discovered an altar and a sacrifice, and where they'd fought their way out of an ambush by four strange warriors.

Even from a distance they could see the area had been disturbed. When they reached it, they found that all five graves, the victim's and the ambushers', had been dug up. No bodies were to be seen.

"So much for discovering any more of those gem hearts," Henri said.

A plethora of tracks surrounded the site — horses both shod and unshod and footprints ranging from bare to moccasined to booted.

"Your El Tigre must have sent someone to check on his little trap and found it sprung," Lina said.

"Not *my* El Tigre," Henri said. "I just don't know what else to call him."

"Murdering bandit works fine for me," Lina replied dryly.

"Tigre is shorter," Henri said. "But yes, it was probably him that did this."

Lina stared at Henri. "Has to be him," she said. "Or someone who follows his orders. Some other party might have dug up the graves looking for loot, but they wouldn't have taken the bodies with them."

"Maybe they dug themselves up and walked off," Henri murmured.

Lina gave him the stink eye. "Don't joke about such things."

"Who's jokin'," Henri said, with a smile that indicated he was indeed joking. He added, though, "This whole situation is weird enough to raise the hackles."

"I'll agree with you there," Lina said.

She studied the empty graves while she listened

to the lonely wind carrying dust. Something made her turn her head and glance back along the trail they'd covered. Heat waves shimmered in the heavy air under the gold shield of the sun. Her eyes burned with sweat. A few miles off, a thirty-foot tall dust devil churned its way across the barren land. As it passed, a wink of light from the low hills behind it caught in Lina's eyes, then was gone.

"I think we're being followed," Lina said.

"Not really surprised," Henri replied. "But maybe we better keep moving. Stay ahead of them."

"Or find a place to let them catch up," Lina said. "So we'll know whether we need to kill them or not."

Henri had no response to that but was ready for whatever might come.

CHAPTER 15

They reached the lava field a few hours later and camped for the night. As they'd feared, the tracks they'd followed weeks before were largely obscured by now. There must have been some rain and other riders and critters such as deer and cattle had passed this way. The only thing they could do was stay close to the edge of the lava as they rode and hope the raiders they followed had continued along it like before.

It couldn't be far to the Rio Grande border with Mexico. Both travelers were sure they'd have to cross that border to find El Tigre and his troop of bandits. The army might not want to send men into Mexico because of political reasons, but Lina and Henri had no compunction about ignoring the border. They did have an understandable reluctance to let themselves be surprised by whoever was following them along the way.

After hobbling the horses and moving them toward the lava field and away from the campsite, they built a fire and heated coffee and stew for supper. After, they rolled into their blankets as if to sleep. Lina took off her cape and draped it over her bed, but only lay beneath it until full dark. As soon as night shadows cloaked them, the two slid from their blankets, stuffed saddlebags underneath to simulate sleeping bodies, then crept into the lava field itself where there were ample outcroppings to hide behind.

Several hours passed; the two took turns dozing. Lina was on sentry when stealthy sounds arose from the dark desert landscape beyond their camp. She dropped a hand to Henri's shoulder. He awoke instantly and silently, rising to kneel beside her. Both had rifles, Henri his Sharps and Lina her Winchester.

The campfire had burned almost to embers. The last bits of flickering light created an impression that the bedrolls shifted occasionally, making them look even more like sleeping people than they had before. Only a sliver of moon cast down any light and it and the uncaring stars were often obscured by drifting clouds. Lina detected no movement but the sounds from the night inched closer, coming from several locations.

Not Comanche, Lina thought. *They wouldn't make so much noise.*

An owl that wasn't an owl hooted. Bullets immediately slammed into the camp. The bedrolls puffed dust. The coffeepot went spinning. Ricochets spanged off into darkness. The attackers continued to pour fire into their targets, an act of savage over-kill — if there had been any victims in the bedrolls to *be* killed.

Using the almost continuous muzzle flashes to guide their aim, Lina and Henri both fired at the same time. Lina swung her Winchester to a fresh target and fired again. Henri's Sharps was a single shot; he dropped it and drew his two Peacemakers. Two men were already screaming in pain as Henri began emptying his revolvers into every shadow that might contain an enemy.

All shooting from the desert stopped. Lina and Henri held their own fire. But the night wasn't silent. One man continued to scream; another moaned long and low. Crawling sounds came from the direction of the moans. Lina pumped three quick slugs from her Winchester into those sounds. A sigh rattled in the darkness, then melted away.

A bullet whined off the lava near Lina's head, stinging her cheek with stone splinters. Henri had gotten one of his Peacemakers reloaded and emptied it again toward the shooter. A curse followed, but it sounded mad rather than hurt.

Someone yelled in English for the screaming man to shut up. The yell was followed an instant later by a shot that must have been shielded in some way because there was no discernable muzzle flash. The screams cut off. The night fell silent.

Lina and Henri split up. Lina went to the right, working her way carefully through the outcroppings of lava. Tomorrow, she'd have a few cuts and scrapes from the sharp black rock, but for to-night it provided great cover. Reaching the edge of the lava field, she slipped back into the desert proper and began to dart from mesquite bush to mesquite bush, circling out into the desert and back to come in behind the enemy that sought to murder from ambush.

A real owl swept over her head on soft wings; coyotes yipped in the distance. She heard small rodents nosing through the rocks and bushes but nothing bigger that might represent her enemies. Then a faint scent brushed her nostrils — drifting gun smoke and scorched wadding. With focused patience, she inched closer to that scent.

Gunfire erupted about a hundred yards to her north. Lina recognized the sound of Henri's Peace-makers. A man cried out, high-pitched in pain. It wasn't Henri. Almost immediately, Lina heard a big body crashing through the brush. A man burst into the open a dozen feet in front of her, indistinct in the gloom. One of the attackers was running, afraid of dying or just figuring to cut his losses.

Lina could have shot him but wanted a prisoner to question. Who were these men? Why had they tried to kill her and Henri? Her right hand dropped to the handle of her urumi. She snapped the sword belt free, but the man was too far away. She drew the flexible blade back behind her, whipped it forward and let it fly.

The urumi spun through the air like a bizarre steel-edged bola and caught the fleeing man in the legs. He went down, shouting in shock and pain. Lina leaped toward him. The man twisted onto his back. His gun had gone flying but he grabbed for a knife at his belt. Lina snapped the butt of her Winchester into his face, knocking him unconscious.

She soon had him on his belly with his arms bound behind him by his own belt. The urumi still entangled his legs and would cut them deeply if he tried to move. He wouldn't get free of that without the use of his hands.

Lina couldn't describe the feeling but the night felt empty of danger to her now. She needed to find Henri. Still moving cautiously, she snuck toward where she'd heard her companion shooting. Ten minutes passed. Henri called out low:

"Lina?"

"Here," she called back.

Henri came gracefully through the brush, joined her. "Found three of them," he said. "All dead. Thought I heard a fourth one running off in your direction."

"Met him," Lina replied. "Got him tied up. We can ask him some questions. Maybe we've got our own guide for a change. Like Joseph Craft has Bolanger."

"Maybe," Henri agreed. "Pretty sure it's the others who were with Bolanger when they set that trap with the kids and the land mines. Don't think there were more than four."

"That makes the most sense," Lina agreed.

Remaining wary but moving with more confidence, Henri and Lina returned to their camp and built up the fire. They dragged the three dead men into the light. One was dressed like your average Texas cowboy. Another resembled a peasant who'd walked right in off a dirt-poor Mexican farm. The third had the waxed mustachios, ornamented vest and crossed bandoliers of a bandito.

"El Tigre employees all kinds," Lina said.

"So it seems," Henri agreed. "I figure we shot all three. But that one." He pointed at the man dressed like a peasant. "One of his own shot him in the back of the head and did the final killing. That's not from our guns."

"The one who wouldn't stop screaming," Lina added.

"Right. Let's go get the one you tied up."

Lina plucked her cape off her bedroll and swung it around her shoulders, tsk-tsking at the new holes she'd have to sew up in the garment, then led the way. They found the man lying on his belly. He didn't appear to have moved or struggled against his bonds. He shouldn't still be unconscious from the blow of her Winchester, though.

"OK," Lina said loudly. "Your friends are dead but you don't have to be if you tell us what you know."

No response came. And no movement. Lina frowned, started toward the prisoner. Henri caught her arm.

"Something's wrong," Henri said.

Lina lifted her Winchester into firing position. Henri drew his Colts. They spread out, walking in carefully on the bound man. He still didn't move.

Lina stepped close enough to poke him with her rifle barrel. Nothing. She poked harder. The man's flesh was yielding, unresponsive.

"He's dead," she said. "But I don't know how."

Henri holstered his pistols, struck a match and crouched by the man's side. He grasped a limp shoulder and rolled the fellow over. Something scuttled from beneath him and Henri leaped back with a curse, dropping his match.

"A scorpion," Lina said.

Henri lit another match, leaned close to the man again. The fellow's face and neck were discolored and swollen. Two more yellow-black scorpions crawled out of his shirt and dropped to the earth before waddling off into the brush.

"Must have been…a whole nest of them," Henri said, rising to his feet and spitting.

Lina shook her head as she leaned over and pulled her urumi loose from around the corpse's legs. "No, there weren't any here when I tied him up. And even a dozen scorpion stings shouldn't have killed him so fast."

Henri shrugged. "I don't know what to tell you. There's no tracks near him except for ours."

Lina looked around. The moon was hidden behind clouds but starlight limned the bushes. It showed no threat. A breeze rattled through the mesquite and fluttered the cactus. There were no other sounds, no smells. She felt no sense of "presence," which she sometimes got when other people were nearby, but the night desert certainly did not feel friendly. Though it was far from chilly, she briefly shivered.

"Another weird thing to raise the hackles," Lina said. "I'm getting tired of such."

"You and me both," agreed Henri. He leaned down and grabbed one leg of the dead man. "Let's get this one back to the fire with the others and see what we can see."

Lina slung her Winchester under one arm and grabbed the man's other boot. "And after, we'll burn them," she said. "I don't want anyone digging them up like they did the last bunch we killed. Who knows what sick rituals this El Tigre might have in his arsenal? We give him *nothing* more to work with. He's got too much already."

CHAPTER 16

Lina and Henri didn't burn the dead. There wasn't enough wood in the local desert to build that hot of a fire. They searched the bodies carefully and laid aside their finds. It was getting close to dawn by then and the sky was graying. They carried the corpses into the lava field to a big lava blister that had broken open to reveal a dark, tomb-like hole. After hauling the dead men inside, they covered the opening with loose blocks of black rock.

Returning to their camp, they studied the little trove of objects they'd uncovered. The pile included weapons such as rifles, pistols and knives, a few greenbacks and some varied coinage, two wallets without any identification, a mouth harp, a plug of chewing tobacco, some rolling tobacco with papers, matches, a rabbit's foot, a picture of what appeared to be a prostitute in a locket, a green glass eye even though the man who carried it had owned two brown ones of his own and exactly one jade heart with veins of filigreed gold.

"I was expecting them all to have the hearts," Henri said.

"Me too," Lina replied.

"Kind of odd," Henri said, "that the only fellow with a heart was the one we didn't shoot, the one the scorpions got. You reckon he was the leader?"

"I'm sure he was. And leaders are *usually* the last ones to get shot."

"Guess you're right there. What next?"

Lina glanced up at the sky. Light was coming swiftly. "We ride on," she said.

Leaning down, she picked up the jade heart. Almost as an afterthought, she also plucked up the glass eye and the locket with the picture of the prostitute. Henri arched an eyebrow at her as she straightened.

"The eye and the locket are the kind of things people remember," she explained. "Might help us identify these men later. Help us find out where they came from. If we need to."

Henri nodded. "Good thinking." For his part, he picked up the matches and the rolling tobacco and papers. "You know these boys got horses somewhere. They might have left a guard with them."

"Horses yes," Lina said. "I doubt the guard. They came after us with everything they had. We'll give a quick look around for their mounts before we continue south. But let's get some food in us now and then get loaded. I want to move!"

******

In a shallow arroyo marked by a line of cactus, Lina and Henri found the mounts of the men who'd tried to murder them, four saddle horses and two more loaded with supply packs. A search of the gear revealed no more jade hearts. They took the canteens and some coffee and grub. Henri found a bag of .45 shells that would fit his Peacemakers. They stripped the animals of saddles and packs and turned them loose. There was no way they could herd a whole pack of horses with them and the animals would find their way to whatever home they'd known before.

Going south along the line of the lava field, they noted that the rough, darkly porous rock began to bury itself beneath soil and dust that had been washed or blown in from elsewhere. Soon the lava completely disappeared under the desert. Shortly after that, as they came over a rise thick with mesquite, they glimpsed the Rio Grande below them. Brush and grass grew tangled along the waterway, much of it yellow-brown from lack of rain.

The river was shallow but running clear. A few fish finned their way along the deeper pools. Lina and Henri let their horses water themselves as they forded. Hardly any bank marked the Rio Grande here, only sandbars that the horses left deep, wet tracks in as they crossed. Just like that, they were in Mexico. It didn't look or feel any different.

"Here's where the hard part begins," Henri said as they paused to take stock. "We could follow that lava field and have a good idea we were traveling in the same general direction as El Tigre and his bandits. But once they crossed the river, they could have turned in any direction. This is where we really needed to have that Bolanger as a guide. And we don't. So, what now?"

Lina had been studying their surroundings. "We ask whoever lives beneath the crows," she said.

Henri raised both eyebrows. "The...what? The heat getting to you, is it?"

Lina pointed to the sky to the south. Henri's gaze followed the thrust of her finger. A few miles ahead, he saw a scattering of black shapes rioting back and forth in the air. They were too small to be buzzards, too large to be blackbirds. Though he couldn't hear any identifying calls this far away, he knew what he was seeing.

"Crows," he said.

"Yes," Lina said. "And from how they're acting, there's food around that area, but something is making them too nervous to settle. I expect it's people."

Henri said nothing, just booted his horse into motion toward their newest goal.

A short ride later, they came to a stream and a small wood. The stream burbled up from a hidden spring, filled a pool worn out over years, then rushed away to the east as if on an important errand no human could fathom. Oak and willow trees clustered close to the banks, their leaves fluttering with the movements of small birds. A small, grassy meadow lay dotted with the pink, yellow and white bursts of wildflowers. A roadrunner leaped away almost beneath their feet but the crows that had led them here had moved on.

Henri spotted a shack hidden among pin oaks some seventy-five yards back from the stream. It looked to be made of wattle and daub, which was not a common building material for this part of the world. While Henri watered the horses, Lina crossed the stream and approached the shack. She moved cautiously. Whoever lived here might think they owned the water and graze. They might not like trespassers and Lina didn't want to get shot, or to shoot anyone without good reason.

"Hello, the house," Lina called. "Anyone there?"

Three scrawny guinea hens scratched and pecked at the ground in front of the shack. They startled at Lina's voice and scattered, then began the obnoxious clucking of their breed, which grated on the ears like sandpaper.

"Hello!" Lina called again.

The door of the shack stood open, revealing a shadowy interior. Lina heard the patter of footsteps and a striking young woman materialized in the doorway. She was barefoot and wore a draped garment of purple-dyed cotton. Lina could not guess at her ancestry. She had deeply dark hair, thickly curled and wild enough to suggest a blackberry bramble around her face.

Her skin was strangely mottled, with large copper patches next to paler splotches of either light pink or almost pure white. Some of the splotches were regular enough to look painted on while others were as irregular as spilled milk. Lina at first thought the marks might be tattoos, but as the woman stepped fully into the sunlight it became clear they were natural blemishes on her skin, albeit something Lina had never seen before.

"What is it you want?" the woman asked, her voice rough and at odds with her appearance.

"My friend and I are passing through," Lina explained. "We want only water for ourselves and our horses and a few yards of ground to cast our blankets on. We'll be gone in the morning."

"You are welcome. But with one requirement."

"And that is?"

"You both join me for the evening meal. I have so little company here."

Lina wanted to smile but kept her lips taut. Normally in meeting a stranger under such circumstances, she would have preferred to eat the food they'd brought with them. She did not know this woman, or where her loyalties and sentiments might lie. But they needed information and this might be the perfect opportunity to learn about this area and the people who passed through. She'd wanted a chance to talk to whoever lived here. It was better to be asked than to have to ask and arouse suspicion. They'd just have to be cautious.

"We will," Lina said. "Tell me when."

The woman gazed up at the sky and said, "It's about an hour until dark. Come to the cabin just before last light."

Lina nodded. "Thank you," she said. "It'll be good to have food we don't have to prepare ourselves."

The woman chuckled. "Oh, you will pay for your food, of course."

Lina frowned. The woman laughed again. "Pay with news of the outside world," she said. "That's the only coin I require." She turned away and shut the door behind her.

Lina returned to Henri, explained to him about their dinner invitation and the woman who had proffered it. They watered the horses and staked them out on some grass for grazing. The evening gathered, painted away the sunset with black.

CHAPTER 17

The day's last sliver of red light was bleeding away when Lina and Henri knocked on the door to the shack in the woods. It opened. The woman Lina had met earlier stood there. She still wore her clinging robe of purple but had paired it with a white lace shawl. Button-up boots encased her feet now. Lina nodded by way of greeting; Henri doffed his faded felt hat.

"Welcome," the woman said. "I was afraid you'd waited too long."

"Too long?" Henri asked.

The woman's eyes were much lighter than Lina had imagined they'd be — almost a yellow amber. Those eyes focused on Henri, drilled into him.

"Until it was completely dark," she said.

"Is that a problem?" Lina asked, frowning.

"Not necessarily," the woman said.

Lina was about to ask for further clarification of the woman's meaning but she turned away with a:

"Please come in and shut the door."

Henri stepped inside; Lina followed and closed the door. The woman swayed across the room to the fireplace and picked up a wooden stirring spoon. Two cast iron pots were suspended on standing iron cranes above the crackling flames. Both bubbled and wafted delicious smells into the air.

Without turning her head from her pots, the woman offered a lazy gesture with her hand that encompassed most of the rest of the room. "Please seat yourselves," she said. "Supper will be ready soon."

Lina gazed around. The shack was a single large, squarish room, although a slanted ladder at one side led upward to what was probably a sleeping loft. Board planks covered the floor, dotted here and there with woven grass rugs. The walls were peeled logs pierced with nails from which a strange mixture of materials hung. Some were tools. Many were useful no doubt — an axe, hammer, scythe. Others were so rusted they looked to have been dug up out of Rio Grande mud.

Displayed weapons included a shotgun with a broken stock, an old blunderbuss that might have ridden across the ocean with the Conquistadors and a range of edged weapons from spears to machetes. Other items were interspersed with the tools and weapons — pieces of pottery with images painted or carved on them, odd shaped sticks of driftwood, the cleaned white skulls of birds and coyotes and cattle and other critters.

A heavy wooden table, badly scarred and black-ened from years of use, squatted in the center of the room. What looked like a solid silver candelabrum with seven lit candles of golden beeswax occupied the center of the table. Three places had been set for the diners. The plates were of fine porcelain while the utensils — knife, fork, spoon — were plain tin. A wooden bowl sat next to each plate.

Lina moved to the setting at the left of the table's head while Henri took the one on the right. This allowed them both to keep one eye on the door and the other on their host. Lina carefully examined her bowl and utensils to make sure no residue of any-thing unusual clung to them. She saw Henri doing the same. It was a precaution against poisoning. They had no reason to suspect the woman of that but wariness became a habit.

A basket covered in yellow cloth sat on the table; Lina smelled fresh bread. A large golden bowl next to the basket held a fern and a variety of stones and feathers. There was also a tortoise shell, a rattle-snake's rattle and a feathered mask the likes of which Lina had never seen before. It was carved from some heavy brown wood and had large, slitted eyes, a long nose, and prominent lips pursed into a kiss.

Finally, there was a tin pitcher of water and three cups. Lina poured for herself and Henri, then took a tiny sip of the water. It was clear and pure, with no contaminants. She took a bigger swallow, enjoying the feel of her mouth and tongue rehydrating after a long dry day.

The woman cooking at the fire turned the two cranes holding her pots further away from the flames. She came to the table and picked up the three bowls, then used a dipper to fill them with fragrant liquid from the pot. She brought two of the bowls to Lina and Henri and set them on the plates in front of them before returning to fetch her own.

"Soup to begin," she said, after seating herself. "And." She pulled back the cloth on the basket to reveal a pile of rolls.

Lina hesitated to see if there was any ritual to perform before eating, but the woman merely picked up her spoon and dipped into her bowl. She blew lightly on the large spoonful before sliding it between her lips. The smell was intense but stimulating. Saliva burst in Lina's mouth.

Comforted by the gusto with which their host slurped her soup, Lina and Henri followed her example. Lina tasted salt, egg, onion, sage and a few other ingredients she recognized but couldn't name. It was delicious. Her stomach rumbled and she spooned more into her mouth. She reached for a roll and the woman pushed a small porcelain container toward her.

"Butter," she said. "I have a few goats. I make it."

Lina took the top off the container and used her knife to spread some of the butter on her roll. Henri took two rolls and slathered them with butter. They both moved into their eating.

"May I ask your names?" the woman said after a bit.

"Henri is mine."

"And I'm called the Black Rose," Lina said.

"Ah," the woman said. "A thorny bloom of the night."

"Nothing so poetic," Lina said. "But what do we call you?"

"Painted Crow."

"Are you...Indian?" Henri asked.

"I'm no one thing. I'm many things."

"And you live out here," Henri waved a hand full of roll around, "alone?"

"No people trouble me."

"Is that because you have power?" Lina asked.

"Everyone has power," Painted Crow said. "Whether guns, or knives, or fists, or...knowledge."

"What if you meet someone with *more* power?" Lina asked.

Painted Crow's amber eyes studied Lina. "Are you speaking of yourself?" she asked.

Lina was surprised. "I have no power. Other than the guns and knives and fists you mentioned."

Painted Crow laughed. It was a pleasant laugh, more feminine and merrier than her speaking voice. It brought a frown to Lina's face, though and Painted Crow saw it and sought to explain.

"You can't believe that, honestly. You have great power. But," the woman's smile faded, "you also carry a curse." She glanced around at Henri, to include him in her words. "You both do. And they are not ones I can lift."

Lina saw that Henri did not seem particularly

surprised at Painted Crow's words. She was and was about to protest when she heard a creaking sound from overhead, either from the shack's sleeping loft, or from its roof. She looked up; her hand fell to the hilt of her urumi.

The front wall of the shack boomed as something heavy struck it viciously from the other side.

CHAPTER 18

Henri leaped to his feet with an oath, dropping his buttered roll and drawing his Colts. His gaze locked on the front door as a low sound, something between a moan and a snarl, followed the booming impact against the outside of the shack.

Painted Crow also leaped up, but stepped in front of Henri.

"Don't shoot!" she pleaded. "He can't get in."

"What can't get in?" Henri demanded.

Another impact rattled the door itself. Henri reached to push the woman aside but she backed up, keeping her distance and staying between the man and the door. Her hands were up, palms out.

"I tell you he can't get in. We're safe in here!"

"Henri!" Lina said. She too had risen and stepped around the table. Her gaze focused on Painted Crow. "You better explain," she said.

Henri's gaze darted to Lina and then back to the front door. He licked his lips and lowered his pistols slightly.

"Explain!" Lina said again to Painted Crow.

The woman dropped her hands. She glanced at the door but everything was silent. She looked back at Lina. "You won't believe me."

"I'll hear it anyway," Lina snapped. Her hand still rested on the hilt of her sword-belt.

"Local people call it the 'beast,'" Painted Crow said. "But it's not."

Henri gave a faint gasp; his eyes sought Lina. She met his gaze, nodded. To Painted Crow, she said:

"You're saying it's a man?"

"Not a man. Just not a beast. Not exactly."

"Some kind of shape changer?"

Painted Crow heard the skepticism in Lina's voice. "I said you wouldn't believe me."

"You're right. Whatever it was out there, that moan sounded like an angry animal. Nothing more exotic than that."

"Might have been a panther," Henri added. "I've heard them make such sounds."

"Really?" Painted Crow asked. "The sound! When he struck the wall. How high on the wall was it? Did you hear?"

"Not high enough to indicate a beast standing on its hind legs," Lina said. "But maybe we'll just have a look." She started across the planks toward the door.

Painted Crow stepped quickly in Lina's way. "Don't!" she commanded. Her eyes brightened. "If you let him in, we won't be able to stop him." Before Lina could say anything in response, the woman spun toward the front of the cabin and lifted her hands, "Go from here!" she shouted.

Lina felt surprise on her face. Henri showed it too and moved his guns to cover the woman as well as the front door.

Painted Crow lowered her hands. "He's going now," she said.

Lina turned her head, listening. Maybe she heard the sound of clawed feet padding away. Maybe she didn't.

"So, you protect it?" Lina asked. "Why?"

"I protected us."

"You didn't want Henri to shoot it," Lina countered.

Painted Crow shook her head. "Bullets won't hurt him. But they'll enrage him. He might have broken through the door. And if he were angry enough he wouldn't respond to my commands."

"What about the horses?" Henri blurted. "A panther might go after the horses."

"He won't harm your mounts," Painted Crow said, straightening her body and speaking as if she were defending her child. "And I told you, he's not an animal!"

Lina shook her head. "Do you expect us to fall for this farce?"

"What are you talking about?" Painted Crow demanded. "I'm telling you the truth."

"Henri," Lina said. "Put her in her chair."

Henri turned his guns on the woman, gestured toward the table where they'd all been sitting moments before.

Painted crow chuckled, though it sounded forced. "You won't shoot me. You are not such barbarians."

Lina drew her urumi free, shook it out on the plank floor. "Henri might not shoot you but I'll make some marks with this. Sit!"

Painted Crow's pupils dilated. She seemed to consider resistance and decide against it. Walking back to the dinner table, she dropped into her chair. Lina jerked a length of twine off a wall display and pulled the woman's hands behind her and bound them through the slats of the chair.

"And this is how gringos repay hospitality!" Painted Crow spat.

Lina ignored her. "Watch her," she said to Henri. "And if you don't want to kill her, shoot her in the leg."

Henri nodded. "What are you going to do?"

Lina pulled one of the lit candles out of the candelabrum on the table. "Have a look upstairs," she said. "I thought I heard something there just a bit ago."

"You—" Painted Crow began, then stopped herself and bit her lip.

Lina strode over to the ladder that she suspected led to a sleeping loft. She went up it cautiously, found that she was correct as her candle revealed a small twelve by twelve space tucked under the eaves. It contained a low bed and a small table with an unlit lantern standing on it. Some wooden crates had been turned on their sides against the wall to serve as bookshelves and storage for clothes. Otherwise, the room was empty.

Bent over to avoid the rafters, Lina slipped over

to the bed. There didn't appear to be anything under it but dust, and nothing on it but blankets and pillows. On an impulse, she lay down on the bed and glanced up at the ceiling. A smile flitted across her lips. A broad, flat piece of wood had been nailed to the ceiling. Drawn upon it was a map.

The Rio Grande was clearly recognizable, as were the creek and wood where they'd found Painted Crow's shack. Other lines represented mountains, hills and streams that lay to the south. Several unusual symbols marked the map, including one that reminded her of the stylized skull of a big cat such as a panther or jaguar. She noted that one very carefully and memorized every curve and landmark she could.

Trouble erupted from downstairs. "Stop!" Henri yelled. A shot cracked. The front door slammed open

Lina rolled from the bed and leaped toward the ladder. A glance over the side showed Henri standing alone in the middle of the shack with a smoking Peacemaker in his hand. There was no sign of Painted Crow but the front door stood agape, letting in the scent of night blooming flowers.

Lina swung down the ladder, dropped the last few feet to land with a thud on the planks. Henri glanced over at her, his face full of anguish.

"Sorry," he said. "She managed to get out of her bonds. By the time I noticed she was halfway across the room."

"And the shot?"

Henri sighed. "I fired into the wall, hoping she'd stop. I couldn't...shoot her."

"I understand," Lina said. "My fault really. Should have tied her better."

"Reckon she's pretty good at escaping," Henri said. "What did you find upstairs?"

"Something important but I'll have to tell you later. We better get back to the horses. She might try to run them off."

"The Appaloosa will kill her if she gets too close," Henri said. "Or anyone else that isn't one of us." He holstered his pistol and quickly moved toward the door. "There is that panther, though. Or whatever it was."

"It was a man who banged on the door," Lina said. "One that works with her."

"But that moaning?" Henri protested. "It didn't sound quite human. Certainly not like a man. And I've heard panthers in the mountains do something similar."

"She did it. Now stay with me," Lina said. "Stay close. They might have a gun out there."

She darted through the door and to the left. A thick group of bushes grew at the edge of the shack's rickety porch. Lina ducked behind them, with Henri right behind her.

"No shots," Lina said. "But they might still be able to strike at us from cover. Maybe with a bow. Or a spear."

"What did you mean by 'she did it'?" Henri asked in a whisper.

"The moaning was hers. I could see her throat vibrating when it happened. She can throw her voice. I've seen it done before."

"But you said it sounded like an animal."

"I lied," Lina said. "To throw her off. Listen!"

Lina parted her lips; her cheeks puffed full of air. A rumble of sound purled up from her chest, bled into the air. A savage growl fluttered leaves on the bushes they hid behind. Lina followed it with a deep, lion-like grunt that would have scared Henri out of his boots if he hadn't been squatting beside her as she made it. It scared him a little even though he watched her doing it.

"There," Lina said, smiling, "maybe that'll give them something to think about. Let them wonder if there's a real beast here. One that's worse than theirs."

CHAPTER 19

The moon made barely a sliver in the sky and at times disappeared completely behind clouds. Lina and Henri crept slowly through the woods and across the stream to reach the grassy area where their horses were staked. Pausing at wood's edge, they stared out at the dark bulks of the four horses grazing in the field.

"They didn't try to ambush us coming out of the shack," Lina whispered, "This is the only other place it could happen. And I feel them out there."

"But how many?" Henri whispered back. "And do any of them have guns?"

"We'll know soon enough. We can't wait here all night."

"You want to split up?"

"Not this time," Lina said. "We'll circle the field, take out anyone we find."

Henri nodded, but before they could move a voice called out from the dark.

"I see you, Black Rose!" Painted Crow yelled. "Got you in my sights. And you too, Henri." She laughed. "Though I appreciate you not shooting me when you had the chance, I'm not sure I can return the favor."

Both Lina and Henri remained completely still. The woman *wanted* them to move, to give themselves away. They weren't about to do it. Lina pointed to the north and made a slashing motion. Henri understood. The voice may have sounded like it came from that direction but it was almost certainly a lie. Painted Crow would use her vocal talents to throw them off. When they finally did move, the companions headed south around the field, keeping to a low squat and traveling only inches at a time.

"*He* sees you too," Painted Crow shouted. "The Beast!"

This time, the voice seemed to arise from the middle of the grassy field. An instant later, a loud snarl erupted from the woods behind Lina and Henri. They didn't bother to turn and though the horses in the field perked their ears up at the sound they didn't act unduly alarmed.

"The horses agree with you that it's not a real panther," Henri whispered. "She has the sound but not the smell, I guess."

"We still have to find her and shut her up. Before she does something more to run them off."

Keeping their hands close to their weapons, Lina and Henri continued working their way to the south. The horses were intensely alert, their nostrils flared as they sniffed the air. They were smelling something besides Lina and Henri, another human who was a stranger to them. The Appaloosa was just ahead. Its white patterned rump shone under the rind of the moon.

Lina grabbed Henri's arm; they both froze. A clot of shadow rose from the ground a dozen feet from the Appaloosa and leaped toward the stake that tethered it. The big stallion startled but did not try to flee. It spun toward the charging figure and reared, ripping its picket from the ground. Its front hooves lashed out.

The shadow wasn't prepared for the stallion to break free. It tried to dodge and didn't quite manage to. The hooves connected; the shadowy figure went flying, struck the ground and rolled. It didn't rise.

Lina sensed movement behind her; she spun around. A man-shaped shadow lunged toward her with a spear. She swayed aside, caught the shaft of the weapon with both hands and drove it into the ground next to her feet. The sudden violent twisting of the spear tore the handle out of the attacker's hands. He grabbed for a knife instead, but by this time Henri had turned and swung up his Colt.

The mountain man fired point-blank into the attacker's chest, igniting the fellow's cotton shirt around the impact site. The man cried out, stumbled forward. Lina half rose from her crouch, slapped her palms against the man's stomach and leg and flipped him over the bushes where they hid into the meadow. He came down with a thud and didn't rise either.

Running footsteps sounded from Lina's right. Next came the splash of water as someone trampled swiftly through the creek and away from the field.

"Painted Crow," Lina said to Henri. She exploded from her crouch into pursuit of the fleeing woman. "See to the horses and the camp," she called over her shoulder. "I'll get her!"

Henri shouted something Lina didn't hear. It didn't matter. He would do what she asked him to. She could hear footsteps and panting breaths just in front of her. She began to gain. The other woman was fast but was wearing a skirt that snagged at brush and slowed her ever so slightly. Lina bundled her own cape around her arm to keep it from doing the same.

The shack was barely fifty yards away. They reached a lane through the trees, with Painted Crow only a few lengths ahead of Lina. The woman cast a glance behind her. Lina caught the brief shine of her face. When Painted Crow turned to run even harder, Lina cut away from the lane, leaped a short bush and barreled on toward the shack.

The shack's door stood open; Painted Crow reached it two steps ahead of Lina. She hurled herself through, slammed the door behind her but had no time to fasten it. Lina smashed the door out of the way with her shoulder and crossed the threshold. Painted Crow grabbed the broken-stocked shotgun off the wall and spun toward Lina. But the Black Rose had drawn her urumi. She whipped the tip forward, caught the barrel of the shotgun and drove it aside.

A shot exploded, tore a hole in the wall. Lina was upon Painted Crow then. She punched with her left hand, with her fingers extended and stiff. The blow hammered into the soft hollow of Painted Crow's neck, knocking her backward. The woman dropped the shotgun as she grabbed her throat with both hands.

Lina swept her leg out, kicked the other woman's feet from under her. Painted Crow crashed down on her back with a loud, "oomph!" Dust spurted up. Lina stood over her and drew back her sword-belt for a strike.

Painted Crow threw up her hands. "No!" she croaked.

"Tell me where to find him!" Lina snapped.

"I...I—"

"The Beast!" Lina said. "The real one. You know who I mean. I've heard him called El Tigre."

Painted Crow shook her head back and forth. "I don't know what you're talking about. I made up the Beast. I don't know the name El Tigre."

"You're lying. I can't allow that. Too many people I care about depend on me finding the truth."

The woman looked stricken. "I can't. I dare not!"

"If you're worried about him killing you, you ought to worry about me killing you first."

Painted Crow's eyes were like amber pools aswim with flashing thoughts. "No," she finally said. "Kill me if you must."

Lina changed her tactics. "What were you hoping to accomplish here?" She nodded around the room.

"Inviting us in? Feeding us? Was the food poisoned? Maybe the drinks after the meal? Why the ruse with the 'beast?'"

"No! I wouldn't...poison anyone. The main dish. I would have given you...something to make you see. To make you understand the Beast. But the others; they revealed themselves too soon."

"Given us something?" Lina asked. "A drug no doubt. Peyote maybe?"

"Yes."

"And that would have made us believe...what? That the Beast was real?"

"He *is* real. You, also, have power. If you were to believe in him. To serve him!"

"Never," Lina said. "Not anyone who hurts the innocent."

"He does not!"

Lina eased her grip on the sword-belt. "You're in love with him! Aren't you?"

The woman's eyes slowly lost their outraged flare. She nodded. "He's...magnificent."

"How so?"

Painted Crow hesitated, then spoke haltingly, choosing her words carefully to avoid anything that could be used against a man she loved. "He...came from nowhere. He led the people. Led us against the masters who beat the poor into the dirt they made them farm. He is strong and has given that strength to those who follow him. He gave such strength to me. My life...was not good before him."

Lina's eyes narrowed. "You say he freed people!

Well now he *takes* slaves. Women. Even children. No one with true strength abuses that power in the way he has."

Painted Crow shook her head. "You don't understand. The women and the children. He'll not harm them. He *needs* them. They will become part of his tribe. A new nation he is building."

A harsh chuckle broke from Lina's mouth. "I know better. I saw four children used as bait by the Beast's men. They were set up to die in an explosion, only for the cause of killing those who wanted to free them."

"I don't.... I don't know how that could be. But if it is true it must have been a decision made by one of his followers. Not by him. He would not do such a thing."

"You're a fool!" Lina spat.

"You, he *will* kill!" Painted Crow spat back. "You and your friend. *All* your friends!"

Lina lifted her urumi. Painted Crow shrank back. Lina stared thorns at the woman before slowly lowering her weapon. She shook her head and slung the urumi back around her waist as a belt.

"Won't happen," she said, turning away.

Lina took three steps and heard the sound behind her that she'd hoped not to hear. She turned, ripping a long Bowie knife from a sheath at her waist. In a final desperate gamble to protect her lover, Painted Crow had thrown herself toward the shotgun on the floor. The woman grabbed the weapon, twisted it toward Lina. The Black Rose flung her knife. The flashing silver blade streaked over the top of the shotgun's barrel and buried itself in Painted Crow' throat.

Painted Crow's hand tightened on the shotgun, then fell away. The gun clattered back to the floor. Above the bone handle of the knife, the woman's face turned ashen where it was not speckled by droplets of spraying blood. Painted Crow grabbed the knife's hilt, jerked it free without thought. Arterial blood pumped like red tea down the front of her purple gown. She fell over. The wall caught her, held her partially in a sitting position. Her eyes remained open.

The Black Rose noticed a machete hanging on the wall over Painted Crow's body. She took it down, slid it beneath her sword-belt. She bent over and picked up her knife. It was sticky with blood and she walked to the table and rinsed it off with water from the pitcher there. The last thing she did before leaving was blow out the lit wicks on the candelabrum.

CHAPTER 20

"What happened?" Henri asked when Lina materialized out of the woods and joined him in the meadow.

"She tried to shoot me in the back," Lina explained.

"And I don't guess she talked?" Henri asked.

"Not about much that really helps us. She knew the 'Beast,' though. Turns out she was his lover. Or wanted to be anyway. She found him 'magnificent.'"

Henri had packed up their gear and saddled their horses. Lina swung aboard the Appaloosa: "We'd best ride. I don't think she had more than two men with her here, but she was an ally of this El Tigre and he might have more men around. They could show up at any time."

"Maybe we ought to wait," Henri said. "Capture one of them. We still need a guide."

"I know where to go," Lina replied. "In a way, Painted Crow *did* tell us how to find him. When I was upstairs in her shack, someone had drawn a map above her bed. There was a jaguar symbol.

Something like it anyway. I'm pretty sure that's where we need to look."

"Ah," Henri said. He pulled up into the saddle as well. "Lead on."

Lina did one last thing before they left the meadow behind forever. She guided her Appaloosa over to a slender oak growing near the outside edge of the field where anyone approaching would see it. Drawing the liberated machete from her belt, she applied it to the tree. A moment later and she was done.

"Whatever help Mother Mercy is sending after us from Santo Tomas," she said. "They know about following the lava field toward the Rio Grande from my telegraph messages. But from here on we'll have to blaze our trail."

"Right," Henri said, as Lina turned her mount away and kicked it into motion.

Henri lingered to study the mark on the tree in the dim moonlight. It was shaped like a rose with an arrow above it pointing south. Then he followed Lina into the night.

******

The bow twanged; the arrow sped. The big jackrabbit flipped head over heels and dropped. Lina rose from behind the cover of a large boulder and stalked forward. Four days had passed since they'd crossed the Rio Grande. She and Henri had traveled well south of the river, into the foothills of mountains marked on the map found in Painted Crow's shack. They'd begun to run low on supplies and had stopped briefly to hunt. The hare was Lina's contribution. Earlier, Henri had snared a few quail for their supper.

Slinging the bow and quiver of arrows over her shoulder, she grasped the hare by the large hind limbs and carried it back toward camp. Henri was already cooking, using a small hot fire built with mesquite.

"Fifteen minutes until we eat," Henri said as Lina entered the camp.

"That'll give me just enough time to dress this and salt it," Lina said. "Breakfast tomorrow."

The two companions had thrown up camp beneath a shallow overhang in a sandstone cliff, which served to diffuse the smoke from their fire. A small stream flowed past it about a dozen yards down a gentle slope. Lina could hear it trickling along through a screen of brush and stunted trees.

Grabbing a bag of salt from one of her saddlebags, Lina headed for the stream. She quickly gutted the hare and pulled off the hide. After washing the meat and her knife in the creek, she laid the hare out on a flat, dry rock and rubbed it thoroughly with salt.

Lina returned to camp just as Henri was taking two spits of fresh green wood off the flames, each stick holding a roasted quail that dripped golden juices. The smell teased and tantalized. She sat down with her back to the inside wall of the overhang as Henri handed her a bird, stick and all. He poured her a brimful, tin cup of coffee and sat next to her to eat his own meal.

Lina devoured as much of the quail straight off the stick as she could before using her fingers to pull the remaining meat off and feeding it to her mouth. She didn't speak during this operation. Nor did Henri. The only sounds were the smacking of lips, licking of fingers and the gulping of coffee.

"Good!" Lina finally said, as she plucked a last little morsel of white meat off the quail and swallowed it down. She tossed the bones down toward the creek where the critters could find them without getting close to the humans' fire.

"Thanks," Henri said. "Looking forward to your rabbit tomorrow. I didn't know you could use a bow and arrow." He grinned. "Course, there doesn't seem to be any weapon you haven't mastered."

Lina glanced at the bow she'd leaned against the overhang wall. She'd confiscated it back in the desert when El Tigre's men had first tried to ambush them.

"My father, Aquiles, taught me how to use many different weapons," Lina said.

"Isn't that a little unusual?" Henri asked. "I mean, for a young woman?"

Lina grinned. "You don't know many Texas women. Most learn to shoot at an early age. At least in the rural areas. Some learn a lot more. The only unusual thing about my training is the breadth of it." She touched the handle of her sword-belt. "I don't know any other women who use the urumi, for example."

"Or men either," Henri added. "Where did you get it?"

"A family heirloom," Lina said.

"From an unusual family," Henri replied.

Lina chuckled. "That's true. But let's talk about you and your family, Henri. We've ridden together a lot lately and yet I know nothing of your childhood. Tell me."

"Pretty boring," Henri said. "I grew up in Massachusetts. My parents were…well off. Father was a lawyer and wanted me to be. But it didn't interest me. I'd read too much about Jim Bridger, Kit Carson, James Beckwourth. The mountain men. I went out to the Rockies when I was seventeen. But the mountain man era was coming to an end by then. The fur trade was dying out. There was still plenty of wilderness but less of it every year and a lot more people around than in the heyday of Beckwourth and Carson."

Licking a last droplet of quail grease off her fingers, Lina said, "Doesn't sound boring at all. Bet there was still plenty of adventure to be had."

"Oh, don't get me wrong. It was still a great life and a lot better than lawyering." He grinned. "And adventures? Well, enough of those so as to take a month of Sundays to tell."

Lina glanced around. Night had fallen while they'd eaten. The campfire was warm against the chilly edge of the dark. A wistfulness filled her thoughts as she listened to sticks crackle in the flames and watched shadows born of fire dance around their campsite.

"Maybe when this mission is done," she said, "we'll go camping out just to camp out. For no other reason than to sit around a fire and eat and tell those stories."

"I like that idea," Henri said. "I'd like to hear *your* story."

Lina became aware that Henri was leaning toward her. Casually, she straightened her back and stretched, which shifted her a little farther away from her companion. She didn't think he had any intention of trying to kiss her but didn't want to invite it. It would be tough on their friendship if she had to reject him. She tried not to think about the part of her that didn't *want* to reject him.

"I need to step down to the creek for a moment," she said. "If you want to sleep, I'll take first watch."

"When you get back, I will," Henri said.

Did his voice suddenly seem flatter, emotionless? Lina wasn't sure. She offered him a smile but the floppy brim of his old hat shadowed his face and she couldn't see if he returned it. She rose, picked up her Winchester and slipped away.

No moon yet but the last gray light of day guided Lina's way to the stream. She crossed the water, did her business quickly behind a cedar tree, then retraced her steps. Pausing at the creek, she glanced up and down the waterway. A few stars sent glimmers of silver-white spattering along the rippling stream. The world was beautiful, but an uneasiness gripped her.

No birds were calling, though the first night birds should have been waking up. And earlier when she'd been here, she'd heard frogs. Now they were silent, too. She drew the Winchester across her body, slipped her firing finger into the trigger guard.

She sniffed the air but smelled nothing unusual. Yet, a presence waited somewhere in the night around her. She was sure of it. Right along the creek, it was relatively open and she would see anything that came out of the brush to attack her. But when she crossed the stream and entered the mass of bushes beyond, visibility would be cut to inches. She knew then where the presence had to be. And she wouldn't smell it there because the wind was blowing from her *toward* the camp. She was being hunted.

A high-pitched shriek tore the night. It wasn't Henri. It sounded like a woman. Not a human woman but something she'd read about in ancient lore — a banshee. And it was close, between her and the camp.

CHAPTER 21

The agitation of the horses caught Henri's attention just before a horrendous scream burst in his ears. Goosebumps erupted all over his body. He lunged to his feet and out from the beneath the rocky overhang. Peacemaker Colts filled his hands. The campfire had died down but still cast out a circle of reddish light that pushed back the dark in front of the overhang. Henri could *see* no sign of trouble but the horses had gone wild, stamping their feet and jerking at their picket line.

And, of course, there was the scream.

"Lina!" Henri shouted. "Lina! Where are you?"

"I'm here! By the creek," Lina called back. "But stay put. That wasn't my scream but there's something in the bushes between here and the camp."

"It's a panther, I think!" Henri called back. "From the way the horses are acting, it's a real one this time. Watch out!"

Lina didn't answer; Henri cast about desperately

for some way to help. Suddenly, he holstered his pistols and tore off his shirt. Grabbing at the undershirt beneath, he ripped it over his head. He yanked up a long thick branch they'd gathered for firewood and quickly tied the undershirt around it, then dipped it into the campfire. As soon as it caught flame, he rushed with his makeshift torch toward the screen of bushes that stood between him and Lina.

The brush was chaparral, shoulder high. It was taller here where it got plenty of water than out in the desert. But right now it was still a little dry from lack of rain, with its tightly bunched green leaves faintly yellowed against its rough gray stems. It grew densely, not enough to stop someone from weaving around it but enough to hide many dangers.

Henri thrust his torch into the first bush he came to. Chaparral bushes were full of resin. They even smelled a little like tar, although not unpleasantly so. And with their woody branches and the leaf litter that often accumulated beneath them, they were highly flammable.

This one exploded into a torch of its own, sending thick smoke roiling. Henri stepped past it, put the fire to another and another. The flames spread. Henri caught a whiff of something rank, not from the burning chaparral. This scent was alive. A loud yowling sounded. Something big but low to the ground tore off downstream through the bushes, sending leaves flying.

Henri rushed forward, yelling to Lina that he was coming so she wouldn't shoot him. He burst out of the bushes to see the Black Rose standing stock-still in the middle of the creek, her Winchester leveled and ready. Black and red war paint turned her face savage. The hem of her cape nearly brushed the water.

"The thing took off," Henri shouted. "But who knows how far it went. Come on!"

He turned to run back through the brush, heading upstream slightly to avoid the fire. Lina followed. They burst out of the bushes, reached the relative safety of their campfire. Both drew a breath of relief, though they weren't quite safe yet.

Henri tossed his torch on the fire before adding more bits of wood. The flames leaped up, brightening from deep smoldering red to yellow-orange. Lina watched the night with her rifle handy.

"I don't think it's gone," Lina said when Henri moved from the fire to stand beside her. "Look at the horses."

Henri did so. The animals had stopped pulling at their pickets but were still intensely alert. Their heads were high, their ears pricked. Their eyes rolled. They looked ready to bolt. Except for the Appaloosa stallion, which acted like it wanted to kill something.

The fire in the chaparral had raced its way along the creek to the end of the thick brush. It had not been able to jump the water and was burning itself out. The ground right in front of the camp was mostly rock, with little to no grass or brush. Henri picked up a fiery branch from the campfire and hurled it off into the darkness. It landed and bounced, shedding sparks. Green eyes flashed from some small scuttling creature, which disappeared into a pile of rocks. There was nothing else, no sign of the panther.

"I didn't realize what it was at first," Lina said. "I thought it was a woman in agonizing pain. But it was…different."

"Took me a second, too," Henri said. "And it's still a little strange. I've known panthers to scream like a woman but this wasn't exactly like any I've ever heard. Deeper somehow. Hollow. But I caught a glimpse of it as it ran from the fire. Just a silhouette but it had to be a panther. It's not like them to stalk a full-grown human, though. Not unless they were starving. And there's plenty of game around here."

"So why did it?" Lina asked.

Henri met Lina's gaze. He shrugged, glanced down and shook his head.

Lina gave an exasperated sigh. "Don't tell me you're thinking that El Tigre sent it to stop us. Or to spy on us."

"I didn't say anything," Henri protested.

"No, but I see your look."

"And I see yours. If I'm thinking it, so are you."

"It's not possible," Lina snapped.

"No," Henri said. "Not by any laws of the world we know. But I don't think we know all the laws yet. I don't anyway."

Lina seemed about to respond when a trickle of pebbles came rattling down the cliff under which they stood. The Appaloosa neighed a challenge. Lina and Henri both looked up, swinging their guns to bear. With no moon, there wasn't enough light to see details. All Henri recognized was a sleek, rippling shadow at the very edge of the cliff above them. He fired his right-hand Colt but didn't shoot to kill, only to frighten. For all he knew, the shadow might be human.

The shot did the trick. The shadow disappeared. The horses calmed down almost as swiftly. Lina lowered her Winchester; Henri holstered his pistol.

"I think it's gone," Henri said. "For now anyway."

Lina said nothing, only turned and stalked back to the fire. Henri followed. Neither of them slept more than a few winks the rest of the night.

CHAPTER 22

Lina and Henri sat their mounts and looked down at what the morning light had revealed in the dust barely twenty yards from last night's fire, a set of pawprints. Henri dismounted and leaned over to place his hand next to one of the tracks.

"Biggest cat I've ever seen," he said when he straightened again. "Likely a seven-footer. If you include the tail."

"That's comforting," Lina replied.

"Even better, it's headed south. Just like us."

"Don't panthers have a range?"

"They do," Henri said. "But it can be pretty large. This cat isn't acting quite normal anyway. We need to ride carefully. Stay away from any place it might take cover. And no riding under trees or rocky out-croppings where it could spring on us."

Lina studied the rugged land to their south. They were already in the foothills of a mountain range and the landscape was becoming steeper and more broken. A set of three largely barren peaks loomed ahead of them. Lina had seen their likeness on the map in Painted Crow's shack. Somewhere among those peaks they'd find the location marked on the map with a stylized jaguar or panther skull. There, she believed, they'd discover the hideout of the bandit they were calling El Tigre, or sometimes "The Beast."

"I don't see many trees ahead," Lina said. "But lots of rock formations for the thing to hide behind."

"We'll go slow," Henri said, swinging back into his saddle. "Even if it galls us."

Lina nodded, booted the Appaloosa forward. Henri followed. Both carried their rifles across their laps. Behind them they left a small pile of rocks shaped like a rose, with a stone arrow pointing due south.

****

The day passed, followed by another night. This one went by without incident. By dawn they were on the trail. The landscape continued to rise toward the mountains. It remained mostly rocky but here and there greens and splashes of other colors began to streak the ridges and canyons. Dryland scrub brush and cacti made up most of the color, but occasional bursts of purple and yellow flowers sprouted wherever topsoil had gathered.

Lina and Henri rode side by side. Lina noticed Henri scanning every little bit of soil or flowered ground they passed.

"Looking for panther tracks?" she asked.

Henri shook his head. "Was hoping to see some sign of Joseph Craft and that Bolanger fellow. We've traveled fast. I doubt they can be too far ahead of us. If we could find their trail we might be able to use Bolanger as our guide, too."

"It'd also help us know we were steering the right way," Lina said.

"That too," Henri acknowledged.

Lina drew her Appaloosa to a stop. Henri pulled his gelding to a halt as well and glanced over curiously. Lina dismounted and began to strip her stallion of gear and saddle.

"What are you doing?" Henri asked.

"Going to switch my saddle over to that dappled gray we brought along. If the mare considers El Tigre's hideout to be home, she might return there if I give her the reins and let her go where she wants."

"Worth a try," Henri said. He dismounted, moved to help Lina.

Between the two of them, they quickly got Lina's saddle and blanket roll onto the mare and she mounted. She clucked it forward and as soon as it started moving, she let the reins dangle loose to see which direction it would go. Henri followed, leading the Appaloosa, as well as the dun gelding they'd brought along as a second remount.

It took the gray a while to figure out what was happening. Without the pressure of any reins, she kept slowing and stopping and would have to be booted into motion again. Finally, though, she got the idea that she had some choice here. She lifted her head into the wind, which was blowing from the south, then began a steady trot in that direction. Gradually, though, she veered more to the southwest.

Lina studied the landscape ahead. The three peaks she'd been aiming for were still in front of them and beginning to loom large. She'd been heading generally toward the central peak, but the gray mare was angling toward a spot between the central one and the one on the far right.

Lina looked over at Henri and shrugged. "She's definitely headed somewhere. And the map showed the hideout in that general direction."

"Could be she's just smelling water," Henri said.

"We'll know soon enough, I think," Lina replied.

Twenty minutes passed. They crossed a barren ridge and below them saw a little oasis. A pool of clear water nestled in a hollow at the foot of a broken cliff. The overflow rilled away in a small stream toward the north. Brush and grass and a few small trees clustered around the pool and stream. Three deer leaped away at sight of the riders coming; a host of birds flung themselves skyward.

The gray mare picked up her pace, headed directly toward the pool. Lina guided her to the stream part instead and dismounted while the horse sunk her muzzle into the creek. Henri swung from his saddle as well and led the other three horses to drink. He used rocks in the stream as steppingstones to cross to the other side and drink in a small rocky bowl where cool water eddied and burbled.

Lina walked a few feet up the stream to stand by the pool. Bubbles churned upward through the clear water, indicating a spring beneath the surface. She knelt, cupped her hands in the pool and brought them to her mouth. The fresh water, faintly tangy with dissolved minerals, tasted incredibly sweet to her after the lukewarm offerings of their canteens.

After drinking deep, Lina rose to study the cliff under which the pool had formed. It was no more than twenty feet high and made up of distinct layers of varicolored rock, much of it cracked and broken. Debris had fallen from the cliff to litter the edge of the pool. Lina picked up a piece of stone about the size of her fist with some kind of markings on the flattest side of it.

A gasp of wonder escaped her lips. The "markings" were actually an image of a tiny fish embedded in the stone. It was about the length of her little finger. The back fin and tail were perfectly identifiable. She could even make out the scales. The head was odd, seemingly put together from tiny bone plates. She could see where the eye had been.

Lina had certainly read about fossils and had seen some in Texas, particularly around the Caddo Peaks in the central part of the state. Those had mostly been shelled animals, though. She'd never seen a fish like this, nor anything so delicate and yet well preserved.

As she looked around, Lina saw a number of other fossils in the debris at the base of the cliff. Some were of shelled creatures and a few even resembled pieces of fern. There were other fish but none so complete as the first one. She saw a fin here, a back part of a tail there.

"Lina!" Henri called. She turned in surprise; her mind had drifted toward an ancient past when a sea had flowed here where dry stone dominated now. What a different world it must have been.

"What?" she replied.

"Come have a look at this."

Still carrying the fossil fish with her, she went upstream and crossed to where Henri stood next to a broadly branched willow tree. He pointed and she saw the tracks in the soft soil by the tree. They were partially overlain by the marks of deer but were clear enough to recognize.

"Horses!" she said.

"Yep," Henri said. "Shod too. And I'm pretty sure this is Joseph Craft's and Bolanger's mounts."

"What makes you say so?"

"That black horse Bolanger rode. Its horseshoes were badly worn. Like it had seen a lot of traveling. One set of these tracks is just the same. The other was freshly shod. And the markings. Well, see for yourself."

He pointed at the top curve of the shoe she was looking at. A word had been incised into the iron and had left an impression in the dirt. It was hard to read but she thought she knew it.

"Cavalry!" she said.

"Pretty sure," Henri said. "That shoe here would

have to be from Craft."

"How recent?"

"I make these to be no more than a few hours old," Henri replied.

"So if we rode hard we might catch them before nightfall."

"Might," Henri agreed. "If they left enough sign for us to follow at speed."

"I was a little disappointed when the mare led us to water instead of El Tigre's hideout," Lina said. "But maybe she led us to both."

"Maybe," Henri agreed.

After quickly filling their bellies and canteens with water, the two companions remounted and headed south on the trail of Craft and Bolanger. Lina switched her saddle back to the Appaloosa in case she needed its speed. They rode hard, with a little more hope in their expressions than they'd had before. Lina took the fossil with her, though she could not have said why.

CHAPTER 23

Knowing that Craft and Bolanger were in the area helped Henri track them. Overturned pebbles, scuffs on stone, broken flower stems, bent branches on mesquite. All these provided Henri with information and for several hours they followed this makeshift trail, riding at speed when they could. Henry told Lina they were gaining on their targets.

They came to an open ascent of smooth rock. The upward grade was only about twenty percent but still too steep and slick to chance just riding up it. They dismounted, led their horses up. At the top they came into a canyon. A wide stream ran through it. Not quite a river, but more than a creek. And where there was water, there was life. An armadillo snuffled through a grassy meadow dotted with bushes and wildflowers that filled the bed of the canyon. Immediately, Henri located Craft and Bolanger's tracks again.

"Fresh!" Henri said. "They might still be here. In

the canyon."

Swinging into their saddles, the two sent their mounts galloping into the meadow. They splashed through the little river, sending icy cold sprays of water flying. The ground rose on the other side of the stream. As they came up the rise they both smelled smoke and saw dark puffs of it weaving into the sky. Glances crossed between the two; each knew the other's thoughts. Why would cautious men build such a big fire where one's enemies might see?

A shout and gunfire surprised them. Both urged their mounts to greater speed. They raced toward the fire, burst through a screening thicket of chaparral and saw what lay ahead. A camp had been thrown up in the lee of an old rockslide. It had been planned for concealment, with only a hatful of fire, but someone had thrown a big pile of chaparral onto the flames. As the dried brush caught fire, it sent palls of grayish-white smoke roiling into the air.

Lina veered her Appaloosa around the smoke, which was pouring down the meadow directly toward them. Henri followed. Lina saw Joseph Craft lying twisted against a pile of rocks. He was alive but blood stained his shirt in a wide fan of red. He cried out as he saw the two of them, then began to shout and wave the rifle in his hands toward the south. Lina couldn't make out what the man was saying. Jerking the Appaloosa to a stop, she started to throw herself out of the saddle. Craft's words got through first.

"Bolanger! He's getting away!"

Lina turned in the direction Craft was pointing. She saw dust lingering in the air and glimpsed a dark shape fleeing in the distance. Maybe half a mile away, Bolanger raced for freedom on his black horse, leading another horse — Craft's cavalry mount.

"Stay with him!" Lina shouted to Henri, who'd ridden up behind her to the fire. She booted her Appaloosa in pursuit of the fleeing outlaw.

Bolanger was riding fast but must have slowed down slightly as he got out of gunshot range from the campfire. He knew Craft didn't have a horse and didn't yet know he was being pursued by newcomers on the scene.

Lina leaned over the neck of her Appaloosa, whispered encouragement to it. Her cape whipped behind her. They began to eat the distance. Bolanger finally glanced over his shoulder and saw Lina coming with a line of dust purling up behind her. Barely a couple of hundred yards separated them.

The outlaw threw the reins to Craft's mount away from him and kicked heel and wooden leg brutally into his own horse. The black gave a squeal but leaped forward, then settled into a hard run.

Lina leaned her face almost into the Appaloosa's mane, her words and hands and feet doing everything they could to urge more speed from the stallion. They closed the gap.

The meadow narrowed. It ended in a pass between the rounded shoulders of two peaks. Bolanger remained ahead but was losing a step out of every three. The black was a beautiful animal but no match for the Appaloosa stallion in a race. Lina pulled closer, almost to the flying tail of the other horse.

Bolanger glanced around. Lina saw his eyes wide and scared; he was beating the reins against his mount's neck with his right hand while he whipped the horse's flanks with his other — his hook, Lina saw. Blood streaked the black's side.

Lina snarled. She whispered a last time to the Appaloosa. They pulled up next to Bolanger. The pass continued to narrow. Rough walls of rock closed in to either side of the two horses. Bolanger swerved, trying to run Lina's mount into the rock. She leaned into the attempt.

The horses banged together. Lina felt her knee brush against the peg leg of Bolanger. They were neck and neck. The rock walls to either side clawed at them. Any false step would send both mounts crashing to the ground, likely killing their riders.

Bolanger stopped whipping his horse and swung a backhand blow at Lina's face with his artificial arm. The wickedly tipped hook winked in the light as it flashed at her. She leaned to the side; her shoulder brushed stone but the hook missed by an inch.

As Bolanger tried to swing his arm back forward, Lina reached out and grabbed it behind the hook. The pass they were in abruptly widened. Bolanger tried to pull away but Lina hung on and twisted savagely. The arm was solidly attached by leather straps at the shoulder. It didn't come loose but Bolanger cried out in pain.

Bolanger's peg leg fitted solidly into a bowl-shaped leather stirrup specifically designed for it. Using that leg as an anchor to hold him on his horse, Bolanger let go of the reins with his right hand and grabbed for a pistol stuck in his belt.

Lina saw her danger. As Bolanger swung the pistol toward her, she let go of the man's arm, leaned low to her left and kicked out with her right leg. Bolanger was shorter than Lina and the black was shorter than the Appaloosa. Her boot caught Bolanger under the left shoulder, lifting him up in his saddle. His peg leg came free of its stirrup with a little sucking sound. He flailed wildly and went head over heels backward off his horse.

Lina heard the whump as Bolanger hit the ground. She sawed on the Appaloosa's reins, trying to bring the big animal around. The stallion squealed as it turned. It banged into the black, sent the other horse reeling. They'd made it all the way through the pass, Lina saw, and entered another canyon and another valley.

Bolanger was down on his back in a stretch of grass but was already starting to twist over onto his hands and knees. The pistol had been knocked from his grip and lay a few feet away. Bolanger scrabbled toward it, grasped the butt and started to swing it around.

Lina drew the Remington over-and-under .41 from beneath her vest. She didn't want to shoot Bolanger. They needed him.

"Stop!" she shouted.

Bolanger saw her gun; he had to know he couldn't beat her to a shot. But he kept lifting his pistol. Lina took aim at the man's shoulder, to wound rather than kill. Before she could pull her trigger, a streak of lithe, ebony rage flashed across her field of vision.

Something struck Bolanger, knocking him flat. His gun went flying; Lina's shot missed and for a fleeting instant she was shocked to stillness. In that frozen moment, a massive black cat had leaped on Bolanger. The beast thrust its muzzle down and ripped the man's throat away in a bright arc of spurting blood.

A sound that might have been intended as a scream but could only come out as a gasp, tore from Bolanger's lips. The big cat didn't even seem to hear. Its gaze had focused on Lina. Eyes of golden-orange blazed at her. The wide muzzle dripped with gore as the lips curled back around vicious canines. A growl rumbled up from its chest like boulders grinding together in an avalanche.

The Appaloosa snorted in a combination of anger and fear. It would have fought a man who threatened it or its rider, but this was a hereditary enemy. Something quailed even inside the big stallion. It backed up. A step. Two steps. The huge black panther's eyes drew down; its shoulders were massively muscled and those muscles bunched in readiness for a charge.

Lina still had her .41 in her hand and she had one bullet left. It wouldn't be enough. She was about to fire anyway when the cat's head lifted. Its ears pricked, as if it heard something calling from far away. Lina thought she heard something too, some faint vibration that tickled in her ear.

The creature turned its head away from Lina. Its muscles rippled along its flanks. And it was gone, darting away into a patch of brush that waved violently and then stilled. Lina lowered her Remington and took a breath. It felt like the first one she'd drawn in ages.

CHAPTER 24

The panther was gone for now. Lina felt sure of it. But she was cautious anyway as she searched Bolanger's body and all around it. She found nothing other than the pistol Bolanger had dropped when attacked. It must have been Craft's cavalry issue weapon, though it certainly wasn't the regulation sidearm. She'd seen its type before though and knew it was called an "automatic." She thought it awkward with its rectangular butt and rectangular barrel, but she didn't take time to study it further as she tucked it in her belt.

The Appaloosa had been well trained by Henri and remained standing almost right where she'd dropped the reins when she'd dismounted to confront Bolanger. Even it had backed up a few steps when the big cat swarmed over the man, though. She climbed back into the saddle and headed for Joseph Craft's camp. Bolanger's black horse wouldn't let her catch it — it seemed mostly afraid of the Appaloosa — but she was able to grab the reins of Craft's cavalry mount.

As Lina reentered the canyon where the campsite lay, she saw that the fire had been put out. A few puffs of smoke still drifted in the afternoon air and that worried her. They'd be seen for miles if anyone were looking. And if *El Tigre* and his men were anywhere near, someone was sure to be looking.

Henri lowered his Sharps with relief as Lina rode up. "Thank God," he said. Then he realized she was alone. "Bolanger got away?" he asked.

Lina shook her head. "Dead," she replied.

Joseph Craft sat propped up against a boulder. He was pale and clearly in pain. Blood had run down his neck to his chest from a deep, ragged cut across his right cheek. His lower body was sodden with blood from a much bigger wound near his waist. Henri must have already treated the latter injury because the bleeding had stopped and a fresh bandage showed through rips in the cavalryman's drenched shirt.

Having his wound treated hadn't helped Craft's mood any. His words were brusque with anger.

"You killed him? He was our one link to the outlaws who have my wife!"

Henri rounded on the cavalry trooper. "You're the one let him escape," the mountain man snapped. "It's your—"

"I didn't kill him," Lina interrupted. "I'd knocked him off his horse. Was about to disarm him. A black panther killed him. Or a big cat of some kind. It came from nowhere."

Both Henri and Joseph Craft stared at her. Craft's mouth hung open. Henri wasn't quite so surprised.

"Not the same big cat?" Henri asked.

Lina took a deep breath, let it out. "Don't know but I don't really believe in coincidences."

"You said 'a big cat of *some* kind,'" Henri pressed her. "What do you mean?"

Lina shrugged. "I've seen a panther before. This thing was bigger. I don't mean just in size. It was bulky. Especially in the shoulders. I think it might have been a jaguar."

Craft was glancing back and forth between them, frowning. "What? A jaguar? A coincidence? What are you talking about?"

Henri explained. "We were stalked by something a couple of nights ago. I figured it was a panther but we never got a good look at it. It disappeared in this direction."

"Surely you don't think it could be the same one?" Craft protested. "That's ridiculous. Panthers don't act like that."

"You friends with a lot of panthers, are you?" Henri asked.

Craft had opened his mouth to respond when Lina interrupted: "Enough!" she said. She gestured at the fire. "I'm glad you got the fire out but that smoke could have been seen from Mexico City. We need to move."

She glanced at Henri. "What about Craft? *Can* he move?"

"I'm fine," Craft snapped.

Lina paid him no mind; her gaze remained on Henri.

"He was lucky," Henri replied. "Bolanger must have shot quickly. The bullet struck the hip before glancing upward through the meat just above. A lot of blood but nothing permanent. I got the bleeding stopped and put in a few stitches. He can move. But we need to take it slow."

"What happened?" Lina asked. She was staring at Craft this time.

"He's sneaky," Craft said. "I tried to watch him close but somehow he got hold of an old stone arrowhead. Maybe from someplace we stopped. Or maybe he had it concealed. Though I searched him. It was almost like a little knife blade. He used that to cut the rope I bound his hands together with.

"I was tired, told him we were stopping early. As I was building the fire, he lunged at me, slashed me across the face with that arrowhead. I'd been leaving the flap of my holster unbuttoned in case I needed my pistol. He grabbed it, shot me. As I went down, he clubbed me over the head.

"I must have been out for a few seconds. Maybe he thought I was dead. When I came to, he'd thrown a pile of chaparral on the fire. To make smoke for his friends, I reckon. And he was riding off with both horses. They'd still been saddled at that point. But he missed the fact I'd taken my carbine out and leaned it against this rock. It didn't matter. I couldn't hold it steady when I shot at him."

"All right," Lina said. "Let's get going before

someone comes to investigate the fire." She walked over to Craft, handed him back his automatic, which he slipped into the holster at his belt. Henri joined her. Between them, they got the man upright and helped him into the saddle. He groaned with pain but managed to take the reins. Lina and Henri saddled up as well.

"Which way?" Henri asked.

"We're still going south," Lina said.

"If any of our enemies saw the fire, that's the direction they'll be coming from," Henri said.

"So be it," Lina replied grimly. "We go forward or we don't go at all."

******

Six rode south from Santo Tomas, Texas. They rode armed. They rode with purpose, first to the destroyed mission of San Javier del Amor and then to the Rio Grande. In a dark line, they crossed the river.

In the lead were two women, nuns of the order of the Sisters of Señora Maria and of the order of the Black Rose, though they were not dressed in their habits now. Instead of the bandeau, felt hats covered their hair and shaded their faces. Their shirts and trousers were of buckskin — the attire of warriors.

Sister Caroline Harp was a little past thirty and could trace her ancestry to a family of slaves from South Carolina. She carried a rifle and pistols, but at her side hung her favorite weapon — the Kpinga. With three sharp blades attached to a wooden haft, the Kpinga was primarily a throwing weapon and

Sister Caroline wielded it with precision.

Sister Sofia Lee was of Spanish descent, a bit older that Sister Caroline. Her dark hair lay close-cropped under her hat. She was a bladeswoman, adept with all forms of swords and knives but particularly enamored of the Facón and the Navaja. She sometimes seemed as cold as the steel she carried. At other times, her temper flared hot enough to melt steel.

The remainder of the six riders were men. All appeared to be of Mexican or mestizo descent, wearing varied dress. One had put on the black trousers, white shirt and short vest of a gunfighter. Others had dressed in fringed buckskin with bandoleers across their chests. Still others wore the white of peasants. All four were heavily armed with lever action rifles, shotguns and pistols at their waists. Their faces were grim after seeing the ruins of San Javier del Amor.

The riders came to a grassy meadow and a small wood where they discovered the mark of a rose blazed into an oak. Beyond that ran a stream and across the stream stood a shack. Sister Caroline and Sister Sofia dismounted in front of the shack and entered. The place stank of death. The body of a dead woman lay half propped against the wall. It was days old. Caroline and Sofia did not know that the woman had been named Painted Crow, but they might have guessed from the unusual markings that mottled her skin.

In the sleeping loft above the cabin's main room, the Sisters located the same map that the

Black Rose had studied. The last telegram they'd received at Santo Tomas had given them enough information to recognize the potential significance of the Jaguar symbol.

"So," Sofia said. "We know where they're going. If not how long it will take to get there."

"Lina will mark the way," Caroline said, her fingers tapping on her Kpinga. "We'll find her."

Sofia's dark eyes met Caroline's even darker ones. "But we are days behind," she said. "Will we be in time?"

Caroline chuckled. "I think you're more worried about missing the action than about having to pull Lina's hide out of the fire. The Black Rose can handle herself."

"Everyone has their limits. Even the Black Rose."

Caroline took a deep breath. She nodded, sobered. "You're right. Let us pray she has not yet reached hers."

CHAPTER 25

Moving forward for Lina, Henri and Joseph Craft meant going back to the meadow where Lina had caught up to Benjamin Bolanger and seen him killed by some kind of big cat. They did not stop to bury the outlaw; all three believed that time was fast running out to save the people kidnapped from the San Javier del Amor mission. They *were* able to capture Bolanger's black horse, which they added to their string of remounts.

Lina had first figured this meadow was like the one where she and Henri had found Craft. But now that she got a chance to look around, it was much bigger. They rode steadily for nearly an hour before they came to the southern end of the great field. By that time the light was turning yellow with late evening.

They'd have to camp soon, especially since Craft, while valiantly striving not to slow them down, was showing his exhaustion. Another pass exited out of the valley to take them deeper into the mountains, but the three riders hesitated to approach it.

"I'd rather go up that pass in the full light of day," Lina said. "To make sure there's no ambush."

"Agreed," Henri said. He took out his binoculars, stood in his stirrups, and gave the valley to the west of them a scan. "There's some trees off to our right," he said after a bit. "We ought to be able to reach them by nightfall."

"All right," Lina said. "That's where we'll camp."

The three rode quickly and reached the trees before the last sunlight faded. The woods turned out to be a patch of willows and oaks growing alongside a small stream. The three dismounted and watered the horses. Henri scouted ahead while Lina got Craft off his mount and seated against a willow next to one of the stream's wider pools. Before she could start to make camp, though, Henri returned with some excitement.

"The woods aren't very thick and there's a small village on the other side," Henri said. "It's nestled in a low spot in the land and you wouldn't see it unless you went through the woods and came out at just the right spot along the creek. It looks like it's abandoned. Might be a good place to spend the night. I wouldn't mind having a door between me and that cat. I've been thinking, you might be right about it being a jaguar. They're not common this far north but there's no real reason they couldn't be here. And they're a lot more dangerous and aggressive than a panther."

Craft snorted in derision. "Whatever it was, it's gotta be long gone," he said. "And it's not gonna attack three armed riders."

"It attacked Bolanger," Henri said. "And he was armed."

"And on foot and hurt," Craft retorted.

"Doesn't matter," Lina snapped. "We need to search this village anyway. We have to know what's in front of us *and* behind us on this journey."

She was about to tell Craft to remain sitting but he'd already struggled to his feet and made off through the woods.

"Let's get it done," he said.

As Henri had indicated, the village looked abandoned. Lina couldn't detect any movement or see any lights in the houses. There should have been light this late — cookfires at the least. Just beyond the town she could make out a few narrow fields clothed in maize. No farmers worked there. She could even see the town's central well. But no people. Not even a goat or donkey.

"All right," Lina said. "We go in. But spread out." She started forward on foot, leading her horse. The others spread out and followed, with Henri bringing the rest of the horses.

Drawing weapons into their hands as they approached the outskirts of the town, the three companions prepared themselves for anything. What they got was nothing. A dozen adobe buildings lined a single street, with a well in the center. Most of the buildings appeared to be family homes, but there was one with a sign outside indicating it as a cantina. The biggest building in town was made mostly of wood and must have been a livestock barn.

The lack of fresh mud around the well indicated that no one had drawn any water lately, but it had been a hot day and mud would have dried quickly. The doors and windows were closed on all the houses except for the cantina, which stood wide open to the world, almost in invitation. The absence of chickens or dogs or any other kind of animal life was conspicuous.

Craft stumbled and nearly fell. Henri caught him. A wood-roofed awning extended out from the cantina, with a few rough tables and chairs sheltering beneath it. Henri led Craft to one of the chairs and Lina ordered him to stay put while she and Henri inspected the other buildings.

They found no sign of villagers and no sign of violence. In a few of the homes, food still waited on the tables for diners who'd never come. It was mostly beans and flat bread, covered with buzzing flies but otherwise still relatively fresh.

"The people haven't been gone more than a day," Henri said.

"Where they went and why are the more interesting questions," Lina added.

Henri shrugged.

The two companions returned to the cantina in puzzlement and joined Joseph Craft. A few unlit paper lanterns hung like sleeping bats from the rafters of the awning. A string of bright red peppers extended across the top of the bar's open doorway. Henri went inside, came back a moment later with a bottle of mescal and three tin cups. He worked the cork out of the bottle with his teeth and poured them each a helping. He and Craft drank theirs and poured another. Lina let hers sit.

"I was thinking that El Tigre must have kidnapped these villagers as well," she said, "but I can't imagine the people would all go so peacefully."

"El Tigre?" Craft asked.

"That's what we're calling the leader of the bandits who have your wife," Henri said. "He seems to like big cats."

"Bolanger told me his name," Craft said. "Or what he calls *himself.* You're pretty close. It's El Tigre sangreedo. Something like that."

"Sangriento?" Lina asked.

"Maybe. Probably. What does it mean?"

"El Tigre Sangriento. Bloodstained Tiger," Lina answered.

"He'll be bloodstained when I get hold of him," Craft said.

Lina studied Craft. His eyes looked bruised. He'd lost his cavalry hat somewhere and his short hair lay matted to his scalp. The skin on his normally gaunt face was loose and ashen. He'd suffered and Lina felt bad for him. But she also had to admit that she didn't much like him. His impulsivity in grabbing Bolanger had cost them all dearly. It might mean the death of his wife and of other innocents. It might mean that little Perla Craft would be left without parents to raise her.

Abruptly, Lina rose and stalked away from the two men into the street. There, she stood surveying the village and its surroundings. The sun was setting swiftly behind the mountain to their west. The mountain to the south was already in shadow. A breeze stirred, fingering her hair and cape. She felt a chill. She wanted to blame it on the breeze. But that wasn't true. The cold in this place was one of spirit, not flesh. At least it felt so to her.

Henri joined her, rested a hand on her shoulder. "We should pick a place to stay and get inside," he said. "I don't like the way things…feel here."

"Agreed," Lina said. "And I don't like having Joseph Craft with us. He'll slow us down. And I don't know what he'll do when we find El Tigre. If he can't control himself he could get us all killed."

"Maybe we could leave him behind in the village," Henri said. "Take all the horses and slip away before dawn. He'll have food here and a place to sleep until we return. We can leave him a note explaining."

"He'd try to follow us on foot."

"Let him. He wouldn't get far.

"Maybe," Lina agreed. "I'll think on it."

Off in the distance, a wolf howled. Others answered and the hills carried the echoes like music from a strange harp.

"You said you thought the villagers had been gone a day?" Lina asked.

"Maybe. Probably less."

"About what I figured. Was it seeing the smoke

from the fire Bolanger set that sent them running?"

"Can't be sure. But it's a good guess."

Lina stood silently for a long moment. Then, "Let's get the horses in the barn. See if it's a place we can defend."

"Defend?"

Lina glanced at Henri. She was glad he was with her. "Something will happen tonight," she said. "It's already on the way."

Henri sighed. "I don't know what it is, but I feel it coming, too."

CHAPTER 26

The barn proved indefensible. The wooden structure was too vulnerable to fire and wasn't sturdy enough to keep a determined enemy from smashing a way in. Lina and Henri decided on the cantina instead. It was the largest of the remaining buildings in the village and was built of fireproof adobe. It had only two doors and four smallish windows that would be difficult to force. Importantly, there was also an enclosed storage room in the back big enough to house the horses. They brought in bales of hay from the barn for the animals.

By the time they'd made the cantina into a temporary fortress, full dark had fallen. Henri lit a couple of kerosene lanterns and hung them from hooks on the wall that were intended for that purpose. He kept the wicks turned low so the light wouldn't destroy their night vision. Outside, the stars were up in myriads. Even without a moon, the whiteness of the village's adobe buildings shone dimly in the starlight. The street made a pale ribbon.

Henri had also located some canned beans in the cantina's storeroom. The small group opened these and ate the contents cold straight from the can while they watched the street and the back entrance to the place. The storeroom had held several cots, too, and these they'd positioned close together in the main part of the building. None of them tried for sleep yet, though. Lina and Henri were convinced that when trouble came, it would come early.

Joseph Craft was propped up on one of the cots with his carbine close to hand. The cavalryman finished most of a can of beans and tossed it clattering onto the floor where it splattered a brown streak of leftovers across the clean swept tiles.

Lina stood near a window at the front of the cantina. She held her Winchester and had slung her recently appropriated bow and quiver of arrows over her shoulder. She turned at the sound of the can hitting the floor, frowning in irritation. They'd certainly created enough disorder in the cantina by making it their camp, but she saw no reason to cause a greater mess than necessary. The people who had fled the village might well be planning to return.

"Perhaps you could have just set the can on a table?" she said, her voice harsh.

"I'm not inclined to consider the hurt feelings of a bunch of Mex bandits," Craft retorted.

"I doubt very much that anyone in this village was a bandit," Lina replied. "The victims of bandits, that I'll grant you."

"They're all greasers to me," Craft said with a sneer.

Lina glared at Craft. "You use that slur again. Or anything like it. And I'll leave you behind."

"You're defending these people?" Craft demanded, his face showing surprise.

"I'm not defending the likes of El Tigre. But not every Mexican is a bandit. No more than every American is. Every type of people has its good and bad. Bolanger and his buddy from Santa Annabella weren't Mexican. How would you like every American to be judged based on Bolanger, a man who used *your* daughter as bait in a trap without regard to the fact that she would die too?"

The heat in Craft's eyes cooled. He took a deep breath, let it out. His chest hitched. "I...I'm sorry," he said. "You're right. Bolanger was American and he was scum. Worse than the me — worse than just about anything."

Lina did not respond, only looked back out the window to study the street.

After a bit, Craft spoke again. "You're the one they call the Black Rose, aren't you?"

"Yes."

"I recognized Henri from Santa Annabella. I thanked him there for saving Perla. But I never got a chance to thank you."

"I didn't do it for you."

"I know. But I'm still grateful. Perla, she's...a special child."

"Maybe you ought to have stayed in Santa Annabella with her. Henri and I, We weren't going to let Bolanger escape. We'd have taken him, or followed him. And we would have held on to him. At least you could have come to us before you decided to kidnap him."

"It's my wife this El Tigre bastard is holding!"

"And it's people I care about, people I'm responsible for, who were also taken. You're not the only one who's suffered a loss. The most important thing is to get those people back, alive and healthy. And to do nothing that might jeopardize that."

Craft bit his lip. For a long few seconds, he struggled with himself, but finally he said, "You're right again. I didn't think. Sometimes I'm a bull in a china shop. I'll…try to do better. Did you…. Did you talk to Perla before you left? How was she?"

"She was worried about her father."

Looking a little numb, Craft nodded. He rubbed his eyes. He started to speak and Lina shushed him with a hand in the air.

"Something's out there," she said.

Craft closed his mouth, then slid out of bed with his carbine in his fists.

"Tell Henri to get ready," Lina said to Craft.

The soldier stepped to the rear of the cantina, leaned through the doorway opening into the room they were using as a makeshift stable. Henri was picking his teeth with the tip of his Bowie knife. Craft gave him the Black Rose's warning. Henri quickly sheathed his blade and readied his rifle.

Craft returned to the front of the cantina, moving

slowly with his wound, and leaned against the wall next to another window. He stared out.

"I don't see anything," he said.

"Something's there anyway. Best be quiet so it doesn't hear us."

Lina held her Winchester across her chest. She wanted to check to make sure it was loaded but did not. She knew it was. The urge was only nerves. She forced herself to patience.

Something raced across her field of vision. There for a moment, then gone. It was the size of a big dog or a small human. She thought it had moved on all fours but couldn't be sure. It might have been a man hunched over. The shadows of the houses across the street had distorted its shape.

"Hoof beats," Craft said from his window.

Lina heard them too. A lot of them. They echoed in the cool night air. She listened as they entered the village and clopped along the road. Horsemen came into view. A dozen of them. They pulled to a stop across the street from the cantina. Several figures dismounted.

Voices speaking low in Spanish came through the window. Lina couldn't make out the words. The small creature or being she'd observed a few moments before returned and joined the dismounted figures. She could see it well enough now to believe it was human, although clearly malformed, with relatively short legs and a hunched and twisted back.

A silhouette of a man bent low to converse with the small being, then straightened again. The silhouette stepped out from among the horses and moved into the middle of the street to face the cantina. Starlight showed him as a heavy fellow with a big belly and a wide sombrero on his head. He bristled with weaponry.

"Gentle men," he pronounced loudly in heavily accented but generally correct English. "We know you are there in the cantina. In the saloon, as you say. The thing for you to do is step out with your hands high and your guns left behind. It will go much easier on you for that."

Lina crossed to the door. She saw Joseph Craft looking at her but gave him no emotion to read. Opening the door slightly, she peered out.

"We've got no quarrel with you," she shouted. "Best you ride on and leave us be."

The man in the sombrero hesitated. Lina imagined it was because he hadn't been expecting his answer to come from a woman.

"That is not possible," the man finally said. "For you see, we *do* have a quarrel with you. You have killed a man of ours and this cannot be taken lightly."

"They must be talking about Bolanger," Craft hissed. "They saw the smoke like we feared and investigated. They probably followed our trail here."

"Probably," Lina said to Craft. She followed that with a shout to the men on the street. "You mean we killed one of El Tigre Sangriento's pets!"

Again, there was a pause before the bandito answered. Again, the Black Rose had surprised him. But finally, "Si. Yes. You killed one of the Tiger's men. But the Tiger is not here this night. He doesn't bother with such petty fools as you. You must answer to us. To me. I am known as El Fuego. You know the meaning, yes?"

"I think so," Lina said. "It's Spanish for egg sucking dog isn't it?"

The delay in response was magnified this time. Lina could almost feel the man who called himself "Fire" struggling against his urge to violence. Eventually, he got control of himself and shouted back. His voice, which had been almost jovial, now cracked with anger.

"It is a good thing I am near to a saint. You try my patience. Come out. Rápido. With your hands up."

"If Benjamin Bolanger was one of you," Lina called in response. "Then I take back what I said earlier. Don't ride on. You most likely need killing too."

A bark of harsh laughter burst from El Fuego. Several of his fellows laughed as well, though whether they'd understood Lina's words or were just responding to their leader's actions was unclear.

El Fuego's words, when they came, though, had nothing of humor in them. "Woman! You talk very tough. But we will see how tough you are when we drag you out of there and make you kneel before us."

"I might kneel at your grave, but even that's not likely," Lina called.

"Are you deliberately provoking them?" Joseph Craft demanded. "Do you think that's a good idea?"

"You think they're going to let us walk out of

here?" Lina snapped back. "The more they talk the more we learn about them and just maybe about El Tigre."

Fuego's voice was clearly angry as he shouted back. "You have three of you in there at most. One is badly wounded. We saw the blood." He turned his head in both directions to indicate his compatriots. "We, on the other hand, are twelve very bad hombres. If we have to come after you, we will kill all three of you slowly. You, the most slowly. The most unpleasantly."

"Couldn't be as unpleasant as listening to you yap," Lina called out.

Even as she said it, Lina knew she'd pushed too hard this time. "Take cover," she ordered Craft as she heard gun hammers being snicked back outside. She slammed the door and slapped the door bar into place.

Gunfire erupted from the street; bullets slammed into the wooden door just as Lina dodged back behind the adobe wall. Splinters flew but the door was thick. It would take a shotgun at close range to smash through it.

As the first fusillade from the bandits ended, Joseph Craft rose from his crouch with a curse. He bashed the window out with the butt of his carbine, fired through it into the street. Lina rushed back to the window on her side of the cantina, bashed out the glass as well and fired through.

The bandits had taken shelter across the street. They answered Lina's shot with a volley of their own, sending remaining shards of glass flying. Lina had ducked back into safety. She waited until the firing paused, then raised up and looked through the window. A shadowy figure darted from behind a watering trough toward the corner of a house. Lina snapped a shot at him from her Winchester, saw him stumble and fall but pull himself to safety.

Footsteps pounded in the dark but Lina saw nothing. From the sound, the enemy was spreading out. Maybe encircling the cantina. A semi-steady fire peppered the front of the building. Lina shot back at muzzle flashes but apparently didn't hit anything important.

A feeling of impending danger whelmed her. She glanced over at Craft, darted over to him and leaned close to whisper. "They're going to try coming in the back. Stay put here. If you're up to it, fire through both these windows. Try to make them think we're both still up front in the building."

Craft fired through his own window, then nodded. He stepped past her toward the second window. Lina rushed toward the storage room of the cantina, reloading her Winchester as she did. She heard Craft fire again as she stepped through the open doorway into the back. A low hiss warned Henri she was coming. He glanced toward her, lifting a hand in acknowledgement.

Henri had done everything he could to make the back room defensible. There was only one door, a wooden one, but it was far flimsier than the front door. A strong kick would wreck it. But Henri had placed candles on the floor around it to light it up. He'd also tied the horses up against the wall farthest from the door. This room must have been used for livestock in the past because iron rings were embedded in the adobe walls for just that purpose.

"I've got a notion they're about to try here," Lina told Henri.

"Right. I've been expecting it. I'm ready. Stay away from the door itself."

"What?"

"Can't you smell it?"

She took a sniff, picked up the scent Henri was talking about.

"You soaked the back door with kerosene," she said.

"Yes. And spread soaked straw there too. Plus..." He fingered the kerosene lamp that barely burned close to his hand. "If they come through, I'll light them up."

"They're coming through," Lina said. "And we need to let them."

Henri arched an eyebrow.

"They're going to want to end this quickly," Lina explained. "They'll try one rush. Here. Because they think there's two of us up front and they probably know this door is a weak spot. It's clear they've been to this village before. It their rush doesn't work they'll surround us and wait us out. They've got the numbers to do it. We need to hurt them badly and this is likely the only chance we'll get."

"So, we let them through the door," Henri said. "A few of them at least. Then we hit them with everything."

"Dead on," Lina said.

CHAPTER 27

Joseph Craft limped back and forth between windows in the cantina's main room, firing through each to make the bandits outside think two people were still on guard. His hip hurt; his side hurt. He felt a trickle of something down the outside of his wounded leg, glanced down to see fresh blood seeping through his shirt from his wound.

Pulling the tail of the shirt up revealed that he'd popped a couple of the stitches Henri had put in. Vertigo seized him. He pressed one palm against the wound and leaned into the wall. The adobe felt cool against his cheek. He was hot and damp; salted sweat beaded his lips.

Needing to keep one hand on his wound made using his carbine difficult. He leaned it against the wall, drew his sidearm instead. It was an unusual weapon, made by Colt Firearms and chambered in .45 caliber. Most people called it a 1911, after the year in which it was first released.

The army had distributed a number of 1911s to its forces. Most had gone to officers. This one had originally been given to Captain Caleb Jefferson, Joseph's commander at Fort Bliss. Jefferson preferred his ivory handled Peacemaker, though and had passed this weapon on to his subordinate.

Joseph had grown up with revolvers but this gun was referred to as a "self-loader." When you pulled the trigger, a slide around the barrel kicked back, ejecting the spent shell casing and automatically loading another round for firing. A magazine fitted into the gun's rectangular butt held seven rounds and you could just keep pulling the trigger until all those rounds were fired. In practice, he'd emptied it in about a second. So far he'd never fired it in anger. He would tonight.

Blood trickled through the fingertips where they lay pressed to his wound. He ignored it. He had a job to do. He had to keep firing. Without looking, he stuck the 1911 out the window and shot off a round, then limped to the other window and repeated that action.

He hadn't told anyone, but it was *his* fault that his wife, Rebecca and his daughter, Perla, had been taken by kidnappers. He should have had them with him at Fort Bliss. They'd been there a while. He'd been the one to encourage them to go visit Rebecca's good friend, Elora, who lately had moved to the mission of San Javier del Amor.

He might not have blamed himself so much if it hadn't been for the reason he'd encouraged that trip — the fiery eyes of a señorita named Juana. So far there'd been nothing with Juana save flirtation, but he'd known exactly what he was doing by getting his family out of the way. If only he could take it back. He fired through the window, cursed himself, fired through the other one.

A small barrel came flying through the window he wasn't standing at. It was about the size of a keg of ale and shattered on the floor when it hit. It wasn't full of booze. Only Hell spilled out.

******

Lina and Henri separated, one to the left, the other to the right. Lina moved behind a wooden support pillar broad enough to break up her outline. Henri crouched behind a stack of hay bales with his kerosene lamp covered under the floppy hat he'd placed beside him. They waited, but not for long.

Without warning, a blast from a double-barreled shotgun tore the back door off its hinges. The candles on the floor snuffed out. Everything went dark. The horses whinnied in fear and began to kick against their ties.

Four men spilled into the room. A fifth followed, breaking open his shotgun to reload. Their attention was caught by the movement from the horses. One man fired. A horse shrieked. Henri grabbed the lantern hidden beneath his hat, whipped it over his head and let it fly. It crashed down among the five invaders and shattered.

The kerosene Henri had splashed across the hay

covered floor ignited. A blue flame gushed upward, set the hay to crackling before leaping onto cotton trousers and shirts. Light was reborn in the room. It came from the burning floor and from the men who'd burst in. A bandito screamed in shock and terror. Another followed.

Henri triggered his Sharps. The .50-90 round caught the shotgunner in the chest and hurled him like a cornhusk doll back out through the door. Lina lever-actioned her Winchester, sent slugs plowing into more of the outlaws. Henri's Peacemakers began to hammer. In a matter of a few breaths, five men lay dead or dying on the cantina floor.

"Stay," Lina ordered Henri.

She leaned her Winchester against the wall but still had her bow and quiver slung across her shoulder. Throwing herself forward, she hurtled the flames and dodged through the door into the night. Henri knew what she was doing, taking the fight to their enemy on their own ground. But he knew the Black Rose. She'd soon make it *her* ground.

A shout from the front room of the cantina brought Henri's head around. Joseph Craft called out something Henri couldn't make out. Behind the shout came wild firing. It sounded as if some enemy had come in the front as well. For an instant, Henri hesitated, not wanting to leave the back door unguarded. But Craft was in trouble.

With an oath, Henri leaped toward the door leading to the cavalryman.

******

As the small barrel hit the floor and burst open, Joseph Craft's pupils dilated in terror. A ropey knot of snakes spilled out into a writhing mass on the floor of the cantina. The musky, urine-thick stench of reptile was overwhelming. He cried out, fired his pistol once into the mass. Blood sprayed but there were dozens of snakes.

The knot broke apart into a hissing, slithering, rattling nightmare. Then something else came scuttling out of the barrel — big dark scorpions the length of his palm with their wicked tales lifted and curved.

Craft backed against the wall. Gunfire continued from outside. Bullets whistled through the windows and thumped into the adobe wall protecting him. He scarcely heard any of it. The scorpions were spreading out fast. He shot at one that looked as big as his fist. The bullet missed a direct hit but the close impact of the .45 slug sent the thing flying.

The snakes were rattlers, Craft saw. Most of them anyway. And they were enraged. They struck at anything near them, at scorpions, at each other. A sidewinder came rowing across the floor toward Craft's boots. He fired twice. The second bullet took the rattle of its tail but didn't stop it. He cried out, fired again. The snake's head exploded; its body thrashed.

Another snake darted toward him. A very strange rattler. It had the coloration but no rattle on its tail. He pulled the trigger on his Colt: click, click, click.

He was empty. He kicked out, caught the snake's upper body with his left boot just as it struck at him. It went flying. But a sudden sharp pain skewered his other leg.

He glanced down in shock, saw a black scorpion on his right boot with its red tail arched. It had stung him right through the thin cloth of his uniform trousers. He shook it off, but more were coming. He opened his mouth to scream.

CHAPTER 28

Lina moved through the dark as if she were born to it. Perhaps she was. Her black clothes blended perfectly. Her cape swirled about her like a piece of night itself. She heard shooting from the front room of the cantina but forced herself to ignore it. Henri and Joseph Craft would have to deal with that concern. She was hunting.

Staying away from areas where starlight gleaming against adobe walls might reveal her, Lina wove a path through the village. Her movements were silent but sure. The breeze shifted. She picked up a scent ahead — fresh horse manure. She circled around it to get downwind.

Ahead of her, horses stomped, whickered, urinated. She began to make out the shapes of individual animals. They were tied on a picket to a bit of wooden fence. She crept closer. The whispering voices of two men came to her, speaking small worries in Spanish. But where were they?

She drifted nearer, like a mist stirred by the faintest wind. The horses must have sensed her. They became restless. Lina moved more quickly, letting the sound of the horses cover her. She saw two men. One pushed away from the adobe wall where he and his companion leaned, started toward the horses with a muttered, "mierda." The other laughed.

As the first man reached the horses and began to check them, the Black Rose drew her knife and took the one who still leaned against the wall. She stepped in close, slapped a hand across his mouth before he knew she was there and cut his throat. She wrenched him away from the wall as he thrashed. The first fellow heard something that caught his attention. He spun around.

"Rafael?"

Lina had taken Rafael's place against the wall. She'd clapped his sombrero on her head and now lifted a hand in a casual wave of acknowledgement to the other man. He came back toward her, unsuspectingly. At half a dozen paces away, he must have recognized something wrong. He paused with an oath. His hand grabbed for the pistol at his belt.

Lina's urumi licked out, snapped around the man's neck. She jerked him toward her; he stumbled and fell to his knees. Lina raised the old long-barreled revolver that Rafael had carried and bashed the fellow over the head with it, knocking him cold. She tucked the revolver into the waistband of her trousers and dragged the man farther into the shadows before binding and gagging him. Later, he would answer questions for her.

A machete and a beaten-up old rifle leaned against the wall where the two bandits had been standing. Lina picked up the machete and hacked through the rope holding the horses to the fence. She tossed both the machete and the rifle onto the roof of the adobe. Leaping up, she grabbed the top of the roof and pulled herself over.

Grasping the blade of the machete, she hurled it butt-first into the closest horse below. Unhurt but startled, the animal reared back with a loud whinny. It knocked into the horse next to it and chaos followed. Realizing that they were no longer tied up, several of the horses bolted in alarm.

The bow over her shoulder was too silent for the work, Lina intended now. She wanted to draw attention. She took up the rifle, checked to make sure it was loaded. It was an old Springfield model bolt-action weapon chambered for the .30-40 caliber. This was an American gun commonly called a "Krag." Who knew how a Mexican bandito had gotten hold of it but a lot of these guns had seen service in the American army. It probably still worked. The Krags were tough weapons.

As Lina had hoped, two men came running to check on the disturbance among the horses. No one in the cantina could see this section of the village so the men weren't worried about being shot. They came right down the middle of the street. The road lay like a pale ribbon beneath the starlight. The men wore dark clothing. Lina waited until they were within twenty yards before shooting the first one. She aimed for center of mass and hit. The man threw up his hands and went down with nothing more than a grunt.

Lina worked the bolt on the Krag, shifted her target, fired again. The second bandit was already diving for cover. She missed, worked the bolt again. The man scrambled behind a water trough. Lina emptied the Krag into it, then set it down so the barrel showed over the edge of the roof. That might distract the enemy for a little bit.

She slipped to the other end of the roof and swung down to the ground, drawing the revolver she'd confiscated from the outlaw named Rafael. It looked like some Mexican copy of the Remington model 1890. When she checked the cylinder, she found it loaded but couldn't see what caliber it was. The barrel was at least eight inches long.

There'd been twelve banditos. Thirteen if you counted the small, twisted being that traveled with them. Six were dead for sure, a seventh captured. An eighth was either dead or badly wounded. Now the hardest part began. The last four or five must be alerted and ready for anything. They couldn't be surprised further.

Or could they?

******

Henri reached the door into the front part of the cantina. The kerosene lanterns were still lit. He could see. The tile floor was alive with rattlesnakes and scorpions. His first thought was, *how?* When he saw the broken remnants of the barrel, he knew.

Joseph Craft was backed against the front wall of the building, between the door and one of the windows. His mouth was wide, his face pale and terrified. He stomped at a snake right in front of him.

"Joseph!" Henri shouted.

The man looked up. His lips worked but nothing came out. Henri did the only thing he could think to do. A straw broom leaned against the wall just inside the door. Henri grabbed it up, threw it toward the cavalryman almost like a spear. Craft caught it, used it to slap the snake away that was right at his feet.

"Get to me!" Henri shouted.

Craft was still holding his empty pistol in his right fist. He stuffed it down into its holster and began using the broom with both hands to sweep a clear path across the deadly floor. The image was ridiculous — the hard-bitten cavalryman sweeping frantically to left and right while snakes and scorpions went flying. Henri felt like laughing and shouting madly at the same time. He did neither.

As Craft worked his way toward Henri, the mountain man realized that the fire had burned out in the back room of the cantina and they'd need light. He darted quickly along the wall to grab one of the lanterns. Most of the snakes were near the front of the room. Henri stomped a few black scorpions before he reached the lamp and pulled it down. He backed up to the door, shouting a "come on" to Craft.

Craft stomped a snake that was too close to him, then batted its body away. A coiled rattler struck at him. He cried out as he twisted to one side. The snake's fangs caught in his pants' leg. Henri saw the spurt of venom darken the cloth but the bite must have missed flesh.

Craft leaped across a sidewinder, turned as he reached Henri. He slapped away a scorpion with the broom but grunted as something hit him hard in the thigh. He fell against Henri and the mountain man dragged him backward across the threshold into the storage room. He dropped Craft, who was grabbing at something with his hands, and slammed the door between the two rooms.

Henri spun back toward Craft and lifted the lantern. The muscular body of a snake almost five feet long slapped against the cavalryman's leg. Its fangs were buried through his pants into his thigh.

Craft wrenched the thing loose and flung it across the room. It hit the back wall and fell stunned to the floor. Henri lifted the lantern high in his left hand to shed light as far as it could reach; his right hand palmed a Colt Peacemaker and blasted one shot. The snake's body jumped as its head disintegrated.

"Bit me, bit me," Craft muttered. He grabbed for the knife at his belt. "Gotta get the venom out."

Henri turned to help Craft but the image of the snake that had struck the cavalryman was shocked into his awareness. He'd seen its tail and knew it wasn't a rattler. *A Fer-de-lance*, he thought. He'd crossed paths with a few before. They were far more deadly than a rattler, deadly enough to kill a healthy full-grown man, much less one who'd already been weakened by a gunshot and blood loss.

******

The Black Rose worked her way along the edge of the village toward the cantina. The firing had dropped off there, both from inside and outside. She didn't know what was happening. She needed to. Were Henri and Joseph Craft still alive?

She froze against a fence as something darted across her field of vision. It was moving fast, low to the ground. It reached the back of one of the houses and stood up straight on its hind legs. She saw that it was the small being with the twisted back who appeared to be a scout for the banditos.

The being crawled up some crates stacked at the back of the house and pulled itself over onto the roof. There was a moment when it was silhouetted against the sky. Lina raised her revolver, took aim, then held her fire. The being vanished below the line of the roof.

Making sure to keep out of sight of that roof, Lina made her way toward the back of the house just across the street from the cantina. This is where all the bandits had been hiding when they started firing. She saw only one foe now, a man hiding behind a water trough who occasionally sent a shot from his rifle slamming into the cantina wall. Thankfully, the fellow had brought along a small candle, which burned on the ground near his feet. It made enough light for what Lina intended.

Sticking her confiscated pistol through her belt, Lina finally drew the bow over her shoulder. She plucked an arrow from the quiver and seated it firmly.

The man fired again and before he could work the bolt on his rifle, Lina made a meowing sound, like a small kitten. The bandit turned. Lina repeated the sound.

Apparently curious, the fellow picked up his candle, held it up slightly so he could see. As the light fell across his face, Lina put an arrow through his throat. The man gave a gurgle and fell back against the water trough. His rifle clunked in the empty trough. The candle dropped to the ground, snuffed itself on dirt.

"Manuel!" a voice shouted.

Gunfire tattered the night all around Lina. She hit the ground, hugged herself against the dirt. Someone must have seen the man Lina had arrowed go down. They were firing wildly, but without knowing her exact location.

Three shots, four. No more. She heard cursing in Spanish and the sound of metal grinding on metal. She knew what had happened. A rifle had jammed. The bandit was jerking at the bolt to loosen it.

Lina rose to her knees. She'd seen the muzzle flashes. They came from the roof of the house she'd been working her way toward. It was barely fifteen feet away. A parapet rimmed the roof, with a man hiding behind it. She saw the solid blackness of the roof and just over the top of it a lighter shadow that had to be a person.

Drawing the bow back, she loosed. The arrow caught the man high in the shoulder. He screamed and dropped his rifle. Before he could think to throw himself down behind the parapet to hide, Lina released a second arrow. This one punched through the man's left cheek. It didn't go all the way through. The feathers caught on the jaw while the arrowhead skewered through the right cheek and out.

The man couldn't scream with his mouth nailed open. He tried to turn and run but tripped and fell. The roof must have had a soft spot. Lina heard the wounded man crash through and thump to the floor inside. Someone shouted wildly from within the house.

Lina had only a few arrows left and wanted to save them. She slung her bow over her shoulder, drew the pistol from her belt. The front door of the adobe crashed open and the big man with the big belly who'd first tried to get her and the others to surrender, leaped out. He carried a shotgun. Light from lanterns inside limned him.

Lina raised the pistol, pulled the trigger. The old gun misfired. Or maybe the cartridges were corroded. The shotgunner heard the impotent click and spun in her direction, swinging his big barreled weapon to bear.

A gun blast from inside the house caught the man in the back and side. He cried out, dropping his weapon and staggering farther away from the door. Lina took aim, pulled the trigger on her pistol a second time. This time it discharged. The bullet caught her enemy in the forehead and knocked him down. He wouldn't get up from that.

But who was inside the house now? And what would be *their* next move?

CHAPTER 29

"Don't shoot!" a voice from inside the house called. "Friend here!"

"Come out," Lina called back, keeping her gun steady.

A man stepped into the doorway. He had a thick mustache and wore dirt stained clothes of white cotton — the clothes of a Mexican farmer. His hands were up. In the left was an old bolt-action rifle with his finger nowhere near the trigger.

"Friend," the man said again. He had very little accent and Lina thought he must have learned to speak English as a child. And probably in the United States. She still wasn't sure if she could trust him.

"Put the rifle down," she ordered.

The man bent slowly and leaned the rifle against the wall of the adobe, then straightened. His brown eyes combined intelligence with curiosity and a hint of fear.

"You're one of the villagers," Lina said.

The man nodded. "I'm Eduardo. An enemy of El Tigre and his men."

"There are two of them left around, I think."

Eduardo shook his head. "Only one was left but he has been taken care of by another friend." He pointed down the street behind her.

Lina moved to look where Eduardo pointed but kept him in sight as well. Her hand tightened on her pistol but then she lowered it. Trotting crookedly down the street came the hunched over being she'd seen climb onto a roof a few minutes before. As he got closer, she got her first clear glimpse of him.

He was male, of indeterminate age, with a spine that would not straighten and a hump on his right shoulder. His arms were long for his size, his legs short. His face lacked any symmetry. His eyes were offset from each other, with the right one larger and higher on his face. His nose was barely there, with slits for nostrils. He had a bad underbite with his lower jaw extending out past his upper lip by a couple of inches. This kept him from being able to completely close his mouth and his teeth were revealed as yellow and irregular. Someone had dressed him in a fur garment and a collar that seemed to be meant to make him look more animalistic.

A bad taste filled Lina's mouth. Who would have clothed a human being thus, no matter how twisted his body might be from an accident of birth? She glanced down at the dead leader of the banditos and thought she knew the answer to her question.

"I thought he was a scout for El Tigre's men,"

Lina said.

Eduardo smiled. "That is what they thought, too. But he is truly our friend. And yours. He is called 'Solo.'"

Solo straightened his back as much as he could. He was barely four feet tall but certainly no child. He reached up to his collar and unbuckled it, hurled it angrily aside. When he looked back at Lina, though, he smiled with crooked and protruding teeth.

"Greetings, Solo," Lina said.

Solo's mouth worked but no words came out. He inclined his head in what was clearly meant to be a bow.

"Solo does not speak," Eduardo said. "His tongue was removed as a child. But he understands both Spanish and English."

Lina nodded, met Eduardo's gaze. "I also captured a bandit for questioning," she said. "He's tied up behind a house a few doors down."

Eduardo glanced at Solo, who gave his head a shake. Lina saw the movement and frowned.

"What," she demanded.

"I'm afraid Solo has a great deal of anger directed at his recent abusers," Eduardo said. "The man you mention will not be able to answer any questions."

Lina glanced at Solo, who gave her a grand shrug.

Releasing a long sigh, the Black Rose turned back to Eduardo. "We need to talk," she said, "but I have friends in the cantina. I have to check on them."

"Of course," Eduardo said, nodding. "Do what you must. After, we will talk."

Lina uncocked the hammer of her old revolver and tucked it in her belt, then trotted across the street toward the cantina, calling out as she advanced so Henri would know it was her. No answer came from inside, though.

Fear clutched at Lina's heart. She didn't even try the door, which she knew had been locked, but looked through one of the shattered windows. Dismay struck her as she saw the snakes. But there were no bodies and the door to the storage area was closed. That gave her a little hope. She called out loudly:

"Henri! Henri!"

"We're back here!" Henri returned, his voice muffled.

Lina's breath came easier. "I'm coming around," she shouted. "It's clear out here."

She reached the back of the cantina a minute later. The rear door had a huge hole blown in it and hung on one hinge. Scorch marks adorned the wall and the floor around the door, but only the straw Henri had scattered had burned. Wisps of smoke rose from the clothes of the men she and Henri had slain. They all still lay piled where they'd fallen.

"Henri," Lina called, stepping over the bodies into the storage room.

A single kerosene lantern burned inside but it had been turned up high. Lina saw Henri rise from beside a set of hay bales where he'd been squatting. He strode toward her. She could see that Joseph Craft lay stretched out on the hay and knew something was badly wrong.

"Was he shot again?" Lina asked as Henri stopped in front of her.

The mountain man shook his head. "No. Bitten. By one of the snakes up front. And not a Rattlesnake. A Fer-de-lance."

Lina hissed in her throat, knowing how deadly the Fer-de-lance could be.

"I opened the wound a little, sucked out some of the venom. But he's already lost a lot of blood, so...." He shrugged.

"Will he live?"

Henri shook his head. "You should...should speak to him."

"What do I say?"

"You'll have to figure it out. But he was asking for you. Did you say it was clear outside?"

"Yes. And we've gotten a little help from the villagers."

Henri raised an eyebrow. "Guess I'll wait for an explanation," he said. "I'll take care of the horses. Take them outside. One of them got hit by a bullet."

"Thanks, Henri," Lina said, resting her hand on his shoulder.

He put his hand over hers for a moment before turning toward the horses. Lina walked over to Craft and stood looking down. Henri had pulled a blanket up to the man's chin but she could smell the blood and an acid sweat on him. His eyes were closed, with deep blue-black circles underneath them. His face already wore the waxy pallor of death, but she could see his chest still rising and falling.

Thinking he was asleep, she started to turn away. His hand leaped from beneath the blanket, the fingers curved like talons. He grabbed her wrist in a death grip.

"Wait!"

Craft's blue eyes were open and feverish. She met his gaze. His pupils were dilated.

"I have to...tell you something," he said. "Something critical."

******

Six riders topped a rise and saw the crime taking place below. Four bandits surrounded an open farm wagon. One had already climbed in the back of the wagon to tear through a pitiful list of belongings, ranging from clothes, to cooking gear, to stocks of food stuffs. Two others were dragging an older man and woman off the wagon seat, kicking and slapping them as they did so. A fourth held the reins of the bandits' ponies. The outlaws hadn't yet seen the riders on the ridge above them.

Sister Caroline Harp jerked her Winchester from its sheath beside her saddle, threw it to her shoulder just as one of the bandits pulled his pistol and pointed it at the old man's forehead. She fired. It was nearly a four-hundred-yard shot but she hit the bandit in the shoulder, sent him staggering back.

Sister Sofia Lee pulled her own Winchester and fired. The outlaw in the rear of the wagon pitched over the side into the dirt. Shouting wildly, the other two outlaws on the ground, including the one Caroline had wounded, ran for their mounts and swung aboard. They wheeled hard and tore off at a gallop.

"Let's get them!" Sister Sofia shouted as she spurred her horse down the hill toward the scene.

Sister Caroline sheathed her rifle again and spurred after Sofia. The four men with them followed. Caroline shouted to one to check on the farm couple and the outlaw Sofia had shot.

The fleeing outlaws had a lead but their pursuers were headed downhill at first and had better horses. They quickly began to gain. Caroline pulled ahead of Sofia until Sofia stabbed her rifle back into its sheath and leaned forward over her mount to encourage it. In another moment the two nuns were galloping neck and neck, several paces ahead of the men who followed them.

The ground ahead was flat and dry, covered mostly by brittle grass and a few clumps of mesquite and cactus. The outlaws' horses kicked up dust as their riders lashed them brutally. Their hearts were in the run but they didn't have the strength of their pursuers' mounts.

Caroline gained steadily on the outlaw in front of her. The world was alive with the pound of hooves. Her horse's mane whipped across her face; dust stung her cheeks. This was the man she'd wounded. Blood stained his whole right arm but he clung grimly to the saddle as he strove to escape.

Caroline let her right fist close around the wooden haft of her Kpinga, which hung at her side. She drew it, pushed up with her feet in the stirrups to give herself a little height, then whipped the three-bladed weapon forward and let it fly.

Sister Sofia closed on a second bandit. The man turned his head in time to see his danger. He jerked at the pistol in his belt, swung it back and fired. The bullet seared past Sofia's shoulder, plucking at the cloth of her shirt. But the action cost the bandit. His horse slowed a fraction.

Sofia pulled alongside the man. She was on his left while he held his gun in his right hand. Sofia drew her Facón, with its bone hilt and razor sharp twelve-inch blade. As the man tried to twist his body around to bring his pistol to bear, Sofia leaned out from her horse and swung the Facón down in a back-hand slash.

The sharpened steel sliced nearly through the horse's girth strap and continued across the man's leg, cutting cloth and flesh with equal ease. The outlaw screamed. The horse, feeling the rasp of the long blade's tip against its flank, shied violently away. The girth strap broke. Saddle and man came loose and crashed to the earth in a thick shower of dirt and rock.

At nearly the same instant as Sofia struck, Sister Caroline's Kpinga smacked the wounded outlaw squarely between the shoulders and buried itself spine deep. He cried out, flung up his head and arms. The horse ran right out from under him and he thudded like a sack of wet grain to the ground.

The last of the fleeing outlaws had gained a few feet while the Sisters were taking out his companions. He might as well have committed suicide. Now that the two nuns were not in the way, the three riders who followed them had an open target. As one, they pulled their pistols. As one they fired. The volley of lead tore the last bandit from his saddle and sent him tumbling to his death.

The five riders pulled their horses to a gradual stop and rode back to investigate the downed outlaws. Two were dead; the third still lived, though his leg bled badly from Sister Sofia's knife cut. He clutched at the wound with both hands but could not staunch the blood flow.

Sofia and Caroline dismounted and approached the man. He put his hands up. They shook.

"Por favor, por favor!" he shouted.

Sofia crouched and drew her Navaja, her other knife. She let the wounded man study the elaborately worked handle before unfolding the blade and showing him the sharp steel blade. His pupils dilated.

"Te suplico!" he begged.

"El Tigre?" Sofia demanded.

"No, no, no."

Sofia leaned closer, asked again if the outlaw knew of, or served El Tigre. The man denied it in a burst of Spanish. Sofia folded her knife, put it away and rose. Sister Caroline had retrieved her Kpinga and joined the other nun.

"What do you think?" Caroline asked. "Is he lying?"

Sofia shook her head. "I don't think so. These weren't El Tigre's men. Just standard bandits, standard scum robbing and killing indiscriminately."

The man who Sister Caroline had ordered to stop at the wagon was called Rico — a gunfighter it was rumored by some. He certainly dressed the part, in black trousers and a short vest outlined with silver braid, with a tied down gun on his left hip. He rode up just then and overheard Sofia's words.

"At least they didn't get a chance to kill those two farmers," he said, gesturing back over his shoulder at the wagon and the old man and woman who were at work reloading it.

"The other outlaw dead?" Caroline asked.

"Shot right through the heart at a great distance," Rico replied, as proud as if he had made the shot himself.

"So only one left," Sofia said, turning her head to glance at the wounded bandit near her feet.

The man still held his wound though the bleeding seemed to be stopping. He was youngish, probably in his early twenties, with greasy, unkempt hair and beard. He looked up, aware that all attention had fallen on him.

"What will we do with him, Señora?" Rico asked. "This is the one who was kicking the old woman. Had we been a momento later he would have become a murderer. Likely he is already."

"We can't afford to lose time," Sofia said. "The Black Rose needs us." She studied the landscape around them. About half a mile distant stood a bare and twisted old oak. Sofia pointed toward it.

"Hang him high," she said.

CHAPTER 30

"What do you want to tell me?" Lina asked Joseph Craft as she sat down on the hay bale next to him.

"In my saddlebags," Craft said. "There's a green stone."

"Like a jade heart?" Lina asked.

"Yes! You know about it? How could you....."

"I've seen several of them. El Tigre gives them to some of his followers. And maybe uses them for other purposes as well. We found one in a dead body. The one you have belonged to Bolanger, I take it?"

Craft swallowed hard and took a few harsh breathes before continuing. "Yes. And he...told me what they were for."

Lina's interest sharpened. "What?"

"Bolanger said...El Tigre uses 'em to 'watch' his followers. Through them, he can see what they see and hear what they hear."

"I don't believe that," Lina said.

"Bolanger does. Did. He said they were full of...

magic."

"I don't doubt El Tigre tells his followers that. Bolanger didn't seem the type to believe such nonsense, though."

"Maybe it don't...seem that way. But he did. I think he saw something, had some kind of experience that...convinced him."

"Did he claim such an experience?"

"Not...specifically. Just the way...he talked."

"Henri and I met one of El Tigre's followers who knew the use of peyote," Lina said. "It's possible Bolanger was exposed to the drug, too. I've been told those experiences can be powerful."

"Must be it," Craft said. "The stone I have. There's a little hollow in it. You pull one of the..." he coughed hard, then forced himself to continue, "one of the golden veins. To open it. There was residue in Bolanger's. Maybe peyote."

"That's something we didn't know," Lina said. "I have a couple more of those stones. I'll check for that hollow."

"Glad...if it helps. Just wanted to tell you about it. Stuffed it in a sock in the bottom of my saddlebags. Just in case. Can't be too careful."

"Thanks."

Craft swallowed again. It was getting harder for him. "Something...else," he said.

"What?"

"I know who you are. Not just the Black Rose, but Sister Catalina Rivera, too."

Lina frowned.

"Don't worry," Craft said. He smiled slightly with ashen lips. "I won't...reveal your secret. Just wanted to...thank you again. For saving my daughter, Perla. If anyone can help my wife, it'll be you and Henri."

"We'll do our best."

"Would you take this?"

Henri must have removed Craft's gun belt for comfort and placed it on the hay next to him. He grasped it with one hand and tried to push it toward Lina. He was too weak. She had to pick it up herself and place it on her lap.

"I don't need your gun," she said.

"It's new. Maybe...you'll like it." He reached out and pressed a button on the side of the gun. A click sounded. Something slid partway out of the handle. "That's the...magazine," Craft continued. "Holds seven shells. Insert it, pull back the slide to load one in the chamber. After that just keep pulling the trigger. It reloads itself."

"I've seen such before and I still don't need it."

"Please," Craft said. His eyes drooped, then snapped opened again. He blinked several times rapidly, managed to wipe his face with his hand. That only smeared the sweat across his features.

"I realize...I'm not gonna make it," Craft continued, turning his gaze directly to the Black Rose's face, "but if you take the gun. If it helps in any little way. Well...maybe it'll be like...*I* helped."

"All right," Lina said. She forced a smile, made a move to stand up.

"Wish I could see Becca once more," Craft whispered. "And give Perla a hug."

Lina could think of nothing to say. She rose silently. Craft's eyes were on her. It took her a moment to realize that he was no longer seeing anything at all.

******

Lina informed Henri that Joseph Craft was dead. He offered to bury the cavalryman while Lina returned to speak with Eduardo, the villager who'd helped them against El Tigre's men. She had a couple of things to do first.

Since she'd told Craft she would, she hooked the man's Colt .45 and its holster on her own belt. She also stopped by his saddlebags and dug out the jade heart he'd confiscated from Bolanger. It turned out to be larger than either of the other two she'd already found. The hollow inside was easily revealed by pulling aside one of the golden threads representing blood veins on the outside of the gem. As Craft had indicated, the inside was empty except for a faint brownish residue of powder. A sniff revealed a bitter scent, though she had no idea if that was the way peyote was supposed to smell.

Tucking the heart in her pocket, Lina returned to the house where she'd first encountered Eduardo. She found the door open and the inside lit with the flickering light of a kerosene lamp. Eduardo and the small man known as Solo shared a jug of pulque at a table inside. They offered her a cup; she took water instead and sat with them.

"Thank you for the help," Lina said. "But I'm wondering why you gave it?"

Eduardo considered. "Most of my people did not want me to interfere," he said finally. "But I felt I had to."

"Why?"

The man offered a smile. "We've seen no one in a very long time who stood any chance of defeating El Tigre. I sense that you and your friends might. That is worth taking some risks."

"This El Tigre seems to have a big reputation locally. But he's only a man. Any man can fall."

"Many would debate with you about whether El Tigre is 'only a man.' But I do believe you speak true. I may be alone in that here. Even our friend Solo," he smiled at the little fellow, "who has seen El Tigre up close, does not believe he is just a man."

Lina glanced at Solo, who nodded vigorously.

Turning back to Eduardo, Lina said, "You're alone in several things. Your English is the best I've ever encountered south of the border. Why is that?"

"I am not originally *from* south of the border," Eduardo replied. "I was born and raised in Texas. Educated there. My father had a certain amount of wealth but after his death it was leeched away by those who took advantage of my mother. She came from a village just north of here. When her health began to fail, she wished to return. I brought her. But her home was gone. Her family gone. We found this respite. She died here. I buried her here. I stayed."

Lina nodded. "What is this place?"

"A refuge. But not a perfectly safe one. Most of the people here are escapees from El Tigre Sangriento's kingdom of the damned."

"Kingdom?"

"Yes. You must have seen the pass that leads from this canyon higher into the mountains. If you followed it you'd come eventually to a...well, city is what I've heard. I've not been there. But it's where El Tigre lives and enslaves many."

"And those who escape come here?"

"Some."

"Why does he not come and take them back. Surely he knows this place exists?"

"He does. But we have watchers in the peaks around. When we see any sign of men coming, we vanish."

"Where?"

"I hope you'll forgive me if I do not tell you."

Lina considered, nodded. "I understand. Tell me what you know of El Tigre."

"I've never seen him," Eduardo said. "But those who have say he is powerfully built. That he has claws on his hands and feet. And that he has the head of a jaguar. I suspect he wears a mask and some kind of...fixtures on his hands and feet. They must be very convincing, though. People say, also, that he is a sorcerer. That he knows your thoughts. That he can be in many places at once. I have wondered if there might be more than one person who wears the mask."

"What else?"

"Undoubtedly, he has some power, some charisma." Eduardo shook his head. "I imagine he's smart enough to know what people are thinking when they're afraid. I don't believe it is anything magical, though many do. But of those he takes captive, many fall under his spell. Not all, of course. Solo did not, though he pretended too. That has worked well for us."

"If El Tigre sent the men here who were after us, he'll soon begin to miss them," Lina said.

Eduardo shook his head. "Those men were sentries. Up in the pass. They acted on their own. Solo was with them. They saw smoke from a big fire. I imagine you knew about that."

Lina nodded.

"Anyway," Eduardo continued. "They all died here. We made sure of that. No message could be allowed to get out. Eventually, though, they *will* be missed. We'll get rid of the bodies before that. And some of our people will go and brush out their tracks."

"What do you know of this?" Lina asked. Reaching in a pocket, she drew out the jade heart she'd brought along. She laid it on the table in front of Eduardo.

The villager's face filled with surprise and perhaps a touch of alarm. Solo hissed in fear and quickly grabbed a cloth off a nearby chair and flung it over the thing. Eduardo wiped his mouth on the back of his hand.

"That is…not something to play around with," he said.

"I thought you didn't believe in magic," Lina said.

"Not magic. Not exactly. But there is something about those things that raises my hackles."

"We were told that they are supposed to allow El Tigre to see and hear what his followers do. Is that the story the man tells?"

"Part of it," Eduardo said. "But more, it is also supposed to protect one from death. Or, if one is already dead, to raise you again."

Lina frowned. "What? Surely no one believes that."

"I'm afraid some do. El Tigre himself claims he has such a heart. And that is why he cannot die. He is said to have a scar on his chest where his heart was removed and replaced."

Solo slapped the top of the table and Lina glanced over at him. The man nodded and tapped the bony chest over his own heart.

"So," Lina said. "El Tigre wants to make himself a god."

"Or to restore the power of an ancient one. Do you know anything of the Azteca?"

"I've heard of the Aztec. If that's what you mean. They were the rulers of Mexico when the Spaniards arrived. The Spanish conquered them. I believe their capital city lay where Mexico City is now. Why?"

"They were a confederation of tribes, as I understand. And the Spanish did defeat them, but only with the help of local allies who were enemies of the Azteca. Tenochtitlan was their capital. Mexico City was built over and around it, after Hernán Cortés — you may call him Hernando — razed the city. I do not know all their history. No one does. The conquistadors destroyed much. And the monks and priests who came after destroyed more. The Catholic church labeled the Azteca evil. And they certainly engaged in brutality. Even practicing human sacrifices. From which, to appease their gods, they ripped the still beating heart."

"And you think El Tigre is pretending to be one of the Aztec gods?"

"His idea of one. Ever since I became aware of him, I've been trying to find more information about the Azteca. I've pieced together some things. Some of it memories of works I read years ago. The Azteca had many deities. One of them is usually shown as a jaguar — Tepeyollotli. The serpent is common in Aztec mythology as well. Quetzalcoatl is one of their major gods and is called the 'feathered serpent.' The followers of El Tigre certainly like snakes. As you so recently saw."

"Right," Lina said. "We've seen them use rattlesnakes as weapons before, too."

"El Tigre seems to be preaching a return to former days of glory. Such is attractive to many who feel powerless today. Perhaps in any day."

"I imagine so," Lina said. "You're well informed about the Aztec. How is that?"

"I told you I was raised and educated in Texas. And that my father had money. Well, I was *very* well educated. I was to become a teacher of history. But my father died and when people began taking advantage of my mother I had to return home to care for our property." He offered Lina a wry smile. "Obviously, I did not do a very good job of that. It seems a head for history does not go with a head for business."

"I understand," Lina said. "So how do we stop this pretend Aztec god? You say the pass beyond the village leads to his city?"

"It does. But to follow it would be suicide. It is narrow. Perfect for ambushes. And under constant surveillance. An army could not get through."

"We'll have to find a way. He has taken people I owe a debt to."

"I surmised as much," Eduardo said. "And there is another possible route to take."

Lina's voice sharpened as she said, "Tell me!"

Solo knows a back way. One that even El Tigre is not aware of. It's dangerous. You could not take your horses. But on foot, it is possible. It is the way most of those in this village escaped from El Tigre's city."

Lina studied the small man at the table beside her. His bent back left him hunched over his mug of pulque. His feet didn't touch the floor beneath his chair. He met her gaze with eyes of dark brown. He did not smile; his face was serious. Small as he was, strength lived in him.

"All right," Lina said. "When can we leave?"

"Sleep tonight," Eduardo said. "There are things that need to be done to prepare." He gestured around at Lina, Solo and himself. "We'll start in the morning. I'll be going with you as well."

"There's no need of that. Besides, in a week to

ten days, I expect friends of mine to arrive. I've left a marked trail for them but they need to be told about the pass. And the back way. We'll need someone here for that."

"I don't know the back way myself," Eduardo said. "I've never traveled it and could show no one. But there is someone else who might be able to. Can you write?"

"Yes, of course," Lina said. "What has that to do with anything?"

"Write your friends a letter explaining everything, with your signature. I will speak to my wife. She was once a slave of El Tigre. She remembers the way. And I believe I can convince her to greet your friends and guide them. I must be there with you, though. I have waited long to strike at El Tigre. Alone I could do nothing. But I will not waste this opportunity."

Lina thought swiftly. "All right," she said. "I'll write the letter tonight. And before we leave in the morning, I'll mark a way for my friends to find this village. But remember this. If you accompany us, you are under *my* command. Neither you nor Solo will do anything without my approval. Is that clear?"

Eduardo began nodding. "It is."

Lina drained her cup of water and rose. "Let's begin," she said.

CHAPTER 31

By the time Lina returned to Henri, the mountain man had almost finished the grave for Joseph Craft. She pitched in for the last foot or so, then climbed out of the pit and stood beside her friend and a dead man wrapped in an old frayed blanket.

"Maybe we should say some words," Henri said. "Before we put dirt on him."

"You're better with words than I am," Lina said.

"Maybe," Henri agreed. "But I'm not sure the Lord thinks I'm worth hearing."

Lina frowned. "You're a sight better man than I am a woman," she said. "Even if I do go around dressed as a nun sometimes."

"It's more than dress. You're a member of the Sisters of Señora Maria. Surely the Lord listens to his own."

Lina huffed a breath. "All right," she said. "It's not getting us anywhere to argue about it."

Taking a few steps to stand over Craft's body,

Lina tried to gather her thoughts. Half the night had passed. The stars sketched their ancient shapes in the blackness overhead. Henri had chosen a good place for the grave. It was not far outside the village, in an area of softer ground near a stand of cacti. A little breeze cooled their sweat.

Lina's fists clenched. She wished she had a Bible. Maybe a woman who so often dressed as a nun should have one with her all the time. The need hadn't occurred to her before. And there was no place to get one now. At least she had her rosary. It was bound up in her hair. She reached up and touched it. Her thoughts began to flow.

"Joseph Craft was not a man without faults," she started. "But who of us is? In the end, he loved his wife. He risked his life to save her and the risk was too much. The last words he spoke to me were of her. And of his daughter, Perla, who he also loved. I saw the way he was with her in Santa Annabella. He had goodness in him, deeper than any of the sins he may have committed. I pray that mercy be granted to him."

She stopped.

"Amen," Henri said.

He'd placed ropes around the blanket-wrapped body's feet and shoulders. He and Lina each took hold of a rope end and began to lower Craft into his grave. Next came the dirt. They had only one shovel, so they took turns. But soon it was done and the earth patted down. Henri had constructed a rough cross from two pieces of wood; he planted this at the head of the grave.

"We better sleep," Lina said. "We've got a guide in the morning who will lead us a back way to find El Tigre. We'll have to go on foot."

"Right," Henri said.

As they turned away, Lina saw a small figure watching them from atop a nearby boulder. She nodded to Solo; he nodded back. She hoped to God she could trust him.

✳✳✳✳✳✳

Morning arrived far too soon. Lina and Henri joined Eduardo and Solo outside the cantina. A woman stood with them — Eduardo's wife, Dolores. Lina handed Eduardo a letter she'd written for those who would come looking to help her. He passed it on to his wife, a short, trim woman dressed in a colorful skirt and blouse with blue sandals.

Dolores had also prepared tamales for everyone's breakfast and passed these out. Lina decided to save hers for the trail but Henri quickly wolfed down two of his and gave Dolores a dazzling smile.

"Delicious," Henri said, rubbing his belly. "Delicioso!"

"Gracias," Dolores replied, smiling shyly.

"Please take care of our horses, Señora," Henri added, speaking further to Dolores. "I'm kind of fond of a couple of them."

Dolores glanced at her husband. Eduardo translated for her. She turned back to Henri and nodded. "Si," she said. Take care."

"Your animals will be put with ours until you

return," Eduardo said. "They'll get the same care as our own."

Henri nodded and bowed to Dolores, then slung the small pack of supplies he'd put together on his back. Lina already had a pack slung across her back, as did Eduardo. The three carried their rifles and pistols were slung at their belts. Lina carried her bow as well. Because of his hunched back, Solo hauled his supplies in a belt around his waist. For weapons, he had only a knife and a sling.

It was an hour after dawn, already warm and breezy. Solo started off through the village, with Lina and Henri right at his heels. Eduardo kissed his wife and held her dark haired head to his shoulder before hurrying to catch up with the others. Their hike immediately took them into scrub brush that soon hid the village houses from view.

The main pass into the mountains lay in the opposite direction from the one they were taking, Lina noted, but she'd expected that. She had no idea how long their hike would be. Eduardo didn't know and Solo couldn't speak. Joseph Craft's Colt 1911 hung heavy in a holster at her right hip and she shifted it on her belt until it nestled almost against her spine. It rode more comfortably there.

The brush grew thicker and taller as they approached the western end of the canyon. Soon she saw actual trees rising around her, mostly oaks and sycamores. It must be wetter here, right near the edge of the mountain. They came to the edge of the canyon but Solo did not hesitate; he continued along the cliff line until he came to a wide crack in the rock leading up.

Solo fit easily into the crack and climbed up. Lina went next, without much trouble. Henri and Eduardo had to take off their packs and turn sideways at places to make it. They startled lizards and a few small toads, but soon they all stepped out on a ledge at the top of the cliff. Immediately in front of them lay the opening to a cave.

Solo drew a candle from a pouch at his belt and lit it. Eduardo had more candles in his pack. He took out three and handed Lina and Henri each one, lighting it for them as he did so. Solo entered the cave and the others followed. The passage was narrow at first. The walls reflected the candlelight and were dry and cool.

The cave began to widen, although the roof remained within touching distance. Lina saw a glow ahead. She wondered if it could be the sun shining into the cave through some opening, but the light was too greenish in tint. As they reached the glow she saw that it bled from some type of fungus that adorned the walls. Here, the walls were faintly damp and she occasionally heard the sound of water dripping. A bitter, mineral scent filled the air.

They'd been angling downward and continued that way for a bit. Just as their direction began to trouble Lina, though, they headed upward again and the cave widened further. Within minutes the darkness ended and they stepped out under a bright blue morning sky. They stood in an eroded crack between two peaks of the mountain. It was wide enough for a wagon to pass, but steep and full of scree.

"Be careful here," Eduardo said. "A slip could mean your death."

Solo was already scampering up the crack. Eduardo followed, with Lina behind and Henri bringing up the rear. An hour passed. The left wall of the crack shortened while the right wall grew taller and rougher.

They came to a flat area where the scree was almost ankle deep. To their left they could see off the edge of the mountain and down into the canyon they'd recently climbed away from. The white adobe buildings of the village looked tiny and peaceful from here, with no sign of last night's violence.

On their right lay the opening to another cave, with a much bigger mouth. Eduardo called for a pause and they found seats on the rock and drank from their canteens. Lina ate most of her tamales but gave Henri one when she saw him gazing at her food longingly.

After that, they plunged back into the mountain, heading generally down now. This new cave was much bigger than the other one, its air bone dry. The roof receded and receded until they moved as a bubble of faint light through an infinite blackness. The candles began to flicker in a faint breeze. Lina saw a shadow take on thickness and form ahead of them. She slowed. Solo continued on; the light of his candle projected ahead. The shape in the tunnel leaped into relief.

Lina grabbed for her pistol.

******

The six riders pulled to a stop near a shallow over-hang in a sandstone bluff where they could see the marks of a campfire and a set of stones arranged in the shape of a rose. Nearby ran a small stream. A bigger fire had recently burned along its banks. They all dismounted.

"Take the horses for some water," Sister Caroline Harp said to one the men.

Sister Sofia Lee and the rider named Rico were already moving to examine the ashes of the campfire.

"How long?" Sister Caroline asked.

"Several days," Sofia said. "The ashes are cauldron cold. But at least we're still on their trail."

"Sister Sofia, Sister Caroline," a voice called.

Caroline turned. One of their men, a fellow named Francisco, had walked a little way off from the campsite and was studying the ground. Caroline walked over to join him. Sofia came along a moment later.

Francisco had been a farmer until recently. He wore the white cotton trousers and shirt that many dryland farmers wore. He'd added to it a red neckerchief around his throat and a pair of crossed bandoliers with two heavy guns at his sides. He pointed to the ground.

"This is puma track," he said. "Very big. And it follows the Black Rose and Henri."

"What?" Caroline said.

"I see it," Sofia said. "Where the track of the big

cat is impressed over the hoofprints of the riders. That's...unusual."

Sister Caroline saw it then, too. Her voice sounded alarmed as she asked, "You mean a panther is following our friends? Why would it do that? Is it hunting them? Do they do that?"

"Puma no hunt human," Francisco said. "Not on horses with guns. But this very odd."

"I don't like it," Sofia said.

Caroline took a deep breath. "I don't either. I'd thought we might take a break here but as soon as the horses are watered we better be moving on. I want to catch up to our friends as soon as we can."

The others nodded, moved away. Sister Caroline remained staring down at the ground where the print of a huge cat overlay and nearly obliterated the hoofprint of a full-grown horse.

CHAPTER 32

Though Lina's fist closed around the butt of her pistol, she didn't pull it. The shape ahead of her in the tunnel did not move and as she cautiously approached she saw to her amazement that it was a bearded man mounted on a horse. There was no threat, though. Both man and horse had been dead a very long time, long enough to become mummified in the dry cavern air.

Henri gave a small gasp as he came up beside Lina and stopped to stare at the horseman. Eduardo joined them, and even Solo returned to their side, though, having seen it before, he showed no surprise at the figure.

"Unbelievable," Eduardo said. "Solo. Well, we are able to communicate with him somewhat using gestures. But I never thought to ask him about something like this. Who would have suspected it?"

"This body must be hundreds of years old," Henri said. He'd been holding his candle up, studying the horseman from all angles as he walked around it. "Look at the armor. The breastplate. That armor plate for the shoulders. This is the kind of armor worn by the Spanish Conquistadores."

"You know your history," Eduardo said. He pointed to the figure's thighs, then to the shins. "Cuisses for the thighs. Greaves for the lower legs. The helmet is missing but definitely a Conquistador. Probably from the late 1500s or early 1600s. At least three hundred years ago."

Lina felt her shock at the sight fading and gave a nod of agreement to the two men. "I've seen paintings of such. But how did he get here? What is he doing here? And mummified?"

"He might have been mummified by the dry air of the cave," Henri answered. "Or maybe the mummification happened elsewhere. He certainly wasn't killed here. He was…placed here. See the arm."

Lina lifted her candle. The conquistador's right arm was thrust out in front of him, with a finger pointing back into the cave in the direction the four had just come from.

"A warning," Lina said.

"I think so," Henri agreed. "But what's holding him up? Even as a mummy, he should have collapsed long ago."

Lina fell to examining the body with her own candle. "Here," she said after a bit. She pointed to several threads of greenish metal running through the desiccated flesh of the left arm. "It looks like copper wire covered with verdigris. It's been threaded around the arm here for support. I would guess it's the same under the armor. And you can see it in the horse, too. Even thicker."

"So, this is some kind of *display*," Henri said. "A warning indeed. For other Conquistadors, I guess. Or maybe just any other would-be conqueror. It's telling them not to go any further. Who could have made such a thing?"

"The Azteca," Eduardo said. "Or some offshoot of them."

"Pretty far north for them wasn't it?" Henri asked. "I thought their empire was mainly located around Mexico City."

"It was. Supposedly. But…I don't know," Eduardo replied. "That's from the histories written by the Spanish. I've heard rumors of Aztec sites scattered all over Mexico. Probably most of those are fanciful tales of lost Aztec gold. But still."

Lina glanced down. Solo was tugging at her cape and gesturing ahead. He pointed at the horseman, then ahead once more.

"I think Solo is telling us there's something else up in front of us," Lina said to the others.

She nodded to the little man, who let go of her cape and stalked forward. She followed, with Henri and Eduardo at her heels. A few paces on and she saw what Solo wanted to show them. There was more to the display. Or there had been.

Lina saw a pile of bones and pieces of dented and tarnished armor, along with scraps of what might have been clothing or leather. What looked like a metal pot turned out on closer examination to be an old Spanish style helmet. Next to it lay a clump of debris. When Lina toed it with her boot she turned over a rusted dagger.

"No effort was made to preserve any of these bodies," Lina said. "They were dumped here. Maybe as a backup to the warning of the horseman."

"What was the point of putting this here?" Eduardo asked, waving his hand around at the cavern. "Surely this passageway wasn't a major travel route."

"Maybe that was the point," Henri said. "The major ways would have been guarded by living warriors. But imagine if you were sneaking in the backway and came upon this display in the darkness! It would surely give you pause."

"Could be, too," Lina added, "that this passage has altered over three hundred years. It might have been a more prominent road in the past. But right now, I think we need to get moving."

The others agreed and they pushed on a little faster. Solo led the way. The cavern began to angle upward again, though it also narrowed somewhat. The trail made for a steep walk but was clear of debris. The group paused only twice more, once to replace their burned down candles with fresh ones and again to gaze back in curiosity as a distant sound of sliding rock came echoing. The sound wasn't repeated and within another hour they reached the cave's end, their backs and legs tired from the strain.

The outer opening of the cave lay screened behind thick brush. Solo pushed through with the others following and Lina and Henri immediately turned to memorize the location. They'd been in the cave for hours. Early afternoon's light greeted them.

Where they'd come out, the world sloped away from the mouth of the cave, hinting at a valley ahead. But they couldn't see if any such valley existed because they were in the middle of a forest. Towering pines made up the bulk of the wood, but oaks and other hardwoods were mixed in. This was an old growth forest, with very little underbrush.

The four travelers paused to catch their breath and drink a little water. It was quiet except for the sough of the wind and the occasional crack-crack-crack of a woodpecker doing its job.

"How much farther to the city?" Eduardo asked Solo.

Solo pointed to the sun, which was starting to slide down behind the trees, then made a circular motion with his arm.

"About a day," Eduardo interpreted.

"Good," Lina said. "We'll go until nightfall before we camp. Tomorrow we'll try to figure out what we're up against. Everyone make sure I don't forget to blaze a trail for those who'll be following us."

"Do you really think your friends are coming?" Eduardo asked. "Or that they will get this far?"

"No doubt of it," Lina said. She glanced at Solo. "We're ready."

Solo nodded and led off. Lina followed, amazed at the small fellow's stamina. He had to take two or three steps to every one of hers. And the way he had to move, bent over because of his back and legs, he must have had to exert tremendous energy to keep up the pace he'd set. But he'd never flagged nor faltered yet.

The rest of the day passed quickly. They went steadily downhill to the southwest and saw only birds and squirrels and a few snakes. Toward evening they found a small stream that cascaded wildly down the mountain and followed it to a small clearing where they decided to camp.

After building a hatful of fire to cook on, they supped on tortillas with red peppers, beans and rabbit that Eduardo had brought along. The smell of the food brought a fox to sit at the edge of their clearing and Henri tossed it a bite of tortilla. It scarfed the piece down and drifted away. Though they'd lit the fire under the thick branches of a cedar to diffuse the smoke, they still dashed it out as soon as the cooking was done and prepared to sleep cold for the night.

Lina took the first watch. A couple of hours in, as she was making the rounds through the camp, an unpleasant frisson stole over her. Goosebumps multiplied along her arms. She snapped to full alertness. Three dark clumps marked the men in their blankets. Eduardo snored softly. Henri and Solo slept without a sound.

The woods around were almost black. The moon hung high and there were many stars, but the forest canopy was so thick that very little light filtered all the way to the ground. Lina heard no movement among the trees and didn't know what had disturbed her, but she'd learned to trust her instincts.

She walked quickly over to Henri, leaned down and called his name softly. He snapped awake, his hand going to the butt of the revolver he'd laid on the blanket beside him. Not having bothered to get undressed for sleep, he quickly threw back his blankets and rose.

"Something in the woods," Lina whispered. "Don't think it's human. Far too quiet."

Henri wasted no time asking for speculation. He went straight to the fire. They'd covered the ashes with dirt and Henri scraped back some of the soil to find a few still glowing embers. He added some dried leaves and twigs, blew on them gently until the flame caught.

Soon, a red-orange light began to force back the darkness. The crackling of fire was normally comforting but helped Lina little at the moment. While Eduardo slept on, Solo awoke and joined her as she kept an eye on the night.

"An animal," Lina said to Solo. "Something big. A predator, I think. Are there any bears in this valley?"

Solo shook his head, no.

"Panthers?" Lina asked.

Solo nodded and flashed the fingers on his hands to indicate some.

Henri joined them with a few makeshift torches. He handed one to Lina, then drew back another and hurled it off into the woods. The burning stick whipped through the air, shedding sparks.

Where it landed, some night bird sprang into the air. And for an instant beyond the light a set of green-gold eyes winked.

Henri shoved his pistol out to fire but didn't pull the trigger as the eyes disappeared. Lina thought she heard something rush away through the leaf clutter, but the sound was so subtle it might have been imagination. Henri hurled his other torch farther out into the woods past the first one. This one showed nothing.

"Gone for now," Henri said. "Most likely a panther."

While Solo returned to the camp to communicate with Eduardo, who had finally woken up and was calling out for information, Lina and Henri walked out to pick up the torches before they started any fires that couldn't be stamped out. They kept their guns handy too, although Lina felt as if the threat had passed for the moment and told Henri as much.

As Henri plucked up the first torch he'd thrown, he spoke, "Given our recent experiences with panthers or the like, I'm not too happy there's one around again."

"Not the same big cat, surely?" Lina said.

"Normally, I'd say absolutely not. But...." He shrugged.

After stomping out a few flickering flames in the leaf cover, Henri and Lina walked toward the second torch. Both kept an eye open for tracks or any other sign as they did so, but nothing showed until they reached the other torch. As Henri leaned over to pluck that one up, he froze. Lina saw what he saw and gasped.

A big clawed print showed in an area of soft loam where the leaf cover had been knocked away by the passage of something large. Henri placed his hand beside the print and shook his head.

"This is…. This is the same animal from before. The size. I remember it. And I've not seen such a big panther before. I think it *must* be a jaguar." He straightened and stared around him at the forest with worried eyes.

"You mean it followed us to the village?" Lina asked. "And *through* the cave?"

"It must have."

"That's hard to believe."

"Let's get back to the camp," Henri said. They walked together, looking constantly around them and holding their torches up to shed as much light as possible on the darkness.

"We're eventually going to have to kill it," Lina said. "Before it kills one of us."

"Or all of us," Henri added.

CHAPTER 33

"So, what's Solo's story," Henri asked Eduardo.

It was midday; they'd stopped to eat and rest. They'd made good time from the cave but would soon have to start being more cautious. Solo had scouted ahead to make sure of their location in El Tigre's valley.

Eduardo paused with his tortilla halfway to his mouth. Lina stuffed the last bite of hers between her teeth and prepared to listen. She was as curious as Henri about Eduardo's answer.

Eduardo put down his food. "I don't know it all. Or even most of it. The first time we saw him was perhaps five years ago. Our sentinels had seen men come into the valley from the mountain pass. We hid, but were observing, of course. I was one observer. El Tigre's men found us the first time by accident. As I imagine, you did. They'd shot a deer who ran through the woods and collapsed just on the outskirts of town. They searched the village of course. Tore up much. Solo was with them but did not take part in any of the destruction. He was… kept on a leash."

"The leader of the men, the same big man who led the ones the other night, had put the leash on Solo and dragged him around like he was a pet. But not a valued pet. For a while, the men returned frequently. Day, night, dusk, dawn. They tried to surprise us. But we cannot afford to be caught asleep. Each time we were hidden."

"At one point, even El Tigre himself showed up. I was not on watch that time and did not get to see him. By that time, Solo seemed to have earned their trust and was no longer kept on the leash. But I was told that El Tigre treated Solo particularly brutally. I saw him treated that way by others. They thought that since he could not speak, he must be incapable of human thought and feeling. He hid his intelligence from them, so that at some point he might escape."

"Solo discovered our hiding place. We were getting ready to move the whole village as a result. But our enemies never came. We knew then that Solo would not report us. That he was a friend. The next time Solo visited, he communicated with us. Using gestures mostly. We offered him sanctuary, but he refused. He stayed with our enemies so that he could help us. Until now. I believe he recognized, too, that you were a hope that we could become completely free of El Tigre's terror."

"What of his family?" Lina asked. "His origins?"

Eduardo shook his head. "He has never revealed any information about them. I've asked him. He understands but will not communicate on that subject. I've stopped trying to find out. He is a human being. Just as we all are. He deserves his privacy. I will respect that."

"Yes, of course," Henri said. "We all have our secrets."

He glanced over at Lina and winked. She almost laughed out loud but managed to control herself.

"Yes," she said sternly. "Secrets are to be honored. On pain of death!"

******

As soon as Solo returned, the small band of four moved out. Within an hour they reached the floor of the valley. They halted in the woods on the edge of a field of maize, with other fields stretching beyond full of beans, squash and tomatoes. Stands of guava trees grew in some fields, along with rows of the cactus-like agave, which was sometimes called a miracle plant. Its juice was used in the making of pulque, its fronds for thatching houses. Its fibers could be woven into cord and, properly prepared, the roots could be eaten.

"I see workers in the fields," Henri said from behind his binoculars. "And I don't think they're acting under their own free will." He pointed to several places and handed Lina the glasses.

She saw no signs of chains or collars on the people doing the hoeing and weeding, but armed men on foot or horseback kept watch over them. It didn't look like the work was voluntary.

"I'd like to question some of them," Lina said, handing the glasses back to Henri.

Solo and Eduardo had not waited but were forging ahead through the woods along the outskirts of the field. Lina and Henri moved to catch up. They passed a row of beehives that buzzed frenetically with activity and a corral full of burros most likely used for transporting farming supplies and the harvest when it could be picked.

Finally, they came to a large stream that ran from the woods straight through the middle of the fields. Lina could see where irrigation ditches had been dug to provide water to the crops.

"They're organized," Lina said. "And prepared to feed a large population. Do we have any idea how many people live in El Tigre's valley?"

"No," Eduardo said. "Solo indicates that it's quite a few. But many are slaves. Or close to it. He doesn't know how many masters. Many fewer but...." He shrugged.

Solo tugged at Lina's cape.

"He has something important to show you," Eduardo said. "A little farther ahead."

Solo led them up around a bend in the stream where they could cross out of sight from the fields. Then, instead of returning immediately to wood's edge, they cut through the trees for half a mile before angling back to the border of farmed land. This time when they came out on that border, they saw more than cultivated fields in front of them.

The woods here were higher than the fields and they could look down on the scene ahead. Less than a hundred yards away lay a village, but not any typical village. Some thirty huts were arranged in three straight rows with narrow dirt walkways between them. A single wider road cut through the middle. The huts were made of wattle and daub and thatched with agave leaves. A wall of thorns some ten feet high surrounded the whole village. The only gate lay closed and padlocked with iron.

Lina borrowed Henri's binoculars and studied the scene. Smoke rose from most of the huts, indicating that the evening cooking was underway. Only a half dozen children were outside, dressed in burlap clothing. Lina gasped as an adult woman came to the door of one of the huts and called to the children. She was bare headed but wore the tattered blue remnants of a religious habit. Lina lowered the binoculars. Her gaze found Eduardo and Solo.

Solo made several gestures to Eduardo, who nodded and turned to Lina. "I believe he's trying to say this is a slave village. A place where any new captives are brought when they first come to El Tigre's valley."

Solo nodded vigorously.

"If your friends are here, this is the most likely place for them to be," Eduardo continued.

Again, Solo nodded.

"So," Lina said. "How do we get them out?"

******

The six riders who followed the trail of the Black Rose entered the canyon and pulled their horses to a stop. They were getting steadily higher in the mountains and this was the biggest canyon they'd found yet. Ahead, they could see a pass leading even higher into the peaks. To their west, the land stretched out flat to a line of trees in the near distance.

"Looks like we head for the trees," Sister Caroline Harp said, pointing to a rose shaped pile of small rocks on the ground in front of them. An arrow of stones pointed toward the woods.

Sister Sofia Lee didn't bother commenting, only reined her mount to the west and booted it into motion. The others followed. They arrived at the woods to find another rose cut into the bark of a big oak, with a blaze mark indicating they should keep going.

Dismounting, the six riders led their horses through the trees and when they came out on the other side they were all surprised to find a small hidden village that looked abandoned. Remounting, they shucked their weapons and rode in cautiously, wary of an ambush. They stopped around a well in the center of the main dirt street.

"What now?" the man named Rico asked.

Sister Sofia pointed toward the far end of the village. A figure had appeared and was walking toward them, holding up both hands in the universal gesture for, "I'm not carrying weapons."

"Maybe she has a clue," Sofia said.

The figure approaching them was indeed a woman, scarcely five feet tall and wearing a blue blouse with a multi-colored cotton skirt. She walked straight up to the riders without fear. The only thing she had in her hand was a white sheet of paper. A few quick words in Spanish from the woman left Sister Caroline puzzling. Sofia translated for her.

"She says she knows we are friends of the Black Rose."

"Si Senora," Sofia said back to the woman. "Es verdad."

More Spanish and then the woman stepped forward and offered the paper to Sofia. Sofia took it, glanced at it. One eyebrow arched.

"It's from the Black Rose," Sofia said. "Instructions."

"Read it," Caroline said.

"The woman who brings you this letter can be trusted," Sofia read. "The pass that you saw when you entered the canyon leads to the hideout of the bandit called El Tigre, who holds some of our people captive. The pass is guarded but the woman knows a back way into the hideout. Follow her and I'll leave signs for you as before. Signed, The Black Rose."

Sister Caroline nodded and dismounted. "All right," she said to the others. "Check your weapons. It's about time for a fight."

******

In the valley of El Tigre, Lina, the Black Rose, stood hidden among trees with Henri, Eduardo and Solo.

The four studied the village of prisoners below them, their hands on their weapons. As far as they could tell, there were only three guards, all of them located in a rough lean-to shack outside the gate.

"Maybe we shouldn't free them yet," Henri said.

"What do you mean?" Lina asked.

"If we break them out. Even if we get them to the cave leading out of here. The bandits will have a chance to follow and recapture or kill them. Even if we escape, the bandits will certainly learn about the secret way into their hideout. It'll be guarded from then on."

Lina sighed. "You're right. We have to take out El Tigre first. And permanently. If we do that, it'll be a lot easier to free these people. Indeed, all the slaves held here."

"Right," Henri said. "So where do we find El Tigre?"

Solo tapped his chest and stood up as straight as he could. He pointed to the distance beyond the prison village and shook two fingers. Lina still had the binoculars. She looked where Solo pointed.

"I see a pyramid," she said. "One of those 'step' kind. I think they call them ziggurats. It's fairly small. Maybe forty feet high with a roofed in altar area at the top. I see a bunch of huts near the bottom of the pyramid but nothing like a city." She lowered the binoculars and glanced at Solo.

"Does El Tigre live in the pyramid?" she asked

Solo shook his head and gestured again with his hand, waving for her to look beyond the pyramid.

With a frown, Lina put the binoculars back to her eyes and focused past the pyramid. Only a few hundred yards separated the pyramid from the wall of the mountain that rose above this valley. A long section of the wall bulged out from the mountain itself, and the recess below it was mostly in shadow at this time of day. It took Lina a moment to realize what she was seeing in that recess.

"Dios mio!"

"What?" Henri demanded.

Lina studied the scene through the binoculars a little longer, then handed them to Henri. He stared through them, gave a gasp, too, as he recognized what he was seeing.

"Cliff dwellings," he said, as he handed the binoculars to Eduardo. "Seen their like in Arizona and Colorado. But those were old, eroded. These are brand new. There's El Tigre's city."

Solo nodded. He picked up a stick and began scraping away leaves and drawing a rough map of the cliff city in the dirt. He scraped out a rectangular shape at the western end of the map and stabbed the stick in it. Glancing up at his companions, he began nodding rapidly.

"There's the dwelling El Tigre lives in. The biggest one at the west end of the cliff," Eduardo said.

Solo nodded and smiled.

"And that's where we're headed," Henri.

"No," Lina said. "That's where *I'm* headed."

CHAPTER 34

"What are you talking about?" Henri protested. "We're in this together."

"We are," Lina agreed. "But we have to be smart about it. You'd stand out like an apple on a grape vine over there." She gestured toward the city. "You and Solo both. I can pass fine. So can Eduardo. We'll have to do the scouting. Figure out where El Tigre is and where to strike at him."

"He has folks like me in his gang," Henri said. "Bolanger wasn't Mexican or Indio. Nor his friend in Santa Annabella."

"He has a few," Lina agreed. "But you can be sure he and everyone around him knows each one of them. You'd be identified immediately as a trespasser."

Henri started to protest again, then closed his mouth. He understood that she was right. "We're just supposed to cool our heels here?" he demanded finally.

"As long as you stay hidden, you can do a lot. You'll have your binoculars. Map out the whole valley. Find where we can hide and where we can't, where we can get horses, or food if we need it. Figure out the best way to free the people in the prison for when it comes time. And be ready for us when we come back."

"All right," Henri said. "I don't like it."

"Noted, my friend." She studied the sky. It was turning quickly into afternoon. "Come with me for a bit," Lina added to Henri. "There's something else I need you to do." She turned to Eduardo and Solo and told them to, "Wait. We'll be back shortly."

The two men nodded. Lina leaned her Winchester and her bow and arrows against a tree, turned and moved off swiftly through the woods. Henri followed. She led them about a hundred yards up the side of the valley before she came to a small stream they'd crossed before.

Near a little pool between sets of broken rocks, she halted. Drawing a tattered cloth from her pocket, she knelt and began to scrub away the war paint that identified her as the Black Rose. When she straightened again, she was fresh faced and clean, and to Henri — achingly young and hauntingly beautiful. He swallowed, looked away.

"Henri!"

He turned back toward her. Droplets of water glistened on her tanned cheeks. A leaf had caught in her hair. She smiled and he never wanted to see her frown again. His hand lifted, to reach out and pluck away the leaf. He willed it back to his side.

"Yes, Lina," he said. "What is it?"

She undid the cloak at her shoulders, rolled it and handed it to him. She took off her vest next and gave that to him, along with the Remington .41 hideout gun she kept holstered beneath it. Finally, she handed him the machete from her belt.

"You'll watch over all those for me, won't you?"

"Of course, Lina," he said. "But your black shirt and pants are going to stand out still. Not to mention that .45 holstered at your back."

She untucked the shirt so it looked more sloppy and hung over her pants, hiding the pistol. "I'll smear some dirt on my clothes," she said. "And borrow a serape first thing I can. That'll help."

"Right," Henri said, smiling.

"I'm sorry," Lina said. "I know you don't want to stay behind for this. But it's necessary."

"I understand, Lina." He considered something, then added. "You recall that story I told you about the devil in the winter mountains in Montana?"

"That's right. You never finished it. I'll have to come back to hear the end."

"There is no end. I still owe it."

The beating of Lina's heart fluttered her shirt.

"But you gave it blood, you said."

"For one."

"Do I want to know what else? Why don't you save it until I come back?"

Henri shook his head. "I don't want it to wait. I never gave it anything else. That devil in the snow.

But it still left me alone." He turned and stared through the woods as if he could see all the way to the bandit known as El Tigre. "There's a devil over there." He gestured. "Don't let him take you as payment for *my* sins."

"Henri! That's not going to happen. I promise you. And El Tigre is no devil. He's only a man."

"Don't underestimate him, Lina."

"Don't underestimate me, Henri."

Henri blinked, and slowly nodded. "You're right," he said. "El Tigre can't be any match for the Black Rose."

Lina chuckled, though she sensed that Henri was trying to be serious. She slapped him on the shoulder. "Don't you forget it! Now, let's get back to the others."

She turned and led off. Henri followed, wishing he could truly believe the words he'd just uttered.

******

As soon as it was fully dark, Lina and Eduardo slipped out of the woods and started across the cultivated fields toward the distant ziggurat and cliff city. They swung wide around the prison village because of the guard post outside the gate and loped along through fields of maize and tomatoes. A full moon aided them.

An hour took them to the ziggurat. It was unguarded and unattended. It stood some forty feet high, apparently made of adobe brick faced with limestone. The top was flat and had been roofed in with a wood frame covered by agave leaves. A fire burned in a stone bowl beneath that roof.

More cautiously now, Lina and Eduardo moved on toward the city, which was less than a quarter of a mile away. There were no cultivated fields here, only stretches of dirt broken up by well-worn walking trails where the ground had been pounded flat by the passage of many feet. They passed granaries and sheds full of firewood and other supplies. They crossed a brick walled stream that must have provided the city with water. No one was around.

"Must be a curfew," Eduardo whispered to Lina as they paused beside a hut full of farming implements.

"Which will make us too conspicuous to approach closer tonight," Lina responded. "We'll have to hide and wait until daylight. Surely people will be out and about then so we can join them and mingle."

"I can already see from here that El Tigre's dwelling is guarded," Eduardo said.

"Yes," Lina agreed.

She'd been studying the city as they approached. It was a hodgepodge of buildings, all constructed of adobe brick under the great overhang of the cliff above it. Some were cylindrical towers, though no more than two stories high. Other buildings were square or rectangular and here and there lay circular pits she didn't know the purpose of. Stone stairs went up and down, seemingly with little rhyme or reason.

At the western end of the city stood the large rectangular building that Solo had indicated as El

Tigre's dwelling. Three windows broke the build-ing's outline and she could see light through two of them. Only one set of stairs led up to this building and at least four guards patrolled it.

"How are we going to get to him?" Eduardo asked.

"We'll let him come to us," Lina answered. "Or if we have to, we'll *make* him."

******

Henri and Solo ate cold tortillas and drank luke-warm water for their evening meal. They weren't taking any chances on building a fire. Fortunately, the moon was up and bright. It didn't help a lot in the woods but gave them enough glimmering at ground level to help them see their food. Afterward, Solo gestured for Henri to sleep but the mountain man shook his head.

"I'll take the first watch," he told the small fellow. "Doubt I could sleep much yet, anyway."

Solo nodded and sought his blankets. Henri leaned his Sharps against a tree next to Lina's Win-chester and bow, then rose and paced with his hands never far from the butts of his Peacemakers. He knew his worry for Lina was likely overblown. The Black Rose could certainly take care of herself and tonight would not be the most dangerous part of her scouting trip anyway. That would come tomorrow when she ventured out among El Tigre's people and risked detection. He couldn't help his worry, though.

Over many years in the mountains, he'd learned to distance himself from his fears and keep his mind working even during moments of high emotion. But with Lina in danger, all that training failed him. He knew why. With each day, he fell more in love with her — not with the nun, Catalina Rivera, nor with the Black Rose, but with the young woman named Lina who walked a fine line between both.

It didn't matter that he knew the situation made his love hopeless. Lina had committed herself to a different path long before he'd even met her. He couldn't even tell her how he felt. He couldn't put that burden on her.

Eventually his thoughts began to calm. The silence of the dark night helped. Whatever animals lived in this valley, they seemed to keep their distance from the cultivated area. He did hear the calls of Chuck-will's-widows and a few other night birds. None of them were very close. The world felt empty. For a while, he leaned against a tree as he kept watch. Only when he went to awaken Solo for his turn at sentry duty did he find out how alone he really was.

Solo's blanket roll lay cold and empty; the little fellow was gone.

CHAPTER 35

Henri pulled back the blankets on Solo's bed roll but found nothing to help him understand where the small man had disappeared to. He had taken his sling and knife with him, so he was armed.

"Solo!" Henri called softly. "Solo! Where are you?"

No answer came, and it was far too dark to make sense of any tracks the man might have left. Henri strode over and picked up his Sharps. His heart pounded. He'd trusted Solo. They all had. But where had he gone? And why?

Henri made a circuit of their camp and then two more wider circuits, calling Solo's name softly a few more times as he did so. He dared not shout. They were less than a hundred yards from the border of the cultivated area. The thorn-walled village was only seventy to eighty yards further on and men were constantly on guard there.

After a last wasted circuit of the camp, Henri made his way toward the open area beyond the woods. He

moved with the practiced ease of the mountain man.
If Solo had crossed into the open, Henri thought he
might see him beneath the moonlight.

Henri was barely fifteen yards from the end of the
woods when he heard a sound behind him. It was
only the faintest of noises, the slither of leaves across
leaves, but he spun around and brought his rifle up.

"Solo!" he hissed. "Is that you?"

Something answered him but it wasn't human. A
low rumbling sound vibrated the air, like a grizzly
gargling with nails. Henri took a step backward,
pushing his shoulders against a tree. His hands were
suddenly slick on the stock of his rifle. He knew his
eyes were wide.

The rumbling sound came again, from several
feet closer than before. Henri cocked the hammer
on his Sharps. The rifle was too long for close work
in the dark but his Colt Peacemakers didn't have the
stopping power he needed for the creature he knew
was stalking him.

"Come on, Cat," he snarled. "Panther, or Jaguar,
or whatever the hell you are. I'm gonna take a piece
of you with me."

The sound did not repeat. Henri understood why.
The big cat had gone into its final stalk, with its belly
flattened and its legs bunched to spring. It was out
there. Right in front of him. And he couldn't see it.

Then he caught its scent, just a whiff — musk
and old sweat and something feral. He took a risk.
Jumping sideways, he twisted around and darted
three steps to another tree. He spun around the tree

and turned back to face the dark.

A rushing sound closed on his position. But his movements had confused the predator just enough to slow its charge. For an instant he glimpsed a darker shadow coiled within other shadows. With no time for thought, he fired.

Instinct guided him right. A yowl hammered the night. A wild dance of shadows convulsed on the earth no more than half a dozen steps from him. He dropped his rifle, palmed his Colts and fired twice into the knotted darkness. Turning, he ran for the open field beyond the woods. That would be his only chance of refuge now.

Behind him, some heavy body came surging through the trees. He broke free of the woods, threw himself forward onto his left shoulder and rolled onto his back. He looked up with his Peacemakers rising. The moon fell bright into his eyes. The jaguar burst from the woods and sprang. He saw it, black against the moonlight. It seemed to hang in the air before dropping toward him with a snarl curving its lips.

A flash of silver moon winked along the beast's incisors. Henri pulled the triggers on his Colts. Ribbons of flame blossomed from the muzzles of the pistols. The sound hammered Henri's ears as the Colts bucked back against his palms. The cat's heavy body smacked down on Henri, knocking his guns aside, smashing the breath out of his lungs.

Dead, Henri thought. *I'm dead!*

But the cat only landed on him and slid cross his

body into the grass beyond. For a single instant, he smelled its breath full of the stench of old meat and felt the wetness of its shed blood spilling on him.

With a cry half of terror and half of revulsion, Henri thrust his closed hands against the ground and pushed himself away from the beast. He'd lost one Colt; he lifted the other. The fear in him screamed that the thing wasn't dead yet. The click of gun hammers being cocked cut through Henri's primal fear, brought back a cold dash of sanity.

"Well, well," a voice said in heavily accented English. "Look what the cat dragged in."

Henri twisted his head toward the voice and a blow struck him on the back of the skull. He went down on his face, losing his last gun but not quite unconscious. Hands seized him, twisted his arms behind him. He felt ropes being wrapped around his wrists.

As he was jerked roughly to his feet, he shook his head to clear his mind. His eyes focused. He glanced to where the jaguar had landed when it slid past him. Like Solo before it, the beast was gone.

******

Something woke Lina. The echo of a distant sound maybe. It wasn't repeated. Something about the sound bothered her but there was nothing she could do about it from here. She sat up in the hay shed where she and Eduardo had taken cover. Eduardo heard her moving and turned to look at her questioningly. He'd taken last watch and Lina could tell by the gray light creeping into the world that it was almost time to get up.

"Anyone up and out yet?" Lina asked the man.

He shook his head. "Won't be long, though."

Lina crawled to the edge of the shed and peered out. She could make out the outline of the cliff city against the mountain. Candlelight flickered in windows here and there as a few people began their day. She smelled tortillas and tamales cooking.

To wait out the remainder of the night, she and Eduardo had moved to a hay shed just east of the city. A few chickens roosted on its roof, hunkered down against the cool night air. About twenty feet behind it ran a heavy wooden fence and in the fields beyond were knots of resting cattle and horses. The smells of grass and animals and manure were pungent.

Eduardo had slept an hour while Lina watched and had later returned the favor. It wasn't enough. Lina felt bone tired but forced herself to shrug it off. When this was over, she'd need a long, long sleep. But for now, she watched the light growing around them and thought about what she needed to do this day.

Lina picked up a forgotten and somewhat ratty blue poncho, a fortunate find they'd made in one of the stalls of the hay shed that would help with her disguise. In particular, it would hide her urumi belt and the Colt .45 automatic tucked in the waistband at the small of her back. She drew the garment over her head just as the first rooster crowed.

Another rooster answered. And another. Quickly after that came the low of cattle and the bugle of a stallion sensing some threat to his harem. Perhaps it was the cry of the coyotes she heard in the distance.

The city gradually filled up with noise as people rose and coughed and murmured, as they rattled dishes and tools and chamber pots. A young man hurried past the shed where Lina and Eduardo hid. He appeared to be heading for the fields, perhaps to check on the cattle or horses. If so, he'd be wanting to feed them soon, perhaps on the hay in this very shed.

A man walked by carrying a stick and a harness for a horse. Two young girls ran past on some unknown errand. Lina and Eduardo stepped out of the shed and stood beside it as if they belonged here. The city took no notice of them as it awoke from its slumber.

Quite a few women began to amble down the city's stairs to the flat area in front of their dwellings. Fires were built, breakfasts prepared. As the number of people moving about increased, Lina and Eduardo let themselves flow along with the traffic. They earned a few curious glances but no one paid them much heed.

The smells of cooking set Lina's mouth to watering and when she looked at Eduardo she could see he was thinking of food as well. The tantalizing odors of bread and bacon and peppers and cornmeal filled the smoky air. Lina actually turned away from the enticing sight of corn fritters sizzling in an iron skillet.

She reached under her poncho, to a bag hanging at her belt and took out two slices of jerky. She handed one to Eduardo and quickly bit into the other herself. The juices flowed down her throat and quieted the hunger pangs of her belly but didn't satisfy the more emotional need for a hearty meal.

As they moved along their way, they noted three classes of people in the city. First were the peasants who were dressed in simple cotton clothing, mostly white but occasionally splashed with other colors. The majority of the people fell into that category.

The second category consisted of guards, or maybe they should be called soldiers, armed with various types of guns. These weren't wearing any kind of uniform so it was hard to think of them as belonging to an army. They were nearly as varied as their weaponry. Some appeared to be Mexican or mestizo. One might have been Chinese, although he was dressed in the style of a South American gaucho. Others were clearly what the locals would call Norteamericanos, or gringos. There were only five or six of these, two of whom were black.

The third group stood out the most, although there were the fewest of these. Lina recognized them from previous experience. Henri would have, too, if he'd been here. Four such men had tried to ambush Lina and Henri back on the other side of the border. They wore a kind of uniform, breechclouts and fur lined boots and armbands decorated with feathers and colored beads.

Their copper-dark skin tones bespoke Indian rather than Mexican. They had black hair, ranging toward the coarse side, which was shaven at the front and worked through leather headbands at the back into complex interwoven braids. Their weaponry was also unique; they carried no guns, only knives, bows and thick spears armed with obsidian heads.

Eduardo gave a gasp when he saw the last bunch but said nothing until they came to a place where a few quick words would not likely be overheard.

"Azteca!" the villager whispered. "I'd swear it. That is what Aztec warriors looked like."

Lina was about to respond when she became aware of silence falling across the crowd. She glanced around. Heads were turning everywhere toward the cliff city. She followed their guide and for the first time caught a glimpse of El Tigre Sangriento.

CHAPTER 36

The cave seemed endless. Sister Sofia Lee was in the point position, with Caroline Harp and their four men following. Sofia paused and lifted her lantern, letting the light illuminate what lay ahead.

"There's the horseman Dolores warned us about," Caroline said from her position at Sofia's shoulder.

Sofia nodded. Dolores was the woman from the village whose husband had accompanied the Black Rose through this cave. She'd drawn them a map to follow and warned them of the strange mummified corpse they'd find.

"Don't much like being trapped in here with that thing," Caroline added.

"We're not trapped," Sofia replied. "And the dead won't hurt you. It's the living we have to fear."

"Living!" Caroline said. "Well, I smell something living. And it isn't human."

Sofia glanced over at her friend, saw Caroline's lips drawn back in a moue of distaste. She sniffed the air, realized what her friend was talking about. A stench lingered here that could not have come from the Black Rose or from any person who might be with her. It was fetid, animal. She couldn't classify it but it was recent.

"A beast of some kind," she said. "Maybe rats. Or a wild dog."

Caroline shook her head. "I don't think so. I've been smelling it for a while but it's particularly strong near here. It's something big."

"Puma," Francisco said from behind them both. "It is like the smell that hung at the camp where we saw the marks of the puma near those of Henri and the Black Rose."

"Quite a coincidence," Sofia said. "But I have heard that pumas lair in caves. Let us hope it did not cause any concerns for our friends."

"Let's hope it doesn't cause any for us," Caroline added.

"Keep your weapons to hand," Sofia said. She lowered her lantern, continued on.

It took a couple more hours but the small band finally broke free of the cave. They made no sighting of the puma. If that was indeed what they'd smelled. After pushing through some thick brush at the cave's mouth, they found themselves on the forested slope of a mountain. Just down the slope they saw a tree blazoned with the image of a rose cut into the bark. The cut was fresh enough to still be dripping sap.

"We're getting close," Sofia said.

"About time," Caroline added as her hand dropped

to her Kpinga and caressed the smooth-worn hilt.

******

El Tigre Sangriento stood on the stone steps out-side his home in the cliff city. Many guards loitered around him. At his feet, on a leash fashioned from silver chain, lay a pure white jaguar. As Lina stud-ied the man across the distance, she was reminded of how the woman, Painted Crow, had described him — "magnificent."

He wore no shirt, only a cape of yellow and black jaguar hide with the beast's head pulled over his own like a cap. The jaguar's fangs framed the man's face, but that visage was…confusing to Lina. She looked away to study the rest of the man, hoping to understand the face from understanding the whole.

The muscles of El Tigre's chest and lower torso bulged and rippled beneath his deeply tanned skin. A smooth white scar over the heart only empha-sized that musculature. The man wore a loincloth of crimson with a wide black leather belt around it decorated with beads and bright shells. A weapon hung there, something like a club embedded with sharp flakes of obsidian. Bracelets and bands of gold encircled his arms and wrists. There were claws of bright steel on his hands, but they extended over his normal fingers and must have been attached to some kind of glove.

Tigre's lower body was also bare, except for bands of hawk and eagle feathers beneath each knee. His legs were lean but well-muscled. Claws adorned his feet as well. They appeared to be of bone and Lina thought they were attached to the man's moccasins. She couldn't see them well enough to be sure.

And so she came back to El Tigre's face. All the rest of the man looked no more than human. But the face was something else. Even at this distance, it seemed exaggerated. The eyes were large and of a lighter tint than she expected, though she couldn't make out their actual color. The skin was a deep yellow with spots and splotches of black scattered across it. She thought it might have been tattooed, but the rest of the face could not be so easily explained.

The nose was long, broad and flattened, the mouth a wide slash. A massive jaw and chin thrust out from the face. It was almost a muzzle, but not quite. She'd never seen another human being with such a prognathous jaw, though.

A mask, she'd been thinking. El Tigre surely wore a mask to make himself resemble a jaguar. But this was no mask. And no accident could have caused it. He might have used tattooing to enhance it but he must have been born this way.

A thought shouted through Lina's brain. *Solo!*

Solo had also been born with physical deformities. Much worse ones than El Tigre suffered. Was it odd that the two knew each other, that at one point El Tigre had kept Solo on a leash? She'd seen no other signs of such births in the people of the cliff city, but she had not been checking for them.

A woman stepped from the doorway behind

El Tigre. She must have been his wife, his queen. Her straight and shining hair hung so long that it brushed her heels. An older woman, a servant it seemed, came up behind the queen and took her hair, drawing it forward over the woman's shoulder to let it fall like raven feathers against the pure white softness of her gown.

Perhaps the old woman had tugged too familiarly at the queen's hair. She was cuffed to her knees for the affront. Lina's jaw tightened in anger. She glanced back at El Tigre to see how he'd react. But the king of this cliff city was not watching his wife. A chill coursed along Lina's spine as she realized he was staring right at her. Across a distance of over a hundred yards, his gaze had found her and lingered.

"We need to get out of here," Lina whispered to Eduardo. "Right now!"

******

A boot in the back sent Henri Moissant stumbling ahead. He nearly fell but just managed to keep his feet. He didn't complain; it would only make things worse. But he picked up his pace a little along the dirt road leading through the fields from the walled prison village toward the cliff city. It was just after dawn.

The white dust of the road made a stark contrast against the rich greens and yellows of the fields around them. *Life to either side*, he thought; *a likely death ahead*. He would have tried to run if it would have done him any good. A single man guarded him on this journey, but Henri's hands were bound behind him and a long rope ran from his belt to the guard's fist.

"Taking me to El Tigre, I reckon," Henri said over his shoulder.

"Si, si, Gringo," his captor said. "El Tigre most happy to see you. He will want to know where you from and if you have any friends. I am sure you will have a nice little talk."

"I told you, I was hunting in the mountains," Henri said. "Found my way here by accident. And man, I wish I hadn't. Any friends I've got are a long way away."

"Oh, I believe you, Gringo. I have never known such a one as you to lie. I don't know if El Tigre will believe, though. Perhaps so. Perhaps you and he will become best of friends. You will drink pulque together and laugh at your great fortunes."

"Your sarcasm needs a little work," Henri replied. The comment earned him another kick.

"I no comprendo that word, Gringo. Perhaps you call me a peeg, eh? I am no peeg. Though I know how to take care of snakes like you."

"I wouldn't call you a pig. A chacal perhaps."

"No, no, no," the man said. "Lobo." He gave a fake howl that sounded nothing like a wolf.

Henri decided not to push it. He preferred to walk without being kicked. Besides, his thoughts had moved on to the Black Rose. Was she all right? What would she do when she found he'd been taken? The question was rhetorical. He knew what she'd do; she'd risk herself to save him. He needed to escape before that happened.

He forced himself to focus, to keep a constant scan of his surroundings. There had to be some way to free himself. For Lina's sake.

CHAPTER 37

Lina and Eduardo stood close together at the edge of the woods behind the cattle field. As soon as she'd realized that El Tigre was staring at her, she'd grabbed Eduardo's arm and faded into the crowd. They'd first returned to the hay shed where they'd hidden that morning, then crossed the field into the woods when it seemed that El Tigre continued to look for them. At least, he kept turning his head this way and that as he scanned the crowd and at his height, well over six feet, he was easy to see without being seen in turn.

"I don't like that," Eduardo whispered, though they were unlikely to be heard where they were. "How did he pick us out? How could he possibly?"

"Don't start with any of that sorcery bull," Lina snapped. She calmed and apologized. "Sorry. I don't think he knew anything about who we are. Otherwise he'd have sent his guards after us. He probably just recognized that he hadn't seen us before. And that alerted his suspicions."

"Hadn't seen us before?" Eduardo said. "At that distance and out of several hundred people standing around us? You have to admit that's…unusual."

"Maybe," Lina agreed. "But not magic."

Eduardo nodded, though Lina wasn't sure he was convinced. "Yes," he said. "I know you're right. It's just…. What are we going to do now?"

"Talk to Henri and Solo. It's clear we can't get to El Tigre in the city among all his guards. I counted over forty armed men and that number is probably higher."

"More will be protecting the pass," Eduardo agreed. "They can get here quickly if there is trouble. Others may be out on raids."

Now, Lina nodded. "Yes, and who knows when those might return. We need to lure Tigre out. Shorten the odds. And we need to find out when our support is coming."

She turned and led off through the woods. Eduardo trailed her. Taking it slow and staying under cover, it took them almost three hours to get back to the place where they'd left Henri and Solo. They were in for quite a surprise.

As she approached the camp, Lina gave the mockingbird call she and Henri had agreed on. No response came. She eased closer and repeated the call. Again, the woods remained silent.

"Wait here," Lina told Eduardo. "If it's clear, I'll whistle. You can come in then."

Without waiting for the villager's acknowledgement, she quickly moved ahead and scouted a circle around the camp. A third signal call went unanswered. Lina's worry grew. She worked her way closer and finding nothing in the way of a trap awaiting her, slipped silently into the camp itself. Henri and Solo's bedrolls were still laid out on the ground, but she found no sign of either man. Her and Eduardo's rolls remained as well.

She whistled for Eduardo. The man came into camp with fear written large on his face as soon as he saw it lying empty.

"Where could they be?" he asked.

"I don't know yet," Lina said. "Check Solo's bedroll."

While Eduardo did as he was told, Lina searched Henri's bedroll. His weapons were gone but everything else appeared to be there — his canteen and binoculars and the personal things Lina had given him before she left to scout the cliff city. She straightened, frowning and glanced over at Eduardo.

"Nothing here," the man said. "What is going on?"

Lina didn't answer. One more time she threw the mockingbird's cry. The results were no different.

"Could they have been captured while they slept?" Eduardo asked.

Lina shook her head. "If El Tigre's men had found the camp they'd either have taken our gear or they would have set a trap for us. They could see the other two bedrolls so they'd have known there were four of us."

"So Solo and Henri just left?"

"They wouldn't have. Unless something happened. And they should have left some kind of sign for us if they did. Henri and I have done just that before. I don't know what could have occurred that kept him from it. But if they did leave, they might have been captured."

Reaching a decision, Lina picked up the binoculars from Henri's bedroll and slung it around her neck. Most of the trees around them were pine, with no lower limbs to assist a climber. She walked through the forest until she found a tall oak. Up it, she went, with Eduardo remaining below.

At about forty feet above the ground, she topped the heads of many of the nearby pines and was able to get a mostly unobstructed view of the prisoner holding area and the guard shed outside its gates. She studied the scene for several minutes. It was just after noon and the people in the thorn-walled village might have been having a siesta. Only a few folks were in the streets and there didn't seem to be any disturbance.

Checking out the guard shed, which was little more than a lean-to with a roof of agave leaves, she realized that she could see the entire interior. Inside, two men played some kind of card game and drank from bottles of pulque.

Two men. There were three before! So where's the third?

She skinned down the tree faster than she'd come up it and rushed back to camp. Eduardo

followed again, though he acted completely confused as to the why of Lina's actions. She didn't
stop to explain yet, only went to her bedroll and
knelt beside it. She pulled forth a leather pouch and
drew out a small storage tin. Opening it revealed
two compartments, one filled with red warpaint,
the other with black. By feel, without a mirror, she
used the black to draw a cross from her forehead
to her chin and across the bridge of her nose. She
filled in the squares between with scarlet.

Turning to Henri's bedroll, she took up her
vest and black cloak and pulled them on, tugging
the hood over her head. She snugged her over-
and-under .41 caliber Remington beneath the left
side of the vest. When she rose, she was no longer
Lina Rivera, but the night avenger known as the
Black Rose.

"What are you going to do?" Eduardo asked.

"I'm going to visit the two guards out there who
watch the prisoners. I'm going to find out if they
know anything about Henri and Solo. I suspect
they do."

"But they'll kill you. As soon as they see you. You
won't get close."

She turned toward Eduardo, lowered her face so
that the cowl hid her savagely painted features. She
drew the silky material of her cape more closely
around her, emphasizing the litheness of the form
beneath it.

"Do you not understand men better than that?"
she asked. "They'll let me get as close as I want."

******

Henri shook his head rapidly back and forth to get the stinging sweat out of his eyes. With his hands bound behind him, he could do nothing more. From his knees, he looked up. He knelt on top of the ziggurat near the cliff city. The altar stood just to his right. It had been constructed in six pieces, four squared off legs of thick polished wood, a flat and heavy rectangle of smoothed granite to make the altar itself and a thin overlay of midnight black obsidian. The obsidian was stained with unholy splotches of gore.

In front of him, a man stood — thick and wide, with a bull-neck, angry black eyes, and rings of bone and jade through his nose and ears. His head was shaved at the front and greased at the back into the shape of a paddle. He wore only a loincloth and sandals, with bracelets of gold and feathers around his arms and legs. The man slapped Henri across the face, then asked him a question or questions in a swift stream of Spanish.

"Can't speak Spanish," Henri said. He was glad, though, that they'd started *asking* him questions. For the first few minutes they'd just beaten him. To soften him up, he reckoned.

A backhand slap knocked Henri's head to one side. Again, a question was asked. He thought it was the same one. He spat blood on the stone.

"Don't...understand," he gasped out.

The man above him drew his hand back for another blow but a voice from behind him snapped, "Suficiente."

The man with the fists stepped obediently away from Henri. Seated behind him on an ornate chair of polished wood was El Tigre himself. It could be no one else. He was tall, several inches over six feet, with his body slabbed with muscle. He wore a cape of jaguar hide and a loincloth of crimson. Everything about him said human except his face.

The name "tigre" was appropriate for this man. Some of his cat-like features, the broadly flattened nose and underslung jaw, had to be accidents of birth. Other's had been enhanced by tattooing, particularly the black lips and the jaguar-like coloration and spots. To add to the impression, a white jaguar on a silver leash lay next to his chair, watching Henri with a dispassionate red gaze.

"I will honor you by speaking with you in your own tongue," El Tigre said to Henri. "The question is, why are you here?"

Henri let his gaze rest on El Tigre's strange eyes, which were yellowish brown and slanted at the outside edges.

"Hunting," he said. "I crossed into this valley while hunting. Your...man," he jerked his chin over his shoulder toward the fellow who'd prodded him here after his capture, "has my rifle. A Sharps. A hunting rifle. I imagine you know that."

The lip curled at the left side of El Tigre's mouth, revealing a rather long and threatening canine. "This I find difficult to believe."

Henri shrugged. "I can't help that."

El Tigre lifted his hand and appeared to be studying his nails. Henri could see his human fingers, but over that he wore some kind of glove fitted with shining steel claws.

"Who entered my valley with you?" El Tigre asked, without looking away from his hand.

Henri swallowed some blood that had pooled in the back of his throat. "No one," he said.

El Tigre grinned. It wasn't comforting. "You understand," he said, "I could feed you to my companion here." He dropped his hand down to scratch the head of his pet jaguar. The beast's eyes closed and it arched its scalp into its master's touch, much like a cat wanting to be petted.

"You could," Henri agreed. "But that wouldn't change my answers."

El Tigre rose slowly to his feet and stretched like a cat himself. "I won't struggle with you over it." He gestured to several of his men, "Strap him on the altar."

Henri headbutted the first man who approached him in the stomach, then surged up from his knees to his feet. His arms were useless but he swept one man's legs from beneath him with a booted foot, kicked a second in the chest and sent him into a wild tumble down the ziggurat's steps.

He turned, hoping to run. A brutal blow across the back of his neck paralyzed him for an instant. He fell hard, barely got his head turned to the side so that he didn't land on his face. El Tigre stood over him, his eyes furious, his nostrils flared as wide as gun barrels.

Men grabbed Henri, jerked him roughly to his feet and dragged him to the altar. Quickly, he was bound on his back across that altar. He was able to turn his head and nothing more. He prepared himself to die as El Tigre leaned over him. But the man had regained his composure.

"As I was speaking," he said, "I will not struggle with you. This is just a taste of what it's like to lie on my altar. But your death is not quite yet." He gestured magnanimously toward his cliff city. "I will have you taken to a room where you will be bathed and fed. Any sacrifice on this altar must be clean.

"When evening comes. Unless you tell me what I wish to know" He lifted his hand and let the steel claws drop down to cover his fingers. "Unless you tell me...everything. I will tear your heart out through your chest with these. After, I will bring you back as a slave to the jaguar god."

"And who might that be?" Henri snapped.

El Tigre grinned. "Me," he said.

CHAPTER 38

Leaving Eduardo to wait and watch from the shelter of the woods, Lina made her way around the
prisoners' village to approach the guard shed from
the other side. The cloak remained tight around her
upper body. She kept her head down to shadow her
face but let her hair fall loose. The long dark hair
spilled like a silken flag from beneath her hood and
she knew that men found it lovely.

The two guards playing cards in their lean-to did
not notice her until she was within fifty feet. Rising
in surprise, both immediately put down their poker
hands and dropped their hands to their guns. Lina
kept coming, silently but letting her hips sway a bit
as she walked.

The men kept watching her and the surprise
in their eyes turned to some other emotion. They
began to catcall and laugh. Their hands drifted
away from their guns. One put his fingers between
his lips and whistled. Lina paused and gave a very

deliberate tremble.

"No, no, no, Senorita," the whistling guard shouted. "No tengas miedo. Acércate. Ven a Jorge"

Lina heard the leering invitation of the man who called himself "Jorge," and let her tremble subside. She started forward again, slowly at first, then seemingly with more confidence. She let the sway come back into her hips.

Jorge wore a wide, straw-colored sombrero on shaggy, brown hair. An unholstered pistol of unknown make was stuck through his belt. He held his hands out toward Lina as he stalked slowly toward her.

The other man was surely a mestizo. His bare head was covered with reddish hair; his eyes were blue. He wore a brightly colored serape and broad-legged black cotton pants decorated with silver buttons. He leaned casually against one roof pole of the lean-to. Two guns hung tied-down on his hips, but his thumbs were hooked in his gun belt as he let his eyes roam freely over Lina's form.

Jorge stopped squarely in Lina's way and opened his arms. She stepped around him without looking up and continued toward the guard shed. The blue-eyed man standing there straightened and grinned.

He called out, "Si, ven a Mando."

"Mando!" Lina said softly, repeating the man's name as she stopped a few feet in front of him.

She could hear Jorge closing in behind her. She imagined the angry expression on his face at being snubbed. She counted on it. She raised her head, pushed back her hood with her left hand. Her right rested on the handle of her urumi.

Mando's eyes widened as he saw the black and scarlet warpaint spread across the Black Rose's face and the grim tight line of her lips. He gave a gasp and shouted an oath as his hands dropped toward his pistols. At the same instant, Lina heard Jorge lunge toward her from behind. She was ready for it and stepped quickly to one side while jerking the urumi free from around her waist.

Mando palmed his pistols. A surprised Jorge stumbled past Lina right into Mando's line of fire. Mando tried to swing his guns around to cover Lina's movements. She gave him no chance to complete the motion. Her urumi coiled. She whipped it forward. It caught Mando across the left arm and the steel-edged whip-blade coiled all the way around his back to bite deep into the right arm.

Mando screamed as the urumi chewed into him. His pistols went flying and he screamed even louder when the Black Rose gave her weapon a savage jerk that tore the steel fangs out of his flesh and brought it whipping back under her control.

Jorge spun toward Lina in shock, his mouth opened on crooked teeth, his pupils dilated and huge. He grabbed for his own gun. The Black Rose swung her urumi up, linked both hands on the hilt and snapped it down toward Jorge's face with all her might.

The whip blades cut neatly through Jorge's sombrero and struck across the man's head and face with brutal effect. He went down as if axed, knocked unconscious by the blow. That must have been a mercy considering the damage done to his forehead, scalp, nose and lips by the weapon.

Mando's arms and hands were wet with his own blood but he stopped screaming as Jorge went down. Throwing himself on the ground, Mando grabbed for one of his dropped pistols. Lina brought her urumi around and down to strike the bandit's hand as he reached out. Mando shrieked anew and threw himself back and away from that blow, leaving three severed fingers behind in the dirt.

The Black Rose stepped toward Mando as the bandit scuttled backward until his spine pressed against the wall of the lean-to. He cradled the injured hand into his chest while he begged for mercy.

"Por favor, por favor!' No mas!"

"Sit very, very still," Lina ordered.

As Mando nodded vigorously, the Black Rose turned toward the woods and lifted a hand to beckon Eduardo forward. The man came running up and pointed his bolt-action Springfield M1903 almost in Mando's face. Since the weapon was chambered for the .30-06, it made an impressive threat.

Lina rolled Jorge onto his belly and tied his hands and feet behind him. She tied Mando's boots together and tied his hands in front of him, after giving him an old rag she found in the guard shed to wrap around the stumps of his missing fingers.

"Now, Chico," Lina said to Mando. "Do you understand English?"

"Si," Mando said, eager to please.

"I'm looking for a man named Henri. A mountain man. He might have carried a big Sharps rifle. Have you seen him?"

Mando hesitated, licked his lips and nodded. "Si. He wuz...he wuz here," he said in broken English. "We capture. Send to El Tigre."

"When?"

"Morning. Early. Sun...coming up."

"What will El Tigre do with him?" Lina demanded.

Mando's whole body gave a shudder. He brought his injured hand up right beneath his chin, cradling it with his other hand while blood dribbled down the front of his serape.

"He will...offer heem...up. To the...the Gods. To Tezcatlipoca...and Huitzilopochtli."

Lina glanced over at Eduardo to see if he had an explanation of those names. He did.

"Aztec gods," the villager said. "Tezcatlipoca was a major deity. Like Quetzalcoatl. I told you about that one before. The two were rivals as I understand it. Tezcatlipoca had a...a symbol." Eduardo frowned as he tried to remember. "It was like a solid ring made of obsidian. Sometimes called a...'smoking mirror.' The Jaguar god, Tepeyollotli, is one of his aspects. I mentioned that one to you before as well. I don't know much about Huitzilopochtli, but the Aztecs offered human sacrifices to him. Supposedly he carried a magical serpent as a weapon."

"So you were right about the connection between El Tigre and the Aztecs," Lina said.

"Seems so," Eduardo agreed. "Wish I hadn't been."

A knot of muscle worked in Lina's cheek as she turned back to Mando. "When will it happen?" she demanded.

"In evening...usually. At dark. That...is heez time."

"Gives us a few hours," Lina said. "Maybe enough."

She leaned forward over Mando. He flinched away. Grabbing up a corner of his serape, she used it to clean the gore off the blades of her urumi. She folded the weapon again around her waist like a belt and straightened. After spitting at the bandit's feet, she pointed toward the prison village, which stood only thirty feet away.

"Where's the key to the padlock on that gate?" she demanded.

"In...side," Mando said. "Table."

"Watch them!" Lina said to Eduardo, who nodded.

Stepping into the lean-to, she found a big bronze key on the card table where the guards had been playing. Plucking it up, she walked over to the gate of the prison and unlocked the chain that bound it closed. She pulled up the wooden door-bar that stretched across the gate and tossed it aside.

As the gate swung open under her hands, Lina saw several dozen people standing just inside, attracted by the noise of the fight outside. Men — mostly older — women and children made up the crowd. At its head stood a woman with cropped blondish-gray hair wearing the remnants of a religious habit.

With her palms up and open to indicate friendliness, Lina stepped through the gate and approached the group. "Are you all from San Javier del Amor?" she asked the apparent nun.

"Most of us are," the woman replied. "I'm Sister Donna Marie. And you are?"

"People call me the Black Rose," Lina replied.

"I've heard of you. How can we help?"

"I need any who can fight," Lina said. "We have a few weapons to loan. A friend who came with me to help you has been taken by El Tigre. I doubt the tyrant will suffer him to live so I'm going after him. The rest of you can flee. We can tell you about a secret way out of the valley."

"We have heard rumors of such a way," Donna said. "As for fighting, most of us are too young or too old to fight, but I can shoot a gun."

Lina studied the woman, who looked to be in her forties, though she might be older. She nodded. "You'll be welcome. I also have...another question."

"Yes?" Sister Donna said.

"Is there a woman here named Rebecca Craft?"

Sister Donna's face lost some of its composure. She shook her head. "There was. But she was murdered. When she tried to protect her daughter from being taken away. They hit her. Far too hard. She never regained consciousness."

Lina winced, but nodded. "The child. Her name was Perla?"

"Yes."

"She's alive. And safe. But now she's an orphan."

"She has a father in the cavalry," Donna said.

"I'm afraid not," Lina replied. "He was killed recently himself. I saw it."

"I am…very sorry to hear that. For Perla's sake. She is a sweet child."

"Yes," Lina agreed. "I'll…. I know someone who can care for her. It won't be easy to tell her."

"I understand," Donna said. "If I can help…."

"Black Rose!" Eduardo called from outside the gate. "Better get out here. We have visitors!"

******

"If it's the enemy, we can fight," Sister Donna said fiercely. Her blue eyes flamed.

The Black Rose motioned her to silence. "Not yet. Stay here. Until we see."

She turned and rushed back through the gates of the prison. It was almost a relief to have something take her mind away from the orphaned daughter of Joseph and Rebecca Craft. Her right hand slipped around beneath her cape to the butt of the Colt 1911 holstered at the small of her back.

Eduardo stood tensely beside the guard shack with his rifle in his hands. He was trying to keep one eye on his prisoners and the other off toward the edge of the woods about seventy yards away. Several people stood there. Six, in fact. They were armed. Lina could see that.

She noticed that two of the visitors were women. Letting go of the pistol behind her back, she smiled and raised a hand in greeting. Eduardo observed Lina's actions and lowered his rifle.

The six strangers raised hands of their own before striding across the field toward Lina. One of the
women broke into a trot and Lina walked to meet
her. They came together and Sister Caroline Harp
threw her arms around the Black Rose and gave her
a fervid hug. Lina returned it.

"So glad you're all right," Caroline said, as she
pushed Lina back to arm's length and gave her the
once over.

"I'm fine," Lina replied. "But Henri has been captured by El Tigre."

Catherine gave a gasp. "No!" she said.

Sister Sofia arrived, with four men at her back.
Lina recognized them as men from Santo Tomas
who often assisted Mother Mercy and the convent.
She gave them all nods of greeting, then led them
over to meet Eduardo and the freed captives from
San Javier del Amor.

As everyone gathered around, she explained what
she planned to do to save Henri and stop El Tigre.
There were no arguments, even though it seemed
likely that some of those here would soon die.

CHAPTER 39

Sister Donna Marie, five healthy men, and two other women from among the captive villagers volunteered to accompany the Black Rose and the others in their effort to save Henri and stop El Tigre Sangriento. That made a total of sixteen, including Eduardo and the six from Santo Tomas. A pitifully small group to take on a city and would-be god.

Eduardo drew a detailed map for the rest of the villagers to lead them to the cave where they could escape the valley. Lina described the rose shaped marks she'd left behind for that purpose as well.

A search of Mando and Jorge's lean-to turned up Henri's Sharps rifle and his pouch of ammunition for it, as well as both his Peacemaker Colts. Lina found herself nearly overcome with a combination of anger and loss as she held the Colts. She closed her eyes, forced herself to breathe. It took a moment, but she regained control.

The lean-to also held a couple of other rifles, old

military carbines with plenty of bullets. Lina didn't want to carry any of Henri's guns; they'd be too much of a distraction for her. She distributed those and the carbines to make sure that everyone going with them to the pyramid would be armed. One more trip to the campsite let her fetch some other items from her blanket roll. She also grabbed her Winchester and her bow. She gave the rifle to Sister Donna and the bow to a woman prisoner who said she knew how to use it.

After moving the two tied-up guards into the village and rechaining the gate, the small troop was ready and set out through the fields toward the pyramid. It was well into afternoon so they began to hurry to make sure they'd reach the pyramid before dusk when, it seemed, Henri would be sacrificed on the altar to El Tigre's Aztec deities.

They kept to the maize fields where they'd be best hidden. They expected to find workers in the fields but saw none. Maybe El Tigre had called them in for his upcoming ceremony.

The evening sun was failing to darkness by the time they reached the end of the maize fields and peaked out upon the open area surrounding El Tigre's ziggurat. People had already started to gather and there was a festive air. Vendors selling meat on sticks and small sacks of pulque and other beverages moved through the crowd. Lina saw maybe two dozen armed guards patrolling the area. No one noticed the strangers hidden among the rows of maize.

The sky darkened quickly, with the reds, yellows and oranges of the sunset bleeding away into purples and blacks. Two men climbed the ziggurat steps and lit torches around the altar. The light revealed nothing *on* the altar as of yet. A few moments later, though, two more men came from the direction of the cliff city. These were from the group that Eduardo had described as "Aztec warriors," those with the elaborate hair styles who carried no guns, only weapons edged in razor-sharp obsidian. Between the two, they pushed along Henri Moissant dressed in a white robe

The muscles in Lina's legs tensed. It was all she could do not to rise to her feet and charge into the field to free her friend. But that was not the plan she'd shared with the others of her party. For that plan to work, she needed El Tigre on the scene. And so she forced herself to wait while the men pushed Henri up the steps of the ziggurat and bound him on his back to the sleek stone of the altar. Afterward, the men stepped to the side and drew their stabbing spears into their hands. They froze into immobility.

A hush fell across the crowd. Down from the city came El Tigre, with his white jaguar on its leash prowling beside him. He was dressed much as before, in a jaguar cloak and hood and a loincloth of crimson. He'd added a chest plate of bone and bright feathers, and wore more feathers in bands around his arms and legs.

The jaguar worried Lina. If he kept that monster beside him during the ceremony of sacrifice it would be harder to get close to him. She breathed a little easier when the queenly woman she'd seen with El Tigre before came and took the jaguar's leash. She led it over to the side of the pyramid while Tigre continued to the foot of the structure and headed up the steps.

El Tigre reached the top of the ziggurat. Lina saw Henri's head turn to face his captor. Tigre raised his hands and the silence of the crowd deepened. This was what Lina had waited for. Into the silence, the Black Rose hurled a threat and a challenge. She straightened to her full height amid the maize; her lungs expanded; she vented a rumbling snarl that built into a jaguar's jungle roar.

Women screamed in the crowd before the pyramid. Men startled and turned with eyes wide. El Tigre froze and only gradually did he move to face whatever it was that challenged him.

While the others among her companions remained crouched and hidden with weapons ready, Lina strode free of the maize field. She began to cross a grassy open area toward the crowd. At first the people stood their ground, but then Lina raised her hands above her head. Not in surrender. In each of her fists gleamed a chunk of jade in the shape of a heart. They appeared to pulse in the torchlight.

The crowd began to part. Even the guards, with their guns drawn, looked first toward their master — toward El Tigre — to see what command he might give. He gave none, and the guards, too, stepped aside for the woman who marched down upon them holding the sacred stones.

Only as she approached the foot of the pyramid did anyone attempt to intervene. Four Aztec warriors stepped in front of her with their spears at the ready. Lina did not stop. She did not slow. Not until El Tigre himself spoke.

"I know you," the one who many called "the Beast" shouted. "You are she. The heart of the darkest night. The Black Rose!"

******

As El Tigre had promised Henri, he'd been fed and bathed. He'd been questioned but told only the same story — that he was a hunter who stumbled on this valley. They didn't believe him but they did not beat him any further. Instead, he was dressed in a ceremonial robe of snow-white cotton and after a few hours was led out into the gathering dusk and taken to the pyramid where he'd be ritually slaughtered.

Henri had not struggled, not as he was pushed along toward his death, not when he saw the altar again and not when he was tied down upon it. It occurred to him that the food he'd been given might have been drugged. The torches glittered as bright as knives; the world did not seem quite real.

Black cloth had been hung about the altar, falling to the stone floor and whispering in the faint wind. It did not cover the thin surface of obsidian, though. That cold material warmed only as it sucked heat from Henri's body — like a vampire.

The mountain man lay still, smelling the twisting

smoke of the torches and the oil with which his skin had been rubbed. He lay still even as he heard what sounded like the angry snarl of a jaguar and some kind of commotion began in the crowd at the foot of the ziggurat. It all felt distant to him. Until he heard El Tigre call out a name — the Black Rose!

Lina! Henri thought.

It was as if he awoke then. He became aware of his heart beating; it thudded against his ribcage. He twisted his head to the right, trying to see. El Tigre's big body bulked in the way. A scarlet aura flickered like lightning around him. Henri could see nothing beyond that aura, but he heard a voice. *Her* voice, and her words.

"Lina," he murmured. "No, no. You shouldn't be here. You *can't* be here!"

He opened his mouth to shout but strangeness silenced him. At first he wasn't sure if it were real. Some force...some *thing* tugged at the ropes around his body. He heard the faintest murmur of sound. Someone was working at the ropes. Back and forth. From beneath the altar. A surge of hope thundered through him. Someone must have hidden under the cloth that surrounded the altar. They were cutting him free.

******

"I've been expecting you, Black Rose," El Tigre called mockingly.

"You lie!" Lina shouted.

El Tigre laughed in booms, like thunder. "Do I?

Do you think I chose San Javier del Amor by accident? Are there not plenty of villages and missions closer to me that I could have raided? And do you think that I accompany *all* the raids myself that originate here?"

Lina felt herself frowning. Could it be? Had El Tigre targeted San Javier because of her? Was she partly to blame for what had occurred?

"Why then?" Lina called.

Tigre said nothing but a smile crossed his broad face, showing an oddly sharp set of teeth. Lina realized they must have been filed to make them look more predatory.

"Why?" Lina demanded once more.

This time, El Tigre answered. "Even here in poorest Mexico, we have heard of the exploits of the Black Rose. She who rides the night for justice. *Justice*!" He almost spat the word. "Justice for the rich Norteamericanos."

"Again, you lie," Lina said. "The Black Rose's justice is for everyone. But mostly for the very poor you speak of so intimately, but who you clearly do not know personally."

"My people have seen differently," El Tigre said, opening his arms wide as if to encompass the entire valley. "They comprehend who will bring them justice. But, there is no denying that you have a certain amount of power. You will make a most wonderous sacrifice to the ancient gods. That is why I invited you here. After I kill your friend," he waved a lazy hand toward Henri, "I will put you on this altar.

I'll take your heart and eat it. To give my gods the power to return to this earth. To once again grant their people glory."

"You're insane!" the Black Rose shouted. "And you must be stopped!"

"So stop me, Black Rose. Stop me if you can. I believe my warriors will have something to say about that."

CHAPTER 40

The ropes around Henri's arms and legs abruptly lost their tension. He was free. But unarmed. El Tigre's back was turned to him. He could rise, shove the tyrant down the steps of his own pyramid. Or could he? Tigre was a huge fellow and not standing very close to the edge. And would that stop the man anyway? Would it hurt him enough? Henri needed to kill him. He needed a weapon.

Turning his head toward the left sent Henri's awareness swooping, like a kite caught in rough winds. He had to have been drugged and the effects seemed to be growing. Sudden nausea gagged him. He spat, and blinked rapidly to clear his vision of bright, stinging spots of multicolored light.

The two Aztec warrior guards who had tied him to the altar stood like statues. They had auras too, black ones that writhed with eel-like shapes. Those weren't real, his mind told him. But the stabbing spears they each held were real. Those lances were nearly eight feet long, with a palm-wide head of flaked black obsidian.

In an instant, Henri's decision was made. He gathered every ounce of strength he had and threw himself rolling off the altar toward the guards, the remnants of his rope bonds trailing from his wrists and feet. The two men were caught completely by surprise. They'd thought him cowed, totally under the spell of the drugs and El Tigre.

Henri's callused fist slammed into the belly of the closest guard. The man doubled over while Henri plucked the heavy spear out of his hands. A shove from the mountain man sent the fellow reeling over the back edge of the pyramid to fall with a wild cry of terror.

The second guard had recovered his wits; he lunged with his lance held low toward Henri, seeking to impale him. Henri twisted aside and brought his newly confiscated weapon around to smack the other spear away.

The guard took one staggering step toward the altar to regain his balance. Henri slipped past him like a tightrope walker along the edge of the ziggurat. As the warrior spun toward him, slinging his lance in a backhand blow at Henri's head, the mountain man ducked beneath and snapped his own lance upward with both hands on the shaft.

The razor-sharp obsidian blade cut through the guard's upper stomach as if flesh and internal organs were paper. The man grunted with the impact. Henri grunted with effort as he twisted the spearhead in the wound.

The warrior screamed, dropped his own spear to grab at the one protruding from his belly. Henri released it, knowing that if the man pulled the lance free now it would tear out his guts. He hooked a foot under the guard's leg and jerked the man off balance.

As the guard fell hard, Henri squatted to grab the dropped spear off the stone. He lunged up again, looking for El Tigre. And El Tigre was there. Right in front of him. Henri thrust with the lance but his enemy was too close. He batted the weapon from Henri's grip and grabbed Henri by the head with both hands. The steel claws on those hands glittered like alligator teeth.

Tigre was immensely strong. He began to force Henri down into a kneeling position. Henri thrust his forearms up between the other man's arms, strained to force them apart. He didn't see the knee that smashed into his chin. Fresh pinwheels of light exploded through his vision as his head jarred brutally backward.

Henri sagged, felt himself losing consciousness. He tried to claw at Tigre's wrists but the rising strength of the drug and his own pain wouldn't let his hands obey. The night began to roar with the sound of ocean waves battering a beach.

El Tigre's hands tightened around Henri's skull.

******

Taken by surprise, Lina stared in shock as Henri rolled off the altar and attacked the guards behind him. She didn't know how he'd gotten free but she knew her friend. He could handle the guards, but what if El Tigre joined in. Then she saw El Tigre turn away from her. He *was* going after Henri. She had to stop him.

With a shout of rage, the Black Rose shoved the two jade hearts into her pockets and charged straight ahead toward the four Aztec warriors guarding the foot of the ziggurat. The lowered their lances to meet her, with torchlight flinging back from the ebony glass of the spearheads. Lina reached back beneath her cape and drew the Colt .45 that Joseph Craft had given her. Craft had wanted her to use it to help defeat El Tigre; now she would.

The closest warrior lunged toward her, stabbing with his spear; Lina shot him in the face, then fired twice into the body of the next man to attack her. She threw herself to one side as a lance's head grazed her shoulder, slicing away a curl of raven-dark hair. Sweeping her boot out, she took the man's legs from under him. As he crashed down, the fourth warrior dropped his spear and grappled with her.

As the warrior's hands locked around her throat, the Black Rose let herself fall backward, pulling the man down with her. She fired twice into his belly as they landed. The .45 slugs jolted him brutally and she brought her legs up to lever him into the air and over her head.

Not waiting to hear the dead man hit the ground, Lina threw herself into a roll toward the pyramid's steps. She knew better than to lie still for long. A lance stabbed into the ground next to her and she shot the knee out of the man who wielded it. The fellow hopped back on one leg as Lina came to her feet. She had one shot left. She wanted to save it for El Tigre. But the warrior in front of her drew a knife, raised it to throw. Lina shot him point blank in the chest.

The steps of the ziggurat were clear. Lina raced up them, dropping the emptied Colt and drawing the Remington twin-shot .41 from beneath her vest. For the first time, she became aware of gun-fire cracking the air all around. Her people and the soldier-warriors of El Tigre were shooting it out too. She heard the crowd screaming and running. But she couldn't do anything about those concerns.

She reached the top of the pyramid. El Tigre bent over Henri, who looked unconscious. She snapped her pistol up for a shot but Tigre had heard her and spun around, jerking Henri in front of him as a shield. The bandit king was huge but Henri was tall as well and Lina couldn't see any part of Tigre well enough to risk a shot.

"Drop your gun!" the tyrant commanded. "Or I'll kill your friend." He curled one hand across Henri's throat, with the steel claws on his glove set to rip and tear.

"You'll kill him anyway," Lina said. "But I'll kill you after. He's unconscious. Lay him down and I'll put my gun down. We'll fight blade to blade."

Tigre grinned. He took two steps toward Lina, pushing Henri in front of him like a sack of feed.

The mountain man's feet barely touched the ground.

"I don't want to kill him like this," Tigre said. "He needs to die on the altar. So put your gun down first. Slide it away from you. And we'll fight. After I finish you, then I can resume my sacrifice of your friend."

Lina glanced desperately around, seeking some opportunity, some way to take El Tigre without dropping her gun. The cloth that hung in front of the altar twitched. Lina glimpsed a small hand reaching from beneath it. She looked away, not wanting to give any hint to the bandit king of something happening behind him.

"Put...down...your gun!" Tigre snarled. His claws indented the side of Henri's throat. A bright spot of blood trickled from beneath one.

"All right," Lina said, turning the gun palm up in her hand. "But we'll do it at the same time."

She slowly sank into a squat. El Tigre began to sink down himself onto one knee, lowering Henri as he did so.

The cloth around the altar twitched again, and for an instant a face peeked out at Lina.

Solo! What was he doing here? How had he gotten under the altar? Lina didn't know but it was a chance.

She lowered the Remington two-shot to the stone of the ziggurat. Tigre slid his clawed fist up and away from Henri's throat. Lina's friend was lying almost prone on the ground now, with only his head held up by El Tigre's hands.

Lina gave the pistol a quick push so that it slid

away from her and directly under the altar. "Now we fight," she said, as she started to rise.

El Tigre smiled, then gave a brutal twist of his arms. Lina heard Henri's spine snap. She saw her friend spasm into death. The rage came boiling out of her in a scream.

CHAPTER 41

As El Tigre released Henri's head, letting it thud to the floor, Lina whipped the knife from her belt into her fist and lunged forward. Tigre was still in a crouch. He lifted his clawed hands to meet her. Lina slashed; Tigre blocked with the steel claws on his right hand. Sparks flew; the knife caught the tip of one claw with brutal force, snapping one of the leather thongs that bound it to the man's wrist.

Tigre slashed at the Black Rose's legs with his other claw. She leaped over the strike as the man powered to his feet. She spun, cut him across the arm but he was backpedaling away and the wound was shallow. Again, Lina brought her Bowie knife around. Again, El Tigre blocked with his claw. Another thong snapped. The claw hung askew on the bandit king's hand.

Sensing weakness, Lina flung herself into the attack, slashing left, right, across, down. The clawed glove on Tigre's right hand tore loose, dropped to the stone under his feet. The man who many called "The Beast" was driven around the altar, throwing up his steel clawed left hand now in a desperate effort to protect himself.

Not even the Black Rose's anger could sustain her attack forever. She slowed. Tigre bled from several cuts but none were deep enough to incapacitate him. The big man's chest heaved beneath the bone breast plate he wore; his breathing came harsh. But he was not daunted and he finally had time to grab for the weapon hanging at his belt.

This was something like a cross between a club and a sword. It had a polished wood haft and a broad thick head embedded all around with flakes of inhumanly sharp obsidian. Lina had seen this thing hanging at El Tigre's side. Up close, she recognized it, though she'd never used one — a macuahuitl, a weapon of the Aztecs.

Armed anew, Tigre charged Lina. She needed to catch her own breath and dared not try to block his macuahuitl with her knife. That would be a good way to lose the blade and her hand. She dodged a powerful swing, circled back to the altar.

El Tigre followed, began to stalk her around the altar as she retreated. The Beast's smile widened, his teeth wet and white in his overly broad jaws. Solo took a hand in the fight. Just as Tigre reached the eastern side of the altar, Lina saw the cloth that covered the foot of the altar thrown back. Solo rolled from beneath it with Lina's .41 caliber Remington in one small hand.

Tigre couldn't have seen Solo as the little fellow leaped onto the altar and swung the Remington toward his target. But he must have sensed something. He jerked his head back just as Solo fired. The bullet intended for the occiput of Tigre's skull smacked through his left cheek instead and exploded out of the right side of his mouth. Blood and flesh and shards of teeth sprayed from the wound.

Tigre roared, swatted at Solo with his left hand. The claws on Tigre's hand slashed the little fellow across the chest and knocked the Remington to one side. The pistol's last shot discharged harmlessly into the air.

Lina reversed her knife for a throw, but before she could hurl it El Tigre stabbed Solo in the belly with his macuahuitl, then ripped the razor-edged stone blades out sideways. Solo grunted, his eyes going wide. He dropped his pistol and fell to his knees on the altar.

Lina hurled her knife with deadly intent. Tigre was turning back toward her and somehow got his left hand up and in the way. The knife's tip struck him straight through the palm, exiting the back of his hand and jamming itself into the clawed glove that he wore. He did not even cry out but let his left hand fall to his side while he lifted the macuahuitl in his right.

Blood dripped from his lips, purplish in the torchlight. The wound to his face was awful to see but he scarcely seemed to experience the pain. At least not any physical pain. He spoke, chewing the words out like gravel through his torn mouth.

"My son!" he rumbled. "Even my son, you turned against me. You have power indeed. Black Rose!"

Lina stood in shock at El Tigre's words. Solo had been his son! But the stories she'd heard from Eduardo of El Tigre leading Solo around on a leash! How could this man have treated his boy so horribly? And how could he pretend here that it hurt him to have killed his own child?

"I didn't turn him against you," Lina shouted. "You did that!"

El Tigre did not respond, only stalked toward her with his macuahuitl swinging from side to side. He moved like an animated statue of bronze. Lina wrapped her fist around the hilt of her urumi and snapped it free. She let the whip-like blade coil around her feet.

"Your last weapon," Tigre snarled. "It won't be enough to stop me."

"I don't care if we die together," the Black Rose snarled back.

******

While El Tigre and the Black Rose faced off on top of the ziggurat, Sisters Caroline Harp and Sofia Lee, with their companions, shot it out with Tigre's guards. The citizens of the cliff city fled wildly in every direction. Only the armed guards remained, but there were plenty of them.

Caroline and Sofia's group faced one charge of the Aztec warriors with their spears. A barrage of bullets withered it away. Now even those warriors had laid claim to guns and lead flew like sleet.

Caroline and Sofia worked their way with their companions out of the maize field and into the riot of huts rising around the base of the pyramid. Not all of them made it, but more of the enemy had fallen. Sofia and Caroline and the four men from Santo Tomas were cool professionals, trained with all manner of weapons. They made every shot count.

A loincloth clad wild man charged Caroline. His old rifle had jammed and he reversed it, leaping forward with a howl to bring the butt down toward the nun. She saved a bullet by flinging her Kpinga into his chest. He staggered and fell, coughing blood. She used the butt of her own rifle to smack savagely against his skull, dashing his brains from his head.

Spinning the Winchester around in her hands, Caroline shot another guard who made the mistake of momentarily showing himself from behind a hut. She crouched, tore her Kpinga loose from the first man's chest and slung it back at her waist.

As she rose, a woman stepped from behind the ziggurat to face her. She had long and lustrous black hair and eyes like mahogany diamonds. Her queenly face lay twisted in rage and both her hands held tight on a silver leash upon which a white jaguar crouched.

The jaguar snarled at Sister Caroline; its claws extended for an attack. But just as the woman started to release her hold on the big cat, a shrieking band of local wives returned to the field and descended on her with clubs and cutting knives. The woman threw up her arms with a scream. The leash fell from her grip but the startled jaguar only turned and ran as his mistress went down under the blows of those she'd once ruled.

And now the husbands of those local wives found their own courage and began to charge forward against El Tigre's armed guards. Many dropped with bullets in their hearts. But many others sensed the possibility of freedom and joined the fray.

Caroline Harp worked her Winchester's lever, firing until the barrel was red and smoking hot. She spared one glance toward the top of the pyramid where the Black Rose fought for her life.

"Kill him and be done," she begged. "Kill him and let's go home!"

******

El Tigre shouted a war-cry as he leaped toward Lina with his macuahuitl swinging. Lina whipped her urumi forward, let the bladed edge caress Tigre's bare thigh. Blood sprayed but she hadn't struck deep. She dared not.

If her weapon hooked on anything, even bone, and it was not a lethal strike, this monster of a man would be upon her. Lina knew that she was strong, that she had the fire of rage in her belly. But El Tigre was stronger, inches taller than her and with cords and slabs of muscle down his arms and across his chest. If he were able to catch her blade, even at the cost of fingers, he would tear it away from her.

She circled the altar, keeping it between her and the bandit king. Her eyes scanned for an opening. She watched for anything and everything around her that could be used as a weapon. As she stepped past Solo's body, she heard him moan. Her gaze slipped to his face. His eyes were open; his hands cupped his belly where pink viscera shone. He moved his head; she knew he was giving her some kind sign. But she didn't know how to read it.

Unless.

She saw what Solo was trying to show her. She didn't stop, though, just kept backing up until she reached Henri's body. Again, she looked down. There was no doubt that her friend was dead. Her heart surged with both hurt and rage. She stopped backing up. Tigre kept coming.

"It will be *my* justice served now," the man growled. "Not yours!" He raised his macuahuitl.

"It's not about justice anymore," the Black Rose said. "It's about vengeance!"

Lina whipped her urumi up and snapped it forward with all her strength. Tigre jerked his macuahuitl down to block. The whip-blade struck the club, shattered some of the obsidian shards that jutted from it. The very tip of the urumi sliced across Tigre's lower face, doing more damage to his mouth, but the man didn't appear to care.

As black flakes of shrapnel sprayed out from the club, Tigre twisted the weapon, causing the blade of the urumi to lock around it. The Beast gave a tremendous yank and Lina was jerked forward off balance. She let herself be drawn.

From the stone behind Tigre, Solo sat up. The agony on his face showed how much the movement cost him. But he had something in his hand. Lina saw it — El Tigre's broken claw-glove, with the steel hooks of the claw shining as if with a light of their own.

Tigre reeled Lina toward him like a catfish on a line; she didn't let go of the urumi's handle. A bloody grin cracked Tigre's lips; the muscles in his arms tensed with the thought of getting his hands on the Black Rose and breaking her back.

Solo slashed the claw down into his father's left calf and raked it hard. The Beast cried out in surprise, turned to see what had struck him. His damaged leg muscles spasmed. He fell to one knee, with his hands up in the air.

Lina released the urumi. She was close to Tigre. Very close. She reached out, wrapped her fist around the handle of her own knife, which was still embedded in El Tigre's left hand. She ripped it free and as the man who wanted to be thought of as an Aztec god twisted back toward her, she slammed the knife down through his right eye socket and into the brain behind.

An awful thunk sounded as the widest part of the knife's blade caught in bone and grated to a halt. El Tigre grabbed for the Black Rose's arm. His hands flailed, then failed. A single grunt spilled from his torn lips, followed by blood. He remained kneeling, but his life had fled.

Lina left the blade sticking out of El Tigre's eye. She took back her urumi, wrapped it around her waist without even knowing that she did so. Solo had fallen back again. Dead. Lina winced at the awful wound in his stomach.

Reaching into a pocket, the Black Rose took out one of the jade hearts she'd carried with her for many days. She leaned down, pushed the stone through the torn lips of El Tigre, past the shattered teeth, deep into the mouth.

"Even this won't bring you back," she growled.

She lifted her head. Above her, beyond the torchlight, the stars gleamed and the moon was rising. She shouted out, in a voice that echoed.

"It's done! It's done! And cannot be *undone*!"

CHAPTER 42

Sister Caroline heard the Black Rose's voice call out. She knew what the words meant. And so, it seemed, did the men who'd followed El Tigre. The gunfire died away. She heard footsteps fleeing through the night.

Slowly, Caroline straightened behind the shed where she'd hunkered down. The battlefield lay silent, with only the drift of smoke across it. Not even the wounded cried out. She stepped into the open. No one attacked. A few of the city dwellers who'd joined the fight on the side of the Black Rose stood around as if stunned at their victory.

With the scent of blood and gunfire in her nostrils, Caroline called out to those who'd *begun* the fight at her side.

"It's over!"

Sofia joined her. And Eduardo. Sister Donna Marie survived and several others. But their losses had been heavy. Francisco, who'd ridden all the way from Santo Tomas with them, had died with an Aztec spear through his heart. Antonio, a man who'd done the Sisters of Señora Maria many kindnesses, lay shot to pieces.

This moment, though, was for worrying about the living and those who *might* still live. Caroline, Sofia, and Eduardo rushed up the pyramid's steps. At the top, they saw the dead form of El Tigre, still in a kneeling position. And they saw the Black Rose. She sat on the stone flaggings of the ziggurat with Henri's head in her lap. Tears dripped along her cheeks.

Caroline and Sofia walked over to Lina with weighted feet. Eduardo saw Solo's broken body and rushed to the small man's side. He, too, began to sob.

Caroline let her hand fall to Lina's shoulder. "We'll bury them," she said. "Say a thousand prayers in their honor."

"Yes," Lina said, her voice flat. "But not here. Not in this…" she lifted her head and looked around, "this valley. We'll take them back to Eduardo's village. Bury them where we buried Joseph Craft. We'll bury all the ones who died fighting for us there."

"And we'll go home," Sofia said.

"Yes," Lina replied. But her thoughts were elsewhere.

******

With the dawn, the Black Rose and her companions saddled some of El Tigre's horses and rode away from his kingdom. They took their friends who had died with them. Many of the "citizens" of El Tigre's city seemed to be leaving as well. Lina and the others passed carts and burros loaded down with pots and pans and sacks of grain and vegetables.

The mountain pass leading out of the valley was clear. No soldier from the Beast's army remained to guard it. Lina looked back only once. An open field stretched behind her where a few forgotten cattle still grazed. Out in that field, Lina saw a dark shape traveling slowly across the landscape.

The cows shied away from it and she knew why. Even though it limped on three legs and held the other tucked under its belly, this thing was a predator. Nearly, it had preyed on her and Henri.

Lifting her Winchester, Lina squinted along the barrel, placing the bead of her sight on the broad skull of the beast. As if the creature sensed her eyes upon it, the ebony jaguar paused. Across the distance its gaze struck into hers. It blinked; its yellow eyes dimmed and brightened again. It turned to continue its journey, away from Lina and her fellows and toward the mountains beyond El Tigre's lost world.

The Black Rose lowered her rifle. Something had to be left to live in this place.

******

When the burying was done, Lina mounted her horse and prepared to ride north away from Eduardo's village and back to Texas. Sofia and Caroline and a few others sat their horses beside hers, waiting until the word to go was given. Eduardo came forward and reached up to shake Lina's hand.

"We'll tend their graves," he said. "In memory."

"Thank you," Lina replied.

Sister Donna Marie stood beside Eduardo. She was staying here, as were most of the refugees from the burned-out mission of San Javier del Amor. They'd lost one home but found another.

Sister Donna lifted her hand to wave goodbye.

"Vayo con dios," she said. "Go with God."

And so it was.

EPILOGUE

Two people stepped off the train onto the platform at Santo Tomas. It was a little before noon, with the sun hot and gleaming overhead like a new penny. A porter unloaded two suitcases beside them that represented everything young Perla Craft owned in this world. The only other bit of luggage the two had was a carpetbag carried in the hand of Catalina Rivera. Inside were the clothes and weapons of the Black Rose.

Perla stared around curiously. The streets were busy with the comings and goings of people and wagons and horses. A carriage pulled up next to the platform to wait for someone who hadn't exited the train yet. The older man driving it nodded to Catalina and tipped his hat with a smile to Perla. Perla returned the smile with a curtsey, holding up the hem of her short blue dress.

"Catalina! Sister!" a voice called.

Lina glanced down the street to see a dark-haired

boy of thirteen or so running toward them, pushing a wheelbarrow in front of him. He lifted one hand in a quick wave, then returned it to the wheelbarrow's handle before he lost control.

Lina waved back. She glanced down at Perla, whose eyes were wide. The little girl's hand stole into Lina's and the woman smiled.

"That is only Paco," she told Perla. "He is harmless, though something of a charmer."

Paco, who was of Apache ancestry and looked it with his black eyes, sturdy frame, and darkly tanned skin, pushed the wheelbarrow up to the bottom of the stairs leading down from the train platform. He drew off his straw sombrero before offering an elaborate bow.

"Miladys," he said. "Your conveyance awaits."

Lina laughed. Still holding Perla's hand, she walked down the steps and placed her carpetbag in the wheelbarrow. "Those other two suitcases up there are ours as well," she told Paco, who straightened and smiled at her.

"I shall bring them forthwith."

"Have you been reading Shakespeare again?" Lina asked.

"Mother Mercy is quite insistent about my reading, dear Catalina," Paco said. "But I find that I am enjoying the tales. Quite satisfyingly bloody."

"Indeed," Lina said. She turned toward her companion. "And this young lady is Perla Craft. She will be staying with us at the mission for a while. We are all going to make her welcome."

Paco still held his sombrero in one hand. He took a step toward Perla, reached out with his other hand to gently take her wrist. Turning it over, he leaned down and bussed the back of her hand with his lips.

"I am forever your servant, milady Perla," Paco whispered dramatically.

Perla grinned, then giggled out loud. Her blonde curls shook and her blue eyes caught a sparkle from the sun.

Lina's heart gave a quick jump in her chest. This was the first time the little girl had shown spontaneous joy since Lina had picked her up at the mission in Santa Annabella and told her that neither of her parents would be coming home. Lina wanted to hug Paco but that would have destroyed the moment. Instead, she said,

"Let us away then, good squire."

Paco released Perla's hand and laughed. He rushed up the steps to the platform to grab the suitcases. Lina and Perla walked ahead toward the mission. Perla took Lina's hand again and started to swing their arms back and forth. Lina let it happen.

The pinkish tinted adobe wall of the mission loomed in front of them. They reached the gate, an ornate affair of bright steel and carved and polished oak. It stood open, with the holy sanctuary rising just beyond and the bell-gable next to it.

As they crossed the threshold into the mission itself, the four brass bells of the tower began to peal the noon hour. Perla stopped walking and looked up with surprise. A huge smile suddenly curved her lips as the sound rang out with confidence and joy.

"I love it!" Perla said. "And I am to live here?"

"As long as you want," Lina replied. "Forever, if you chose."

Perla laughed. Down a cobblestoned path from the church, Mother Mercy hurried toward them with a welcoming face. Everything seemed right with the world, or as right as it could be after the costs paid to defeat El Tigre Sangriento. Later, Lina would mourn again for Henri Moissant and for a small fellow named Solo. But not now. She put on a smile.

A low voice spoke from beside her shoulder. "Shall I make young Perla a rosary?"

Lina turned. The old man who stood next to her was blind; his flesh lay loose and wrinkled on a thin frame. The white hair on his head gleamed almost angelically against the windburned darkness of his skin.

"It will be years before Perla is old enough to decide whether or not to join the order," Lina replied.

The old man nodded. "I *will* make her a rosary."

"Catalina!" Mother Mercy declared.

Lina turned to be hugged, to be kissed on the cheek. And when she looked around again, the old man was gone. As if he'd never been.

A LOOK AT: AVENGING
ANGELS: VENGEANCE TRAIL

In the first book of this shocking new series, Reno and Sara's farm is burned and their family murdered by a group of ex-Confederate soldiers known as the Devil's Horde. These ex-Confederates have a chip on their shoulders, and they're burning a broad swath across the Yankee north, murdering, pillaging, and raping their way to the Colorado Territory.

But when they burn the Bass farm, they find out not every follower of God is a sheep. Sworn to vengeance, Reno and Sara become black-winged avenging angels on a mission from God. Hounding the Confederate devils' every step, these black-winged angels begin efficiently and bloodily killing them— one by one and two by two—reading to them from the Good Book while sending them back to Hell.

AVAILABLE NOW FROM A.W. HART

ABOUT THE AUTHOR

Charles Gramlich lives amid the piney woods of southern Louisiana and is the author of the Talera fantasy series, the SF novel Under the Ember Star, and the thriller Cold in the Light. His work has appeared in magazines such as Star*Line, Beat to a Pulp, Night to Dawn, Pedestal Magazine, and others. Many of his stories have been collected in the anthologies, Bitter Steel, (fantasy), Midnight in Rosary (Vampires/Werewolves), and In the Language of Scorpions (Horror). Charles also writes westerns under the name Tyler Boone. Although he writes in many different genres, all of his fiction work is known for its intense action and strong visuals.